I0709012

Marina Mews

A CORAL SHORES
VETERINARY MYSTERY

DL Mitchell

Black Rose Writing | Texas

©2026 by DL Mitchell

All rights reserved. No part of this book may be reproduced, stored in a retrieval system or transmitted in any form or by any means without the prior written permission of the publishers, except by a reviewer who may quote brief passages in a review to be printed in a newspaper, magazine or journal.

The author grants the final approval for this literary material.

First printing

This is a work of fiction. Names, characters, businesses, places, events, and incidents are either the products of the author's imagination or used in a fictitious manner. Any resemblance to actual persons, living or dead, or actual events is purely coincidental.

ISBN: 978-1-68513-708-3
LIBRARY OF CONGRESS CONTROL NUMBER: 2025945565
PUBLISHED BY BLACK ROSE WRITING
www.blackrosewriting.com

Printed in the United States of America
Suggested Retail Price (SRP) $19.95

Marina Mews is printed in Baskerville

*As a planet-friendly publisher, Black Rose Writing does its best to eliminate unnecessary waste to reduce paper usage and energy costs, while never compromising the reading experience. As a result, the final word count vs. page count may not meet common expectations.

*In loving memory of Johnny,
the best cat there ever was.*

SPECIAL THANKS

To all the mystery lovers—from sunny Coral Shores to wherever you are now—thank you for reading, for caring, and for believing in stories where even the quietest paw step can leave the biggest clue. Your love of cozies, animals, quirky characters, and small-town secrets keeps this veterinary series alive and thriving.

A heartfelt thank-you to the veterinarians, vet techs, and animal care professionals who work tirelessly to heal, comfort, and advocate for the creatures who can't speak for themselves. Your dedication inspired so many moments in these books.

And to the cat lovers—you understand the power of a well-timed purr, a slow blink of affection, or a sassy tail flick. Whether you've shared your life with one feline or many, your appreciation for their mystery, majesty, and occasional mischief has helped shape the heart of this story.

To my publisher—Black Rose Writing—thank you for believing in this series from the very beginning. Your support, guidance, and commitment to bringing these stories to life have made all the difference. I'm grateful to be one of your authors.

And none of this would be possible without my husband, Blair, and daughter, Maddy. They cheer me on every step of the way with their love and support.

PRAISE FOR
Marina Mews

"I've read all of DL Mitchell's Coral Shores Veterinary mysteries. *Marina Mews* is the best one yet!

The author blends friendship/animal/small-town charm with coastal intrigue in her latest installment in the series. Veterinarian Emily stumbles upon the body of her childhood dive instructor on the beach. What first looks like a tragic accident quickly turns into a full-blown murder investigation, and Emily—never one to sit on the sidelines—dives into the case alongside her ever-loyal sidekick, Anthony. With clues surfacing at the marina and a terrified six-toed cat named Hemingway hinting at deeper secrets, the mystery ripples with cozy tension and heart.

And...my favorite character, Elvis, is back doing his part to keep kids happy, fellow animals company, and bad guys away!"
–Cam Torrens, best-selling author of the Tyler Zahn mystery/suspense series

"Mitchell's *Marina Mews* reunites familiar characters, including Elvis, the plucky terrier with an instinct for solving crime, while creating new ones, like Hemingway, a female cat who holds the key to catching the people who murdered her owner. Mitchell blends themes of friendship and loyalty with a gentle romance that leaves readers eager for the next trip to her charming Florida town. It shows that following the feline along with your heart pays off in a big way."
–Katherine Nichols, author of the Lucy Howard Mystery Series

Marina
Mews

CHAPTER ONE

"Elvis! Come back!"

Emily squinted against the morning sun as the energetic West Highland White Terrier sprinted along the shoreline, spraying wet sand in his wake as he sped away. Regretting her decision to unhook his leash, she kicked off her flip-flops near the breaking surf and chased after him.

"Elvis!"

Thankful for a deserted beach at this early hour, she had no worries he could get into much trouble. It wasn't like Elvis to ignore a command—her niece and nephew had been working hard on his training, but Elvis was a terrier. His instincts were strong, and it had been a few weeks since his last beach day, his favorite place to play. Emily assumed he'd spotted a sandpiper or shorebird along the water's edge, and she knew it would be impossible for him to resist flushing them.

The sun's glare reflecting off the flat-calm Gulf of Mexico made it difficult for Emily to see any distance in front of her. Elvis finally came into view, standing next to a large, dark shape. It was hard to make out, but it looked like a dolphin or turtle had beached itself, so she picked up her pace, prepared to render veterinary first aid.

Elvis turned and ran to meet her, barking. It wasn't his normal, playful bark but rapid and high-pitched. He sounded distressed. He latched onto the leash hanging from Emily's hand and pulled her toward the unmoving mound.

Before he took off again, Emily clipped his leash then struggled to keep pace. As they neared the stranded animal, she gasped upon realizing it wasn't a marine mammal in need but a scuba diver wearing a full-length wet suit, buoyancy vest, and tank.

"Oh, no!" She dropped to her knees beside the body. "Are you okay?" Silence followed.

The diver lay face down and motionless. As she gently turned the body onto its side, she recoiled, falling back into the sand at the sight of the vacant expression. Emily pressed her fingers to the jugular vein, searching for a pulse. Finding none, she understood every second mattered and prepared to administer CPR.

The scuba gear interfered with chest compressions. She had to get his equipment off and fast. Being a certified diver herself, Emily quickly released the remaining air in the BCD vest and detached the tank that impeded her ability to give first aid. Another shock came when she removed the scuba mask and instantly recognized the diver as William Todd, a local resident who owned a marina and dive shop.

Emily pinned Elvis's leash under her knee, dialed 911, set it to speaker, then tossed the phone face up in the sand and began chest compressions.

"Nine-one-one, what's your emergency?" The dispatcher's voice became Emily's lifeline, helping to calm her nerves.

"This is Dr. Emily Benton. I've found an unconscious scuba diver on the beach in front of the Eliza Klein Sea Turtle Center. There's no pulse, and I've started CPR. Please send an ambulance."

"Are you at 8500 Gulf Beach Road?" the operator asked.

"Yes. I need help. Hurry!" Emily's voice came in staccato bursts as she worked hard with each push on his chest. She delivered two compressions per second, the strain of that pace already taking its toll.

"They're on the way. I'll stay on the line with you until they arrive."

"Thank you." Emily glanced at Elvis, who seemed to understand the gravity of the situation as he sat quietly next to her. She paused to check for a pulse but detected nothing, so she resumed compressions.

The sun had risen well above the horizon, and the temperature climbed. The sweat dripped off the tip of Emily's nose as she continued with the grueling task of providing CPR. Though only minutes had passed, she felt as if she was nearing the finish line of a marathon. Doubt crept in—did she have the physical strength to keep going? Then she heard a siren in the distance.

You've got this, Emily said to herself. *Just a little longer.*

The ambulance pulled into the construction lot for the sea turtle center, and two paramedics emerged from the grassy dune. Elvis slipped free from her hold on the end of his leash and ran toward the men, which caused them to slow down as he approached. When Elvis turned to lead them back to Emily, the terrier kept looking over his shoulder as if double-checking they were still following. *Good boy*, Emily thought.

She continued compressions until one paramedic took over, allowing Emily to collapse in exhaustion. His partner assessed vitals, placed a ventilation bag over Mr. Todd's face, and connected a heart monitor. After cutting away the remaining dive vest, he reached for the defibrillator.

"Clear!" the paramedic shouted.

Emily pulled Elvis next to her as the first responders removed their hands and all contact points from the victim before delivering a potentially lifesaving counter-shock. No response. "Clear!" They attempted a second time. Emily held her breath as all three stared at the monitor, hoping for that beeping sound showing a heart rhythm, but the line remained flat.

Everything that came next blurred together. The paramedics took turns providing chest compressions while working to save his life. The fire department and law enforcement arrived on the beach—standard protocol for a 911 emergency call. She vaguely remembered hearing, "Clear!" called one or two more times.

A firefighter took over compressions as the EMTs placed an IV catheter then lifted Mr. Todd onto a stretcher. Within minutes of arriving, they loaded him into the back of the ambulance and sped off with lights flashing and sirens blaring.

Despite feeling overwhelmed, Emily somehow remembered to grab her abandoned flip-flops before making her way to the turtle center parking lot. She sank to the ground in the shade of a palm tree, and when Elvis climbed into her lap, she noticed him trembling.

"It's okay, little buddy." She wrapped her arms around the white terrier. Sirens and loud sounds often triggered a fear response in dogs, and even though she had never seen Elvis react this way, he was a very intuitive dog and could be picking up on her emotions.

She watched as the deputy walked to her vehicle and grabbed a clipboard. A statement would be required, but Emily's focus remained on Elvis. His trembling persisted, despite her reassurances. With no time for a lengthy phone call, she texted the two people she could count on in an emergency.

I'm at the sea turtle center—need your help. I'm safe, but come quick.

CHAPTER TWO

Emily did her best to provide Deputy Garcia a detailed description of the incident. She and Elvis stumbled upon a scuba diver who had apparently drowned during a dive. She felt she had done everything in her power to keep Mr. Todd alive, but deep down, she knew he may be beyond resuscitation. As a Doctor of Veterinary Medicine, Emily understood her actions were unlikely to change the outcome—when he arrived at the hospital, an ER doctor would be tasked with calling "time of death."

William Todd had lived in Coral Shores for as long as she remembered. Everyone in town called him Billy. He owned Blue Water Marina and Dive Shop and operated scuba and snorkel trips, catering to the tourists. He had been her dive master when she earned her scuba certification as a teenager, and she had recently seen him during a veterinary checkup for his cat, Hemingway.

Dr. Emily Benton, the owner of the Coral Shores Veterinary Hospital, had become acquainted with most of the local residents' cats and dogs. After graduating from veterinary school and finishing an internal medicine internship, she had returned to work at her hometown veterinary hospital while supporting her mom through her cancer treatments.

As far as Emily knew, Billy didn't have any other family in town. His only niece, Lauryn, or Lala to her friends on the swim team, moved away from Coral Shores during Emily's years at college. *Who is going to tell Lala what happened?*

As she finished her statement, two separate vehicles simultaneously pulled into the parking lot. The cavalry had arrived.

When Detective Mike Lane stepped out of his unmarked car, Emily sighed. Even after months of dating, he took her breath away. His wavy brown hair was tucked under a ball cap, shading his hazel eyes that Emily swore were flecked with gold. A wrinkled Pittsburgh Steelers T-shirt and gym shorts only accented his tall, lean, athletic build. She waved to signal that she was all right, which prompted him to smile—his most attractive feature. He had responded to her call for help as her boyfriend, not as a law enforcement officer, and she was grateful he was here.

Before Mike cleared the construction barrier next to the road, Anthony raced past him, still wearing his pajamas and waving his arms over his head. Despite the seriousness of the situation, Emily stifled a giggle. His 6'3" robust frame and handsome baby face made Anthony instantly likeable. Her best friend since high school and current hospital manager, she could depend on him in her time of need. They always had each other's back.

"Em! Are you okay?" Anthony shouted.

She rose to her feet, cradling Elvis in her arms. "I'm fine."

Both men embraced her with a hug. Anthony gently took Elvis and stepped back to give Emily a once-over. Mike kept his arm wrapped around her shoulder.

"What's with the police and your 911 emergency text?" Anthony asked. "You had me totally freaking out."

"Sorry. I didn't mean to worry you. It's just that I, uh, found a body."

"What? I mean, where? When?" Anthony squeezed Elvis tight.

Mike's jaw tightened as he turned to face her. "Em, start from the beginning."

"Well, as you know, I'm pet sitting Elvis until Duncan and Jane get back with the kids from Mac's baseball tournament. I combined his morning walk with a check on the progress at the turtle center. We were on the beach and right when we reached the center, Elvis took off toward what I thought was a stranded marine mammal—but it wasn't. A scuba diver, wearing all their gear, had washed ashore. I called 911 and started CPR right away."

"Em, I'm so sorry. That must have been a shock, for you and Elvis." The squirming terrier demanded to be put on the ground, and Anthony obliged, holding his leash tight.

"It was, but there's more. The diver was William Todd."

Anthony drew in a quick breath, his eyes widening. "No."

"Who's William Todd?" Mike directed his question at both of them.

"I've only ever called him Uncle Billy," Anthony said. "A friend of ours, Lala, is his niece and lived with him during high school. He runs the marina." He turned to Emily. "Didn't he teach your scuba diving course?"

She nodded. "And we just saw him a few weeks ago with Hemingway."

"I get that I'm new in town, but who's Hemingway?" Mike asked.

"A cat." Emily and Anthony answered together.

"Actually, a polydactyl cat," Emily said.

Mike looked thoroughly confused. "A *polly-dack-til* what?"

"They're multi-toed cats," Anthony said. "Hemingway has six toes instead of the normal five. Her name was inspired by Ernest Hemingway's famous colony of multi-toed cats that live at his historic home in Key West. The person who fostered her as a kitten got the gender mixed up, so even though she's a girl, it stuck."

Mike raised his eyebrows. "Sounds like you have lots to fill me in on. But first, I'm going to talk with the deputy before she leaves."

Emily watched him cross the parking lot and when she turned back to Anthony, he had a wide grin on his face. "What?" she asked.

"You're so transparent. Not that I advocate playing hard to get."

Emily shrugged. She felt little like talking, especially about her love life. The adrenaline rush after finding Billy and administering CPR had waned, leaving behind a numb exhaustion. She attempted to tuck stray hairs into her pony tail elastic then brushed away the sand covering her arms and legs. "I'm a mess."

"You're fine." Anthony picked a piece of seaweed off her shirt. "You could be wearing a garbage bag, and Mike would still think you're beautiful."

Emily's long, straight, red hair, and blue eyes channeled her Scottish heritage. Freckles dusting her nose were her only adornment, since she rarely fussed with her appearance.

"Do you know where Lala is living or how to get in touch with her? She'll be devastated if he doesn't pull through," Anthony said.

"I have no idea. I haven't seen her or spoken to her since that first year after graduation—at our homecoming football game. What about you?"

"Same."

They noticed Mike and the deputy turn in their direction. Mike dropped his shoulders and stared at the ground.

Anthony grabbed her hand. "That's not good."

"No, it's not." Emily walked toward the road as Anthony followed behind with Elvis.

"I'm sorry," Mike said. "He didn't make it."

"Oh." Emily's eyes welled up. "I guess I'm not surprised, but it's still so sad." This wasn't the first time she had discovered a dead body, but nobody could be prepared for the emotional flood that followed.

Emily and Anthony took a moment to comfort one another before offering Deputy Garcia more details about William Todd, including his niece's name. Before she left, the deputy handed Emily her card, assuring her she could reach out with any questions or new information. Next of kin needed to be contacted before announcing anything to the public. An autopsy would be performed as a standard course of action, but they all agreed accidental drowning would likely be the cause of death.

As a certified scuba diver, Emily understood that many things could go wrong on a dive. He might have suffered a medical emergency while underwater. William Todd had a long career as a dive master and had always stressed the importance of safety to his students, but that didn't make him immune to the risks.

"Em, let me drive you and Elvis home," Mike said, wiping a tear from her cheek.

"Thanks. I'm ready to drop. Both of you are my heroes for showing up the way you did this morning."

"And we always will," Anthony said. "I've got to tell Marc what's going on. I ran out the door right as he returned from a bike ride. I'll check in with you later." He hugged her tight.

As they walked to their cars, Emily stopped suddenly. "Wait," she said. They turned toward her. "We can't go home. We need to find Hemingway."

CHAPTER THREE

"Hemingway, the cat?" Mike asked.

Anthony nodded. "She lives in the dive shop at the marina." He turned to Emily. "Is Uncle Billy married?"

She shook her head. "Don't think so unless it's recent. He never mentioned a wife, and he's the only one to bring Hemingway into the vet hospital. Mike, can someone from the sheriff's department check at the marina? To make sure everything's okay. As her veterinarian, I can go with them, if that helps. I'm concerned since we don't know how long she's been alone."

"After I drop you off, I'll head to the station. I'm sure it can be arranged, but it may take a couple hours."

"I want to go, too. But not dressed like this." Anthony gestured to his tank top and shorts, both covered in a baby sea turtle print.

•   •   •

Air conditioning had never felt so good. Emily stood inside her front door with her arms stretched wide, letting the cool air wash over her. She was thirsty and needed a shower, but all that would have to wait. Bella, her mammoth-sized, gray tabby Maine Coon cat, greeted them at the door, meowing her disapproval at the late breakfast hour.

"Forgive me, Bella." She bent down to pet her head and followed her cat into the kitchen. This morning's menu included tuna feast pate, which Bella devoured with gusto. Elvis stared at her longingly despite having already eaten before their eventful walk.

"You were such a good boy." She asked him to sit then presented him with his dental chew treat. He darted off to his dog bed to enjoy it in private.

Emily drank a large glass of water, hit the start button to brew a fresh pot of coffee, and showered to remove the sand and salt covering her body.

Once refreshed and with a mug in hand, Bella and Elvis pushed past her as she stepped outside onto her beachfront deck. Plopping down in her oversized chaise lounge, Emily took a long sip, closed her eyes, and exhaled.

Images of William Todd's lifeless body were hard to shake, so Emily opened her eyes to focus on the scenery in front of her. The coconut palm trees at the edge of her property framed her ocean views. Rhythmic sounds of a light surf breaking onshore helped calm her nerves. This was her happy place.

Her mom had taken respite in this same chair during her cancer treatments followed by those long weeks of in-home hospice care. Even prior to her mom's death at the beginning of the year, Emily decided to make Coral Shores her permanent home. Her mom left her estate, including Bella and this cottage, to Emily and her brother, Duncan. He lived nearby with his wife, Jane, and their kids, Mac and Ava. Since the kids were established in their schools, he wasn't interested in moving to the beach, and they'd easily sorted out their inheritance.

It had taken time, but Emily could now enjoy this special space without being overwhelmed with grief. The pain from losing her mom never went away but faded into the background, allowing only warm, loving memories to come to the surface.

Elvis sat alert on the deck, keeping an eye out for passing beachgoers, while Bella insisted on claiming her spot on the chair, prompting Emily to scoot over. As she ran her fingers through Bella's luxurious fur, a loud purr rumbled in response. Emily could feel the tension melt from both their bodies.

Minutes later, Emily was startled out of her reverie when her phone announced an incoming text. Mike would meet her at Blue Water Marina in an hour with a deputy from the sheriff's department. What a relief. She updated Anthony and confirmed she would bring Bella's travel carrier in case they needed to take Hemingway with them. A quick check of the time meant she still had fifteen minutes to savor her coffee.

·   ·   ·

The drive from Emily's cottage took her along the sleepy barrier island toward the causeway connecting the beach to the town of Coral Shores. Blue Water Marina was strategically situated on the inland side of the bridge, on the Intracoastal Waterway, and only minutes away from the open waters of the Gulf.

The tropical vistas reminded her how fortunate she was to live in paradise. Coral Shores had maintained its small-town feel despite the seasonal influx of tourists who flocked to the area in search of suntans and keepsake seashells. In another month, the area would be inundated with snowbirds who stayed from Thanksgiving until Easter. Shop owners looked forward to the uptick in revenue, and waiting lists would be common at the local seafood restaurants.

Anthony, who lived closer to town, was waiting by his car when she pulled into the parking lot. The Blue Water Marina and Dive Shop hadn't changed since Emily took her diving course during high school. The weathered blue-gray exterior had survived years of Florida sunshine and the occasional hurricane. The red dive flag with its white diagonal stripe flapped in the wind from a flagpole mounted to the dock. The salty smell of the ocean and the funky odor emanating from a floating blob of sargassum seaweed permeated the air. Gulls cried overhead as stoic pelicans perched on dock pilings, patiently waiting for scraps from the fish-cleaning station. Two chest freezers sat on the dock pushed up against the building—one labeled *Ice,* and the other labeled *Bait.*

Emily counted about a dozen boats docked at the marina, sailboats with their melodic, clanging masts next to fishing boats of varying sizes. She was overwhelmed with sadness about William Todd's death and its impact on the local community. This was the largest marina servicing the town, and Billy had many friends.

A uniformed deputy sheriff and Mike peered in the marina window, while another man holding a toolbag waited at the front door. Emily and Anthony joined them, the cat carrier in hand. Mike introduced everyone, including the locksmith who'd been called to help them gain entry.

Anthony asked, "Do we need a warrant to go inside?"

"Not for a welfare check, even though this is the first time I can remember doing so for a cat." The deputy smiled. "Nobody answered the door, and we can't see or hear anyone moving around."

Mike nodded to the locksmith to start working on the door mechanism. It took only minutes until they heard the telltale click, then he turned the knob to confirm their access.

The deputy entered first, announcing their presence. "Coral Shores Sheriff's Department performing a wellness check."

Silence. Mike thanked the locksmith then turned on the overhead lights as they all stepped inside.

They waited while the deputy completed a quick search of the building. "I don't see a cat."

"She likely got scared after hearing us outside," Anthony said. "Cats are masters at hiding."

"Even cool cats like Hemingway." Emily walked behind the sales counter. "Almost every time I come in here, she's sleeping in this basket next to the swim fins."

They split up and spent ten minutes checking every nook and cranny in the shop, storage area, and adjacent rooms. Emily noticed the back office had a Murphy bed pulled down from the wall. She wondered if Billy had been living at the marina or used it to rest on long workdays. When they gathered together near the masks and snorkels, the deputy received a call on his radio.

Mike, the only other person in the room who could decipher the police codes they overheard, said, "I can handle things here, and we'll lock up when we leave."

"Thanks, Mike." The deputy, who had been summoned to another scene, nodded to Emily and Anthony and then hastily returned to his vehicle.

Anthony wandered over to the large sales counter and stared at the four open bags of cat treats. "That's strange."

"Hemingway." Emily spoke in a calm, gentle voice, followed by short smoochy sounds. "Here kitty, kitty, kitty."

Anthony echoed her calls while he rechecked all likely hiding spots. "Do you think he might have taken her somewhere to board?"

"It's possible, but at our last appointment, he asked me about our cat condos at the hospital and seemed interested. Doesn't mean he didn't choose another place. But we know he didn't leave town."

"Does the cat live here all the time, or does he bring her back and forth from his house?" Mike asked.

"I'm quite certain she lives here." Anthony walked to the middle of the room and looked up to the open ceiling rafters and smiled. "There she is."

CHAPTER FOUR

"How did she get there?" Mike craned his neck upward.

Emily moved next to Anthony to see where he was pointing. "Cats are as good at climbing as they are at hiding," she said.

"There's a stepladder over here, but it's not tall enough to reach the ceiling joists." Mike climbed to the top rung for a better vantage point. "Is she orange?" He squinted toward the back corner of the room.

"Yes, she's a long-haired orange tabby," Emily said. "Very sweet and very fluffy."

Mike stepped down onto something crunchy then lifted his shoe. "I think it's cat food."

Anthony squatted to examine the crumbs. "Those are some of her treats—the same ones that are on the counter." He climbed up the short ladder and stretched to place his hand on top of the only ceiling beam within reach. "There are a bunch more up here. Hemingway, it's okay," he said, repeating Emily's kissing sounds. The orange tabby wasn't budging.

"It looks like someone tried to entice her to come down with food," Mike said. "I'll look around outside for a taller ladder." They continued to call the kitty's name until Mike returned.

"Sorry. No luck," he said.

Anthony asked, "What are we going to do? We can't leave her up there."

"Something's really spooked her. Every time I've been in the store, she either ignores the customers or saunters over to them without a care in the world. She barely reacts when people come in with their dogs. This isn't like her," Emily said.

"I don't think a tall ladder would make a difference right now," Anthony said. "Her pupils are huge. She's scared, and if we try to grab her, I'm worried she'll scramble to get away and could hurt herself—or worse—she could fall."

"I agree. Mike, we should leave her alone right now, and Anthony and I can return later with some canned food to coax her down. We'll have more luck without all this commotion. Do you think that can be arranged?"

"Give me a minute, and I'll find out." He placed a call and walked outside to talk in private. When he came back into the store, he was still on the phone. "Let me check, and I'll get back to you."

"What's that about?" Emily asked.

Mike shared the latest development. The sheriff's office had tracked down William Todd's next of kin—Lauryn Todd. "She lives in Denver. She's quite upset at the news and told them she would be on the next plane and hoped to arrive in Coral Shores by tomorrow."

"I remember them being very close. Something happened between Lala and her mom, and she ended up moving in with him during high school. Uncle Billy never missed a single one of her swim meets," she said.

"I thought if we could find a spare set of keys to the marina, we can ask her for permission to return." He continued to search around the counter.

"Good idea. I'm sure she'd be comfortable with either of us coming back for Hemingway." Anthony motioned between himself and Emily. "Even though we've lost touch over the years, we used to be close friends."

"These might be what we're looking for." Mike shook the keys in his hand and walked over to the door. He tried a few without luck until the last one turned the lock. "Ah ha, got it. We can lock the place until you speak with Lauryn. The deputy gave me her contact info. I'll send it to your phones."

Emily looked at Anthony. "Do you want to call her or should I?"

"I think you were closer with her because of swim team and scuba diving. Tell her how sorry I am about Uncle Billy."

"I will. Let's go so Hemingway can feel safe and come out of hiding. There are enough landing zones for her to climb back down. Cats are smart. If they can get up, they can usually get down on their own." Emily led the men out of the marina store, then Mike locked the door before handing over the keys.

•   •   •

Emily did her best to preserve Sundays for quiet time—to catch up after a hectic week. In over her head when she bought the Coral Shores Veterinary Hospital from Dr. Dinsmore, her learning curve had been steep. A major part of that decision had been convincing Anthony to leave his job as head veterinary technician at a big referral practice in Tampa to return home and take over the role of hospital manager. His talents and support played a key role in going forward with the purchase.

Even with him by her side, there were moments when she'd second-guessed her decision. Hospital ownership came early in her career, fueled by a desperate need for something to ground herself. After her mother's death, Emily was buried by grief and unable to fathom moving away from the beach cottage where they had spent so much time together. Being surrounded by a lifetime of memories—all the holiday dinners and family events—helped her feel connected to her mom, but Bella was the most important link. She had promised her mom she would give Bella a wonderful life.

Working in a big-city referral hospital had been Emily's dream, but she couldn't imagine being far away from her brother and his family after everything they'd been through. As she pulled into her driveway, she thought about Lala and hoped she also had family nearby to lean on.

Elvis ran to greet her at the door, tail wagging as he spun and hopped on his hind feet. "Good boy." She leaned over to rub behind his ears. "Where's Bella?"

"Meow."

"Oh, there you are." Bella stepped out of Emily's bedroom and grabbed the edge of the living room carpet with her front claws before executing an exaggerated kitty stretch. "Let's get some treats."

Cat and dog followed her into the kitchen with clear expectations of snacks to be had. Elvis finished his in two seconds then gave Bella a lick on the side of her head before returning to his nap on the couch. Bella grimaced but resumed eating. Not able to stomach a full meal, Emily added some frozen fruit and coconut milk into a blender and took her smoothie outside to enjoy on her beachfront deck.

Mike had offered to cancel his tennis match to spend the afternoon with Emily. She waved him off but not before making plans for him to return for dinner when Duncan and Jane would be stopping by to pick up Elvis. She needed some time alone to compose herself before calling Lauryn.

The sun was high in the sky, and a fresh cool breeze blew, a rare commodity in south Florida. Both Elvis and Bella joined her on the chaise lounge—Elvis at her feet and Bella next to her hip. Once her four-legged emotional support system had settled in, she picked up her phone. Still uncertain about how much she should share, she wanted to be there for Lauryn as she dealt with the trauma of losing Billy. Especially since she had been the one to find him. In the end, no words could soften the blow from this devastating news.

CHAPTER FIVE

"Lauryn?" Nobody spoke on the other end of the line, so Emily double-checked her phone to ensure the call hadn't dropped. "Lala, are you there?"

"Yes, sorry. It's me." She whispered, her voice sounding scratchy.

"It's Emily Benton."

"Oh, Em."

"I'm so sorry about Billy." She paused, uncertain what to say next. It would be best to follow Lauryn's lead since discussing the gruesome aspects could be overwhelming so soon after receiving the news about her uncle's death.

"Thanks. I just talked to him yesterday. I don't understand what happened. He's an expert diver."

"I'm not sure what they told you, but I wanted you to know I'm the one who found him on the beach."

"That was you? The deputy said a Good Samaritan gave him CPR until the paramedics arrived. Thank you, Em."

"I wish I'd got there sooner."

"You did everything possible. I talked to the doctor at the hospital, and they said there was nothing they could do to revive him."

"Is there anything you need? Anthony was with me this morning after they took Billy in the ambulance. He wanted me to tell you how sorry he was."

"Oh, I could use one of Anthony's bear hugs right about now. I miss seeing you both. It's been way too long. Why does it always take a funeral to bring people together? And Em, I feel horrible I didn't make it back for your mom's celebration of life ceremony. Billy had offered to pay for my flight, but my boss wouldn't give me the time off work."

"It's okay. I understand. Your card and note meant a lot to me." Emily didn't want to make this moment about her loss. Plus, she still found it hard to talk about her mom.

"Well, today, when the police called about Billy, I told my boss I had to leave right away, and he said if I didn't show up for my shift, I'd better not bother coming back. What a jerk. But I'm not surprised. He's a horrible human being. I probably shouldn't have, but I quit. It was a crappy waitressing job anyway. I'm booked on the last flight out tonight."

"Do you want us to pick you up at the airport?"

"No, but thanks. I don't land until after midnight, and I arranged for a car to drive me from the airport to the marina. I can use Billy's truck once I get there."

"You're going to stay at Blue Water? What about Billy's place, or is there any other family in the area?"

"No, it's just Billy and me. He tried to hide it, but he'd been living at the marina for a few months after being forced to sell his condo. Money had been tight, and he got behind on his mortgage payments. The dive shop was his baby—his passion, and he'd rather give up his place than lose the business. Plus, I'm worried about Hemingway."

Now the Murphy bed in the marina office made sense to Emily. "About Hemingway. Anthony and I were worried about her too, so we had the sheriff's department help us get into the store this morning—"

Lala interrupted her. "Is she okay?"

"She's fine, or she will be. We couldn't find her at first because she'd climbed up into the ceiling rafters and wouldn't come down."

"That's not like her. Now I'm really concerned."

"I think all the activity outside and loud knocks on the door scared her. If it's okay with you, Anthony and I plan to go back this afternoon to check on her. The store is locked, but we found a set of keys to the front door. We'll bring some extra tasty canned food to entice her if she's still in hiding. She knows us, so we'll have more luck on our own."

"Yes, please do whatever is best for Hemingway. Billy loved that cat. He thought of her as his mascot for the marina, a talisman that brought him *Fair Winds and Following Seas*. He said the only good thing about losing his condo was that he got to bunk up with Hemingway." Then the line went quiet until Emily heard her friend sobbing.

"Lala?"

"I'm here." She blew her nose and cleared her throat. "I can't believe he's gone. What am I going to do?"

"I don't know, but it helped me to take one day at a time. Otherwise, it can become overwhelming."

"You're right. I started jumping ahead, and it's too much. Finding out you and Anthony are in town is the very best news. I haven't called Coral Shores my home for so many years, but now, I'm desperate to get back."

"Well, don't worry about Hemingway. I'll send you an update on how she's doing as soon as we get there. Do you need me to hide the keys somewhere for you?"

"No, I have my set and can get the spare keys from you later. Thank you again. I'll call you and Anthony in the morning. And Em, I'm really glad to hear your voice."

•   •   •

Emily selected a variety of Bella's favorite cans of food and texted Anthony she'd be leaving soon and should be at the marina in twenty minutes. They'd given Hemingway enough time alone to feel safe, and hopefully, she would be in her regular spot—the kitty bed behind the register.

Walking around the marina this morning brought back a ton of memories from her diving course. Setting up your scuba gear before a dive followed a strict and unchanging sequence of tasks. That muscle memory ensured no important step would be overlooked. Billy had always stressed safety, and whether you were prepping for a first dive or your thousandth dive, the process remained the same.

He was also a stickler for practice and discipline. Once you become a certified scuba diver, your license remains valid for the rest of your life. But Billy required any diver who had not been diving for over a year to buddy up with him. He'd run them through a mini refresher course to ensure they were comfortable below the water and knew what they were doing.

That's what made it so hard to imagine what happened to him on his last dive. He kept his gear in perfect working order, so she had to assume he'd had a medical emergency. A reef wall not far off the beach meant a diver could get to depths beyond a hundred feet without traveling miles offshore.

Emily could have used a wading entry to scuba dive in front of her cottage, but it wasn't safe to go alone. The buddy system ensured there would be someone there to help in case of an emergency. They'd even paired up to practice emergency drills as part of their certification.

"That's it." Emily put her hand across her forehead when she realized why she felt so unsettled. Why was Billy diving by himself? And if he wasn't alone, where was the other diver?

CHAPTER SIX

"Have there been any missing person reports filed in the past day?" Emily asked.

"What?"

She took a deep breath, realizing she'd fired off her question without even saying hello. "Sorry—Hi, Mike."

"What's going on?"

"I've been thinking about scuba diving and my time spent in Billy's shop. That's when it hit me. Why would he be out alone? The buddy system is the most important safety factor in planning a dive. Billy hammered that into our brains over and over again."

"I can check. Give me a few minutes, and I'll call you back."

Emily paced around the room, tapping her finger against her phone. Elvis jumped off the couch, following behind in concentric circles.

She looked down at the enthusiastic terrier. "I promise to take you for another walk when I get back."

He tilted his head from side to side, a dog's way of saying, *I understand* or at least, *I'm trying to understand.*

The buzzing phone in her hand startled her, even though she had expected the call.

"So, nobody has filed a missing person report in Coral Shores or the surrounding counties in the past twenty-four hours," Mike said.

She continued to pace. "How did he get out to his dive location? It didn't dawn on me to check the marina for his boat. It's called *Diver Down*."

"All good questions. The deputy who took your statement is a friend. I'll reach out to her for a status update. Other than collecting basic information surrounding the fatality, she'll be waiting on the autopsy results before taking any further action."

"How long will that be?"

"Likely a couple of days."

"Okay. Thanks for looking into that for me. I'm heading to the marina to meet Anthony, and I talked with Lauryn. She gave us permission to do whatever's necessary to care for Hemingway until she gets to town."

"I'm here to help if you need anything—just let me know."

"I will. Duncan and Jane should be arriving around five o'clock for dinner, but if you want to come early, I should be home by four."

"I'll plan on it."

·　　·　　·

Emily got out of the car and waved at Anthony. She slung a tote bag filled with cans of cat food and feathered toys over her shoulder while holding the carrier in her other hand.

"Hi, Em. I picked up some tins of sardines on my way over. A rescue group I worked with in Tampa used them to lure feral cats for their trap-neuter-release programs. They're disgusting, but I'm not a cat. Hope it works."

"Great idea. Before we go inside, I want to check if Billy's boat is docked in the marina." She shared her concerns about the solo dive. "I'm glad no other diver has gone missing, but it makes his accident more confusing."

A large sailboat obscured their view until they reached the main dock. Emily immediately recognized *Diver Down*, docked in its usual spot. The wide-hulled vessel had an open stern deck lined with benches and racks for divers to stow their gear and secure their tanks. Freshwater buckets used to clean underwater cameras between dives sat under the shaded cabin. Laminated placards mounted on center supports identified the fish, corals, and marine mammals commonly spotted when diving the tropical waters of south Florida. The side entry door was closed, and the gangway and dive platform had been pulled onto the deck.

"I'm not making that jump," Anthony said before Emily tried to talk him into performing the gymnastic-style leap necessary to get onboard.

She had placed her bag and the carrier on the dock to lighten the load, which made the incredulous expression on her face less convincing. "Did I say anything about jumping?"

"I know you, Em. You can't help yourself."

She smiled and shrugged. *How does he always know what I'm thinking?*

"Since his boat is here, that means someone else was with him and drove the boat back to the marina, or he went diving on a different boat. But why would he do that? He loved *Diver Down*."

"I can't imagine someone abandoned him on a dive, but that's for the sheriff's department to figure out. We're here for Hemingway. Come on, Em."

·   ·   ·

They spoke in hushed tones as they unlocked the door to the marina store. Emily hid the carrier from view in case it triggered a fight-or-flight response from Hemingway. Cats hated being put in a carrier since it always signaled a car trip which often ended with a vet visit. Emily and Anthony had instituted changes at the hospital to foster a "Fear-Free" environment for both cats and dogs. During her last appointment, Hemingway had loved the warmed towels placed on the exam table and the computer monitor displaying swimming goldfish.

Anthony shook a bag of treats—a welcoming sound to most cats. Hemingway was nowhere to be seen. He climbed the step ladder to check her previous hiding spot.

"That's not good—she hasn't moved," he said, pointing to the orange tabby huddled in the far corner of the ceiling joists.

"I thought for sure she would have come down by now. Especially since it's been quiet in here."

Emily set her bag of toys and food on the counter, and that's when she noticed an open can of cat food. "Anthony." He turned to see her holding the can. "This wasn't here before, was it?"

He stepped off the ladder and joined her. "No. There were bags of cat treats, but they weren't scattered around like they are now."

"Someone's been here. Let me text Lala to find out if she knows anything about it." Emily typed her message.

"I think we'll have the best chance to get her down if we're quiet, play some classical music—cats love that, and open the can of sardines. If we ignore her, she may feel less threatened," Anthony said.

Emily looked around. "The only chair in here is the stool behind the counter. I'll grab a blanket out of the back office, and we can sit on the floor." She returned with a well-used quilt, its red and white squares forming a scuba diving flag. Anthony found a classical music channel on his phone app and put it on speaker.

"Gross." He placed the open tin of sardines on the other side of the store, closer to where Hemingway would descend, then joined Emily on the quilt. "And now we wait."

Over the next half hour, they reminisced about their high school days and time spent with Lala. It would be great to see her again. Even better if she settled back in town for good.

"Don't look, but I think we have movement," Anthony said, using only his eyes to motion upward.

"Please, please, please, let this work," Emily whispered.

"It will."

They held their breath as Hemingway navigated her way down. After she jumped to the floor, she froze, staring at Emily and Anthony for any signs of threat. They didn't move a muscle. The cat crouched low, then crawled toward the sardines. Once she had her first bite, her body relaxed. In no time, she devoured half the tin.

"She must have been starving," Emily said.

Hemingway groomed herself, starting with her front legs, then licked her oversized paws before wiping her face—a normal cat behavior to signal her comfort with their presence.

"Hemingway." Anthony tossed a few treats in her direction. She followed the trail, eating as she moved along. He lured her to the edge of the quilt, where she stared at them with her beautiful green eyes.

The long-haired orange tabby cat had a thick, shiny coat, and her bottlebrush tail stood straight up, the tip flicking rapidly to show her interest. An ornate kitty collar had *Hemingway* engraved on the pendant. Her unique and defining feature was her oversized front paws. The extra sixth toe made it look as if she had pulled on a pair of fuzzy mittens.

Anthony extended his finger for her to sniff. She approached and rubbed her cheeks along his hand and purred.

Emily exhaled through pursed lips. "Your reputation as a cat whisperer remains intact."

Anthony had been sitting with his legs crossed, giving Hemingway a space to curl up. As he petted her under her chin, she closed her eyes but continued to purr.

"Crisis averted." Emily smiled. Her phone vibrated to signal an incoming text, which she read aloud. "Lala didn't authorize anyone else to come into the store."

The hair on her arms stood on end as she glanced around, half-expecting a bogeyman to emerge from the shadows.

Eyes wide open, Anthony said, "Then who was in here?"

CHAPTER SEVEN

Emily scanned the store, looking for anything out of place.

"Stay here with Hemingway. I want to double-check if all the windows and doors are locked."

She started with the front door, as she couldn't remember if they had secured it upon arrival. The windowless storeroom contained limited inventory. Emily assumed Billy kept most of his stock on display. A locked side door led to a small fenced yard that housed the air compressor and equipment used to fill scuba tanks. A padlock secured the gate on the outer fence. Emily jiggled it just to be sure.

She came inside, locked the door, and walked into the office. Nothing stood out, but since she'd only been searching for a cat the last time, she couldn't be certain. There were papers scattered around the desk next to a docking station, but no laptop. The jalousie windows were cranked shut and locked. The far corner of the room had been converted into a makeshift kitchen, including a hot plate, microwave, and shelves stocked with cereal, pasta, tuna, and crackers. The mini bar fridge held a few condiments, two bottles of beer, and a variety of takeout containers. A bathroom with a small shower completed the space. Definite signs that Billy Todd had been living at the marina.

"So?" Anthony asked, still trapped on the quilt with Hemingway fast asleep in his lap.

"Everything is secure and looks as you'd expect. Wait, let me check the till." She walked behind the sales counter and pressed the release button on the register. The inner tray contained basic change and a few bills in small denominations.

"There isn't much money in the drawer, like how we set up our cash tray after pulling the day's sales for deposit."

"That makes me feel better. Obviously, a burglar wasn't in here. Besides, what type of criminal brings canned cat food to a heist? Maybe Billy planned to be away and hired a pet sitter to feed and check on Hemingway."

"That makes sense. Lala wouldn't necessarily be aware of those arrangements. Plus, none of the doors look tampered with, and the windows are locked. Whoever came in here had a key."

"They were probably trying to do exactly what we did—entice Hemingway out of hiding." Anthony looked down at the tabby. "She's the sweetest thing, but my legs are falling asleep sitting like this. I don't want to disturb her, but I need to get up. Can you help me?"

"Let me fluff her favorite bed on the back of the counter first." Emily refolded the cushy blanket to create a nest then lifted the sleeping cat into her arms. Hemingway hung loose like a rag doll, and as soon as Emily placed her in her bed, she curled up, tucked her paws under her chin, and resumed her nap.

"That's more like it. She must be exhausted after her ordeal. Let me find out what Lala wants us to do." Emily exchanged texts while Anthony walked around to stretch his legs. He scooped the litter box, filled the water bowl, and placed a fresh can of food in a dish he found in the kitchen. She still had lots of kibble, so he tossed the remaining sardines. They were stinking up the place.

"Lala asked if we could come back one more time today. She should arrive sometime after midnight."

"Don't you have Duncan and the kids coming for dinner and to pick up Elvis?"

Emily nodded. "And Mike, too."

"Well, in that case, I'll check on her later. Marc and I had planned to eat out at the Thirsty Pelican—it's trivia night, and you know how much he loves that. We won't be late since tomorrow is a work day."

"Thanks. I told Lala we'll hold on to the keys in case she's delayed. She's going to stop by the hospital once she's settled." Emily looked at the sleeping feline. "I feel better about everything now. It would be more stressful for Hemingway to put her in the carrier and take her home with us or to the kitty condos at the hospital. Plus, she's used to being alone overnight."

"She seemed to respond to my music. Did you see a stereo in the office?"

"There was a small marine radio above the desk. It looks like an old-fashioned car radio. Let me grab it."

With the channel tuned to a local easy listening station, Emily and Anthony tiptoed out, double-checking the lock before leaving their separate ways.

•   •   •

"Okay, Elvis. I promised you a walk, and I never break my promises. Bella, we'll be back soon." She clipped the leash onto the eager terrier and stepped onto her beachfront deck. Emily ran with Elvis while he chased the waves breaking onshore. Once he'd burned some of his excess energy, they turned back for the cottage. Always grateful her mom had installed an outdoor shower with a handheld wand, she washed Elvis so he would be clean and fluffy to greet his family.

"It's my turn now." She had an hour until Mike arrived. Just thinking about it caused her heart to flutter. They'd been dating for a few months now, and despite an early hiccup over some miscommunication, things were getting more serious. They hadn't made any grand declarations, but that was okay since she preferred to take things slow. Mike seemed to be on the same page, and they had been spending more time together lately. Things were good right now. No need to mess with it.

•   •   •

Mike knocked on the door then let himself in. "Em," he called out into the cottage.

"I'm on the deck," she replied. "Hanging with Bella and Elvis."

He walked through the patio doors, a wide smile on his face. "Any room for me on that chair?"

Elvis jumped down to greet him in the usual over-the-top friendly way, followed by Bella.

"She barely acknowledges me when I come home unless she wants food," Emily said. The giant cat stepped in front of Elvis, then flopped over at Mike's feet, inviting him to rub her belly. "She's shameless."

Once they wrapped up their greeting, Mike moved fast to fill the empty spot next to Emily before the cat, dog, or both got there first.

"This is more like it." He wrapped his arms around her, and she turned toward him, melting into his body. They kissed, gently at first, then with more intensity until Elvis interrupted with a "*Yip.*" He stared at them from the foot of the chair.

They both laughed and invited him to settle in between them.

"Duncan and Jane should be here soon. I've got a tray of chicken enchiladas in the oven for dinner."

"When did you find time to cook?"

"Oh, I didn't. It's from Agave Sol—I love their food." Emily always had aspirations about making homemade meals, but the hectic pace of her life seemed to get in the way.

"Em, I didn't tell Duncan about William Todd. He had his hands full this weekend coaching Mac's baseball team at the tournament. Thought it would be better if he heard it from you, since I wasn't sure how well he knew him."

"Oh, boy." Emily exhaled. "I'll tell him. I don't think he interacted with Billy much since he was never interested in scuba diving. At least this time, there's no murder involved."

More than once, she had to call her brother after stumbling into a crime scene. She never went looking for trouble, but it never stopped him from bristling at her involvement. Duncan and Emily were close—they always had been, and even more so after their mom died. But her older brother often forgot she was a capable young professional and continued to treat her like his little sister. That dynamic had created conflict in the past when Emily inserted herself in his investigations. Always looking out for the victim, she refused to stand by as the criminal justice system moved along at what felt like a snail's pace to an outside observer.

"Promise to have my back if he gets upset?" she asked.

"I got you." He held her tight, nuzzling her neck until Elvis popped up, ears forward, wagging his tail.

"They must be here."

Emily held Elvis in her arms so he wouldn't dart out the door to greet his favorite two people on earth—Mac and Ava, her niece and nephew. Emily had been watching over Elvis ever since that fateful veterinary house call when she found him distraught, sitting next to his deceased owner, Mrs. Eliza Klein. Mrs. Klein had been her and Anthony's piano teacher when they were kids and a mentor during their high school days. She worked tirelessly for every animal related charity in Coral Shores, most notably with sea turtle rescue. Emily immediately fell in love with the little terrier and had been ecstatic when her brother and his wife, Jane, adopted him into their family.

"Elvis!" Mac and Ava shouted as they stormed through the front door. The kids' red hair marked them as Bentons. While Duncan was more strawberry blond growing up, nobody doubted they were all related.

Mac had recently celebrated his eighth birthday at a Tampa Bay Rays baseball game. He was obsessed with all things baseball. Ava, his little sister and the artistic one in the family, kept everyone laughing with her already well-developed comedic timing.

Emily struggled to hold the wiggling terrier and had to set him on the floor. He inundated the kids with dog kisses and demands for belly rubs, resulting in squeals of delight.

"He's all they've been talking about the entire way home from the tournament," Jane said as she stepped into the cottage. "Em, thanks again for taking care of him."

"Are you kidding me? I love having him here."

Her brother closed the door behind him. "Does Bella agree with you?"

"I think so. Sometimes she acts put off, but deep down, she loves him, too."

Emily checked on the enchiladas then stood with the fridge door open. "Anyone want a drink?"

"I could use a cold beer." Duncan joined her in the kitchen.

"How was the tournament?" Emily asked.

"We made it to the playoffs, but lost in a nail-biter. The kids did amazing, especially considering it was the first tournament for most of them."

Emily extended a bottle to her brother and as he reached for it, she held on, forcing him to lock eyes with her. Under her breath, she whispered, "I have something I need to tell you." She let go of Duncan's beer and motioned for him to follow her onto the deck, out of earshot of the kids.

CHAPTER EIGHT

"Again! You found a dead body, again," Duncan said after hearing the news.

"Yes and no." Emily recounted her early morning walk on the beach with Elvis, administering CPR, and William Todd's apparent diving accident.

"Why didn't you call me?"

"You were busy coaching the kids and besides, Mike and Anthony were on speed dial."

"I'm sorry, Em. I know you were close with Lala and admired her uncle."

"I'm just really sad, and my heart breaks for Lala. Do you remember how much time she spent at our house back in high school?"

"I do. Didn't her mom have some problems and ended up leaving town?"

"Yeah. I think she had been in and out of rehab, and that's when Billy took Lala in. He really stepped up for her. We haven't been in touch for years, but Anthony and I are here to help her with anything she needs."

When Mike joined them on the deck, Duncan asked him, "Who's handling the case?"

"Deputy Garcia."

Duncan nodded. "I'll check with her in the morning. See, that's why I never got scuba certified. Too many things can go wrong. Plus, I feel claustrophobic breathing through a snorkel."

Emily wondered how the two Benton siblings could have been raised in the same house. She spent her childhood in and under the water. Duncan preferred the security of a fishing boat.

"Scuba is safe if you follow the rules, and that includes always diving with a buddy. I don't understand why he would be out there alone—"

Mac poked his head through the sliding door. "Auntie Em. Come quick." He waved her over, putting an end to their conversation about Billy.

"Look." He raised his flat hand in front of the terrier and said, "High five." Elvis tapped it with his paw.

Jane clapped. "Yay! They've been working hard on that one."

Ava moved in front of her brother, asking Elvis to repeat his new trick.

"That deserves a cookie." Emily retrieved a few of Elvis's favorite peanut butter-flavored snacks from the kitchen.

The kids repeated his new skill until the cookies ran out and the terrier lost interest. He ran to retrieve a ball, dropped it at their feet, then danced in anticipation of their throw.

Jane followed Emily into the kitchen. "Need any help with dinner?"

"Can you set the table? Food's ready, and I figured you'd all be tired and want to get home early."

"We are. When Mac made this travel baseball team, we were ecstatic—but these weekends are exhausting. Watching Duncan with the kids makes me fall in love with him all over again. You should see him, Em."

She smiled at Jane. When her brother introduced his college girlfriend to the family, she and Jane bonded immediately. Duncan's attraction had been obvious with Jane's petite frame and beach-blond beauty, but it was her confidence, humor, and brilliant mind that captivated him, leading to a marriage proposal.

Emily finally had the sister she had always wanted, and she and Jane often spent time together without Duncan. She vividly remembered her mother cradling Mac and Ava as newborns, memories she cherished deeply. Staying close to her only family had been one of the main reasons Emily remained in Coral Shores after her mom passed away. Her happiest days were playing with the kids on the beach—she couldn't imagine a life without them.

"Dinner's ready," Emily called out.

Everyone followed her onto the beach deck and within minutes, the table became silent. She'd made a good choice for tonight's menu.

"Auntie Em, I love *en-chip-lapas*." Ava swirled a forkful in the air before shoving it in her mouth with gusto.

Emily giggled. "I'm glad you like them, and I have ice cream sandwiches for dessert, too."

The kids gobbled down their food so they could resume playing with Elvis. Jane gathered up all the dog toys, food, and his bed to load into the car.

"Sorry to eat and run," Duncan said, as he cleared the table. "And thanks again for watching Elvis, and for dinner." He turned toward the kids. "Say good night to Auntie Em and Mr. Mike."

"Will you let me know what you find out about Billy from Deputy Garcia? Lauryn might be stopping by the hospital in the morning."

Mike walked into the kitchen and stood watching the two of them. To Emily, it looked like he was holding his breath. On prior occasions when she had inserted herself in one of her brother's cases, the tension between the Benton siblings spilled over to those around them. Anthony and Mike were often innocent bystanders when Emily pushed for answers or investigated clues on her own.

"Sure," Duncan said. "It sounds like a tragic but routine investigation. There might not be much to share."

Stunned by his capitulation, Emily could only manage a quiet "Thanks"—until small arms wrapped around her legs, catching her off guard.

"I love you, Auntie Em."

Emily lifted her niece and hugged her tight. "I love you, too, Ava the Brave."

"Why do you call me that?"

"Because you're strong, and smart, and fearless." When she set her down, Ava posed in a superhero stance, hands on hips, feet wide, and chin out.

"I am brave," she said. Then she ran to join Mac and Elvis at the front door.

Mike laughed. "I think you've got your hands full, Duncan."

"Don't I know it." He patted Mike on the shoulder and turned to leave.

"Night, Em." Jane waved from across the room. "Okay, kids. Let's go."

•   •   •

"That was fun," Mike said. "How are you holding up? It's been a long, difficult day."

"Actually, I'm sort of numb. Anthony and Marc are stopping by the marina on their way home to check on Hemingway one last time before Lala gets there. I'm eager to hear if everything is okay."

Mike pulled her close and brushed a loose strand of hair away from her eyes, holding her gaze before kissing her softly. "You're good to your friends."

Emily put her arms around his waist, resting her head against his firm chest, and hugged him tight. She stood that way for almost a minute with her eyes closed.

"Are you falling asleep standing up?" Mike stepped back and grinned.

"Maybe—that's a first. Sorry, I'm exhausted."

"Don't apologize. Listen, we both have an early start tomorrow, and even though I'd love nothing more than to spend the evening with you, I'm going to head home. Unless you want me to stay?"

"I always want you to stay, but after Anthony calls with his update, I'm going to crash for the night. Can I get a rain check?"

"You can cash in any time." He kissed her again, this time, more passionately. Emily melted in his embrace and rethought her need for sleep. He gently caressed her face before gathering his keys. Emily watched him walk to his car through the front window, still feeling weak in the knees.

"It's just you and me, Bella." Using both hands, she scooped up her enormous cat, then used her elbows to switch off the lights before moving into the bedroom. After changing and washing up, she checked the time. Anthony should be at the marina by now.

Emily dozed off waiting for his call. She checked for messages. Nothing. As she entered his number, her phone buzzed.

"Hey. I was just calling you. How is Heming—"

Anthony interrupted her. "Em, we've got a problem."

CHAPTER NINE

Emily sprang out of bed, stepped into her flip-flops, grabbed her keys and purse, and bolted out the door. Anthony said it would be easier to show her once she arrived—whatever that meant. During her drive to Blue Water Marina, her mind scurried down a rabbit hole full of things that could have caused him such alarm.

She pulled into the seashell driveway for the marina and parked next to Marc's car. All the lights were on inside the scuba shop, illuminating the nearby docks. Emily sprinted for the door but slowed her entry to avoid startling Hemingway.

Anthony sat on the dive flag quilt in the center of the room but stood to greet her. "That was fast."

"Well, you sounded upset. What's wrong?"

Both men pointed to the rafters. "That's what's wrong,"

Emily saw Hemingway perched on a beam, backed into the far corner of the ceiling.

"Oh, no. Was she up there when you arrived?"

Anthony nodded. "When we got here, I searched for her in her regular spots but didn't find her. Then I noticed that." He pointed to the open can of cat food sitting on the counter near Hemingway's kitty bed. "Something's wrong. We didn't leave that out for her."

Marc said, "Anthony was focused on finding Hemingway, but I'm sure I heard a door closing in the back of the shop when we walked in. The door was locked, but I ran around the outside of the building and saw a truck turning out of the lot, heading toward town. Of course, they could have been parked anywhere at the marina—I wasn't paying attention when we arrived."

"I thought if we sat quietly, like last time, she might come down," Anthony said. "But I don't have any sardines with me, so we pulled some shrimp from our restaurant doggy bag. Hope it works."

Emily nodded, and the three sat on the quilt, listening to the classical music streaming from Marc's phone app.

She said, "I've never known Hemingway to act fearful with the customers in the shop. But something or someone is scaring her."

"I texted Lala," Anthony said. "She was boarding her flight but planned to call a locksmith in the morning to change the locks. Marc and I agreed to stay until her flight lands."

"She's moving." Marc motioned upward.

It took a few minutes, but Hemingway repeated her descent route and headed straight for the shrimp. After polishing off her treat, she walked toward Anthony and didn't hesitate before curling up in his lap.

He rubbed along her cheeks and under her chin. The orange tabby cat stretched her front legs, her loud purrs drowning out the latest concerto.

"Look. She's making biscuits." Marc pointed to the rhythmic motion as she flexed and extended her toes. "That's a good sign."

They heaved a collective sigh of relief.

"I don't understand this. Billy loved Hemingway. I can't imagine any scenario where he would hire a pet sitter if he knew she reacted this way," Emily said.

Anthony slowly shifted his legs but avoided disturbing the cat. "But it's possible he didn't know."

"I guess. I'm glad Lala will be here soon. If this keeps up, Hemingway may hurt herself."

Emily stayed for another hour before heading home. Anthony and Marc would wait until Lala was en route from the airport. Tomorrow's reunion with their friend would be bittersweet. Lala had to navigate her grief after her uncle's death while making decisions about his funeral and whether to reopen the marina and dive shop. Emily understood how daunting that must be, so she planned to be there to support her friend any way possible.

•   •   •

The Coral Shores Veterinary Hospital buzzed with activity. Clients dropping off their cats and dogs for surgery, boarding, and grooming filled the lobby waiting area. Abigail, the head receptionist, handled it all with ease.

Emily had settled into her office to review the schedule for the day when Anthony joined her.

"Any word from Lala?" he asked.

"Not yet. What about you?"

"No. I waited up last night to hear from her. She got to the marina after one o'clock and texted a picture of Hemingway in her kitty bed." Anthony turned his phone to show Emily. "Lala said she's acting like her old self."

"That's a relief. I'm sure they're both exhausted and are probably still sleeping. I'll call later this morning."

"Did you see who's coming in?"

Emily smiled. "Yes, I can't wait."

•   •   •

Phoenix, an eleven-year-old black Border Collie mix with a sprinkling of gray on her muzzle like powdered sugar, was one of Coral Shores' most beloved canine ambassadors. When Elizabeth rescued Phoenix, the sweet pup struggled with many health challenges, including the amputation of her right hind leg. To celebrate Phoenix's adoption or "Gotcha Day" every year, Elizabeth hosted a fundraiser to benefit the Coral Shores Humane Society. So far, Phoenix's annual shindig, the Yappy Barkday Pawty, had raised over twelve thousand dollars. Always in fashion, Phoenix wore a signature flower on her collar and was known for giving heartfelt dog kisses.

"Hi, Dr. Benton. Hi, Anthony," Elizabeth said as they entered the exam room.

Phoenix hopped up to greet them, accepting all their pets and attention.

"I love her collar. It looks like a purple sunflower," Emily said.

"It's an aster. I have them in my garden, and a local artist created the flower for her. Phoenix is partial to purples and reds."

"It's my favorite one so far. Her pansies were cute too."

Anthony continued to pet Phoenix while Emily and Elizabeth discussed the reason for their visit. Phoenix was a lean, athletic dog. Now in her senior years, she occasionally suffered from the equivalent of a sore back. Dogs with a hind limb amputation often adjusted their gait for balance, and that could put a strain on their muscles.

"I want her to feel her best. With the fundraiser less than two weeks away, we have lots of social engagements on the calendar."

Emily completed her exam and agreed that Phoenix had some tightness and discomfort in her lower lumbar or back muscles. Anthony walked the dog down the hallway, and they noticed her placing her left hind leg under the center of her body, creating a curvature of her spine. After only a minute of gentle massage, Emily felt Phoenix relax her muscles.

"Look at her face. She likes that," Elizabeth said.

"When her muscles become strained, it affects her mobility. There's a new veterinary rehab practice in town, and they have a registered canine massage therapist on staff. Phoenix would benefit from some physical therapy." She provided their contact information.

"That's marvelous. She'll be getting a massage for her birthday this year. I'll call them right away and get their first available appointment. Thank you, Dr. Benton. I have to admit, I thought it might be more serious."

"If she's still struggling after consulting with the rehab vet, bring her back for a recheck. I'm going to dispense a few doses of an anti-inflammatory you can give her if she's uncomfortable. Just make sure you give it with food."

Anthony handed Phoenix a dog cookie. "I'll send her referral request through their online portal right now." He petted her again before leaving the room.

"Are you and your staff able to attend the Barkday Pawty?"

"We wouldn't miss it."

· · ·

Emily worked through a morning of routine appointments that included a skin infection, a broken toenail, and annual wellness checkups on healthy cats and dogs. By the lunch break, she joined Anthony in his office to discuss the staff schedule for the upcoming month.

He said, "I still haven't heard from Lala. Should we be worried?"

"Why don't we swing by after work? It's been so long since we've hung out together, she might not feel comfortable asking us for help. Let's make it easy on her—we can show up with dinner. Let her know she's not alone."

"Good idea. Marc is working on a big project and will be late tonight. He wants to meet her, so maybe he can drop by when he's done."

They were debating what takeout to order when Abigail called over the hospital intercom.

"Dr. Benton. Anthony. There's a Lauryn Todd here to see you." Then she whispered into the phone. "She's on her way to your office. She's really upset."

Emily and Anthony turned toward the open doorway. Lala stood before them, her shoulders shaking and tears streaming down her face. Between sobs, she pushed out the words, "I need your help."

CHAPTER TEN

Before Lala slumped to the floor, they pulled her into a group hug, holding her until the sobs subsided. She eventually stood tall and took a step back.

"Look at the two of you." Lala smiled. "It's like only a day has passed since we were hanging out together."

Lala had cut her long black hair into a short bob. She stood two inches shorter than Emily, her frame more delicate than they remembered. But the exhaustion on her face couldn't dim her beauty. Her high cheekbones and dark, expressive eyes reflected her mom's Korean and her dad's South American heritage.

Anthony ran to grab a third chair so they could sit together.

Emily handed her a box of tissues. "Did you get any sleep?"

"An hour or two. I think Hemingway was lonely. She kept pawing at my arm to pet her, but she eventually curled up next to me, and we both fell asleep." Lala's voice trailed off as she stared out the window at the palm tree swaying in the breeze. "After I moved to Denver, I never thought I'd call Florida home again. I guess that's proof you should never say never."

"Well, we're glad you're here." Emily wiped a tear from her own cheek.

"You said you needed our help," Anthony said.

"I'm heartbroken about Billy. He was that person who always had my back and supported me no matter what. Even when I messed up—and I did that a lot. I don't know what I'm going to do without him."

Emily understood. Anthony was her person, and she couldn't imagine life without her best friend by her side. She said, "All I know is that when things seem overwhelming, it helps to take it one day at a time. One task at a time."

"You're right. I called a locksmith this morning, and they've already changed all the locks at the marina. I don't know who's been coming in to feed Hemingway, or who else might have a key to the place. I didn't feel safe until I knew it was secure."

"Good. Finding Hemingway up in the ceiling worried me. She's always so calm and confident around people," Emily said.

"Would it be easier if you had somewhere else to stay?" Anthony asked. "Do you or Billy have any family in the area?"

"No. It's just the two of us. My mom was adopted, and Billy was her only sibling. I never knew my dad, since he passed away when I was a baby. The rest of his family still lives in Columbia, but I don't really have a relationship with any of them."

"What about your mom?" Anthony asked.

Lala shook her head. "We've haven't had contact for a long time, but she reached out to me a few months back, and we've had the occasional text chat. She's living with a friend in Tarpon Springs, and it sounds like she's trying to get her life on track—to get healthy. Of course, I've heard that before."

"Well, consider us your family," Emily said. "We're here for anything you need."

"And I have a guest bedroom that's yours if you want it," Anthony offered. "But unfortunately, the place isn't pet friendly."

"Thanks. The thing is—I'm clueless about what I need or want." She wiped the tears from her face. "I'll have to make arrangements for Billy's funeral. I've been away for so long, I don't even know who to call."

Unfortunately, Emily had been through the process not that long ago. "The people at McIntosh Funeral Home on Bay Avenue are wonderful. They helped me arrange everything for my mom."

"I'm sure they're pretty expensive." Lala looked down as she squeezed the tissue into a little ball. "When I'm ready, will you come with me?"

Emily reached forward and held her hand. "Of course."

Lala stood and gathered her purse. "I'm meeting with Deputy Garcia at the sheriff's office."

"Did they say what they wanted to talk with you about?" Emily asked.

"No, but I got the sense it's a routine formality. After that, I need to get a handle on things at the marina. After all those years working there in high school, I never thought I might be running the place."

"Is that your plan?" Anthony asked.

"I don't know. I'm comfortable managing the shop, so I know what I'm signing up for. Whether I decide to stay and make a go of it or sell it, it needs to reopen or it's going to be worthless. Already this morning, two different boaters knocked on the door, asking to buy fuel."

"Working the pumps is outside my skill set, but how about we bring over dinner? I can inventory all the dive gear," Emily said.

"And I'm good at the paperwork side of a business," Anthony said. "That's a lot of what I do here."

"Thank you. I'd love the help." Lala stepped forward and embraced the two of them. "You know where I'll be."

After Lala left the hospital, Anthony said, "That was intense."

"Can you imagine losing someone you love and dealing with taking over a new business, all at the same time? My brain hurts just thinking about it."

"But that's exactly what you did," Anthony said. "You bought the hospital right after your mom died."

"And I barely survived, and that was with you by my side." She squeezed his arm. "I plan to pay it forward with Lala. She needs us now."

·   ·   ·

At closing time, the staff completed a daily checklist of tasks before locking the doors for the night. Catrinna, the head veterinary technician, placed the lab samples in the outdoor lockbox for pickup. Abigail prepped the medical records for tomorrow's appointments while Emily returned clients' phone calls.

Anthony came into Emily's office and sat down. "I called Bravo Italiano with our order, and it'll be ready by the time we get there. I'm glad I checked with Lala first because she's a vegetarian now. I picked a variety of dishes and thought we could share."

"Perfect. I'm starving. Let's go."

The marina was located halfway between Anthony and Marc's townhouse and the beach where Emily lived, so they drove separately to Lala's.

Low clouds filtered the late-day sun, painting the sky in fiery oranges, soft pinks, and deep purples. Silhouettes of palm trees swaying in the tropical breeze lined the entrance to the causeway connecting the back bay to the barrier islands. Locals fishing from the regularly spaced bump outs in the bridge packed up their coolers and gear for the day.

With only three weeks until Thanksgiving, this sleepy, small town would soon balloon in population as tourists descended into the area to enjoy the powdery, white sand beaches and warm weather. Emily loved this time of year. Hurricane season was in the rearview mirror, but the roads, shops, and restaurants weren't yet inundated with snowbirds. It was still easy to get a table at her favorite waterfront restaurant, Barnacles.

Anthony arrived first and juggled two armfuls of paper bags containing their dinner. Emily got out of her car to help him and glanced in the direction of Billy's boat, *Diver Down*, and smiled. She had fond memories of her many dive trips over the years. As she turned away, a flicker of movement caught her eye. She squinted into the setting sun and thought she saw someone disappear under the boat's canopy into the forward cabin.

"Huh?" she muttered.

Anthony handed her a bag of takeout. "Are you coming?"

"In a minute. I want to check out Billy's boat before it gets dark."

"Why?" Anthony looked confused.

"I thought I saw something." She started across the parking lot, and Anthony followed. "It's probably nothing. It'll only take a sec. You can head inside with the food."

"All right." He turned toward the dive shop until the sound of Emily's voice stopped him.

"Hey, what you doing there?" she shouted.

CHAPTER ELEVEN

A man wearing a baseball cap low on his forehead stepped into view on the stern deck, carrying a small tote bag. He appeared in his twenties, with blonde hair peeking from under his cap.

"Oh, hi." The stranger looked startled.

"What are you doing? That's private property," Emily said.

Anthony now stood next to her. He had one free hand on his hip and a scowl on his face. Before the stranger could answer, he said, "You need to get off the boat."

"Yeah, yeah. Sure. I accidentally left some gear behind from my last dive." He held up the bag in his hand. "Found it."

Emily started to say something about Billy's death but caught herself. It hadn't been announced to the public, and she knew better than to divulge details ahead of the police.

"Can you show us what's inside?" Emily asked. "Please."

"I don't think I need to show you anything," the man said, turning combative. "Who are you anyway?"

"We're friends of Billy's, and I think you do," she replied.

His eyes narrowed, and he paused before reaching into the bag, unzipping a black, soft-sided carrying case, and flashing them a glimpse of the contents. Emily leaned in but could only see a small, three-inch computer screen.

"It's my dive computer. And none of your business." He shut the case.

Emily relaxed her posture when she realized they appeared to be threatening this stranger who was trying to retrieve his lost item. She tugged at Anthony's elbow, backing them away from the boat. The stranger took advantage of the opening and jumped onto the dock, passing by on his way out of the marina.

"Poor guy. Have we become that cynical or suspicious?" Anthony asked.

"Yes, but for good reason. Let's go," she said. "The food is getting cold."

They followed the dock as it wound around the marina. The wind sock mounted atop a No Wake Zone sign indicated an onshore westerly breeze. Rigging clanged against a sailboat mast. All the sights and sounds that brought Emily joy. They waved at a couple sitting on the deck of their catamaran. It had been close to a year since her last dive, and being back at Blue Water Marina reminded her how much she missed the peacefulness she experienced underwater.

Before entering the dive shop, she looked behind her and noticed the stranger walking out of view around the watersports business in the building at the far side of the marina.

· · ·

To avoid startling Hemingway, they knocked softly. Lala had been sitting behind the sales counter and moved to open the door. Her puffy eyes and streaked face made it clear she had been crying.

Emily and Anthony set their bags of food on the floor and enveloped her in their arms, not saying anything. Years had passed since they last connected, but some friendships transcended time.

"I'm okay." Lala wiped her face. "Actually, I'm lying. It's hard. There are so many memories in this place."

Emily understood, having stayed in her mom's cottage after her death. Surrounding herself with her mother's belongings had brought comfort, but also presented challenges. At first, contemplating the movement of the couch or a chair stirred feelings of guilt and betrayal. As the months passed, Emily's small changes allowed her to make the place her own. It took almost a year to move through the stages of grief before she could refer to the cottage as her home and not her mother's.

"Are you sure it's a good idea to stay here?" Anthony asked.

"Probably not, but I don't have a choice. I have some money saved, but it won't last long if I have to pay rent. Plus, moving Hemingway would be a bad idea, and I'm not going to leave her here alone. This is her home."

Emily picked up the bags of takeout and set them on the counter. Hemingway was curled up on her favorite perch and lifted her head to acknowledge the visitors.

"This is how I remember her greeting anyone who came into the shop—with a casual glance. I'm still trying to figure out why she'd hide in the rafters."

"She's been acting normal ever since I got here. Mostly, anyway. A few times I've found her wandering around the office and meowing. But a more drawn-out meow or howl—like she's calling for Billy."

"What if a loud noise or a thunderstorm frightened her? Cats don't normally respond to bad weather like dogs do, but it's not impossible," Anthony said.

"I don't think that's the reason. I've been here to help Billy secure *Diver Down* during a tropical storm, and she didn't seem to care," Lala said.

"Plus, it was a sunny day. Too bad I'm not Doctor Dolittle. We could just ask her." Emily smiled as she opened the containers of pasta and eggplant parmesan and placed three water bottles on the counter. "I forgot to ask for plates."

"I'll grab some dishes from the office. I only had a granola bar and some gummy bears for lunch. I'm starving."

The three friends laughed, recalling stories of their high school graduation trip to Key West. Lala had insisted they tour the Ernest Hemingway House, home to a colony of polydactyl cats. They learned that a ship's captain gave Ernest his first six-toed cat, which he named Snow White, and the colony had since expanded to almost sixty cats. Some even had seven toes on their front feet. Lala often hypothesized that Hemingway was a descendant of Ernest's famous felines.

Emily and Anthony refused to take home the leftovers, so Lala put the food in the small office fridge. When she rejoined them, her eyes looked sad.

"What's wrong?" Emily asked.

"I've been avoiding spending any time in the office. All of Billy's stuff is in there. I can even smell his Old Spice."

Anthony moved behind the counter to pet Hemingway. "My offer still stands to help you sort through everything. All the business stuff, anyway."

"Thanks. I'd appreciate that."

"Have you had any more thoughts about running the dive shop and marina?" Emily asked.

"Yeah. I think I'm going to give it a shot. When Billy sold his condo, he updated his will and sent me a copy. I'm his only benefactor, so it's on me to figure it all out."

"Did Billy have any other employees?"

"Not since he moved in here. At least that's what he told me. He'd been doing it all by himself."

Emily looked around. "There's the shop, fuel dock, and dive charter boat. You can't do that alone."

"I can manage the store and the pumps. I did that job throughout high school. The charter boat business and dive school will be put on hold for now. Billy had encouraged me to get my captain's license, but I never pursued it. Plus, I'm not a dive master. Unless I can find someone to run that part of the business, I may have to sell it."

"When do you plan to reopen?"

"Not until after the funeral. That'll give me a few days to get my head on straight and sort through stuff. I'm exhausted and not up to talking with the public quite yet." Lala wiped away her tears.

"Do you mind if we look in the office—to see what type of system Billy was using?" Anthony asked.

"Sure. His work files are a mess, but you can have at it."

The three of them moved into Lala's living quarters. Anthony sat at the desk while they discussed ways to create a warmer and more inviting place to live.

"I think a new paint color would go a long way to brightening up the room," Emily said.

"I love that idea. A buttery yellow would be much better than this muddy beige."

"New curtains and some seating—it could be comfortable," Emily said. "I have some spare furniture I'm not using that I can lend you. There's an armchair, an ottoman, a small rug, and a side table. If you fold up the Murphy bed during the day, it would feel more like a living room."

"That sounds perfect, and having something to do would take my mind off things."

"I'm not an expert painter, but we can come back tomorrow night with supplies and get started on Operation Apartment."

Lala laughed. "This place needs a good cleaning. That would give me a day to tidy up and get prepped. Let's make it a pizza painting party."

"I think I can enlist a few helpers. But only if you're up to it."

"If they're friends of yours, they're always welcome."

Anthony had his head down at Billy's desk, rummaging through drawers and shelves, while Emily and Lala worked on a list of necessary supplies. A sudden crash shattered the quiet.

"Oh, no." Anthony held up a broken credit card machine. "It fell apart in my hands." He picked the remaining pieces off the floor and attempted to press the front screen onto its base.

Lala patted him on the shoulder. "Don't worry about it. It's likely a spare Billy was trying to fix."

Anthony gave up reassembling the machine and set it aside. "I also found these in Billy's receipts box. Do you know what they are?"

He showed them four keychains, all in the same teardrop shape but in different colors—a red, yellow, white, and blue keychain marked with GA on one side and different numbers imprinted on the back.

They walked over to get a closer look. Lala picked one up in her hand, then her eyes widened.

"I've seen these before. A coworker of mine at the restaurant in Denver had them. They're given out at Gamblers Anonymous to commemorate the number of months a person has stopped gambling. Like sobriety chips from Alcoholics Anonymous. But why did Billy have them in his desk? Unless…"

CHAPTER TWELVE

Lala turned all four keychains over in her hands. On one side, the stylized letters *GA* were set inside a circle, and the other side was engraved with either *Welcome*, *30 Days*, *60 Days*, or *90 Days*.

"Did Billy have a gambling problem?" She stepped back and slumped into the chair next to the desk. "Why didn't he tell me?"

Anthony rested a hand on her shoulder. "Maybe he was ashamed or embarrassed."

"He knew I would never judge him. That's not the type of relationship we had. Do you think this is why he had to sell the condo? To pay off some gambling debts?"

"We're getting ahead of ourselves. They might not even be his keychains," Anthony said.

"You're right. Billy loved all sports and used to play in that fantasy football league, but so do lots of people. At my restaurant, the staff created a bracket every year for the March Madness college basketball tournament. It doesn't mean anything. It was for fun."

Outside Lala's view, Emily looked at Anthony with raised brows.

"Did Billy use a desktop or a laptop?" Anthony asked. "I couldn't find either one."

"He had a laptop." She got on her knees and searched under the desk. "His router is still here. He offers free Wi-Fi service to the marina customers, and this boosts his signal so it reaches the fuel dock." She remained under the desk, like a little kid hiding from the world.

Emily suggested they move outside to the dock for some fresh air.

Lala climbed out. "Good idea. I need to find it, but I don't have the energy to look for the computer right now—it'll have to wait another day. I'm going to pour myself a glass of wine. You want one?"

"Yes," Anthony said, "and I'm sure Emily would like a glass, too."

Under the soft light of the Blue Water Marina sign, they settled in multi-colored Adirondack chairs. Gentle sounds of water lapping against the moorings were interrupted when a large tarpon broke the surface. Two brown pelicans roosted on pilings, their tucked bills and heads resting against their shoulders with tufted feathers to insulate them from the night air.

"Lala, was it normal for Billy to go diving in the morning?"

She nodded. "Calm waters and less boat traffic. But it was for more practical reasons. The marina opened early, so it was his only free time to squeeze in a one-tank dive."

"Which friends did Billy dive with?" Emily asked.

"There have been a few over the years. Why?"

"I was wondering who he might have been out with the day he—" Emily caught herself.

"It's okay. You can say it. The day he died." Lala took a sip of her wine. "The police asked me the same question, and I gave them a list of possible names. I have to wonder if he went out alone, since nobody reported him missing."

Emily shook her head. "Billy stressed the importance of the buddy system every chance he got. He said it didn't matter how experienced you were, anything could happen."

"Well, I'm clueless about diving," Anthony said, "but I assume he had an assistant for the scuba and snorkel charters. If Billy drove the boat, he'd need help to get divers in and out of the water."

"Yeah, that was my job. He always had at least one other person on board for trips. Two for big groups. But I have no idea who he used lately. Of course, I also didn't know he had a gambling problem." She turned away from her friends and wiped a tear.

Emily dropped the subject after seeing how it upset her friend. "I've never been here at night. It's so peaceful."

Lala smiled. "Billy and I loved sitting out after the marina quieted down. He'd ask me all about my day—from swim practice to my last science exam." Her voice trailed off.

"Remember, one day at a time," Emily said.

Lala said, "You're right. Billy always used the analogy that a bike stayed upright as long as the wheels kept rolling. If they stopped, the bike would topple over. All I can do is keep pedaling."

"We're here for you," Anthony said. "You don't have to do it on your own. I'll come back tomorrow after work and begin sorting through the business side of things."

Lala squeezed his hand. "I'll look around for Billy's laptop in the morning, then I'm going to stop in to talk with the funeral director—to find out about what's involved in planning a funeral. Billy made it crystal clear he wanted a sea burial with his ashes spread over the reef. He always complained that funeral services were too sad and stuffy. He wanted a celebration of life, like an Irish wake. I thought I could have it here at the marina."

"I'll come with you to the meeting if you can go during my lunch break," Emily said.

"That would be great. Whenever it works for you. Just text me when you know your schedule, and I'll pick you up at the hospital."

Lala rubbed her eyes and looked up at the sky. "That's enough sad talk for one day. Let's enjoy the moonlight over the marina."

·   ·   ·

Anthony arrived at work first, as usual. Emily dropped her bags on her desk and joined him in his office.

"Morning," she said. "I brought bagels and cream cheese for everyone but saved your latest favorite flavor." Emily handed him a bag.

"Thanks, Em." Anthony smeared cream cheese on his sesame bagel, took a bite, and swallowed. "I woke up thinking about Billy and the marina business and forgot to eat."

"I'm worried about Lala. She's taking on so much."

"She seems pretty determined. Let me show you what I've found so far." He took a second bite and started typing away on his keyboard. Anthony pulled up the website for Blue Water Marina, clicking on the reservation link for scuba and dive charters.

"I'll remind Lala she'll have to contact any bookings to tell them the trips are on hold for now. There's a link to sign up for future scuba certification courses, but no dates were listed—only a mention to check back soon."

"She'll have her hands full running the store and fuel dock. The scuba diving and snorkel charter side of the business will have to wait."

"I also did some investigating about those keychains. There's a different color keychain to mark when a person has stopped gambling for 30, 60, and 90 days, then 6 months and 9 months. After that, they shift from keychains to annual medallions. There's a Gamblers Anonymous group that meets here in Coral Shores twice a week at the church on Center Street, and it's open to the public."

"Gambling could explain how Billy got into financial trouble. But I hope not for Lala's sake. She seemed upset he would keep that from her."

"Looks like you have routine appointments, and I've blocked off the last one before lunch so you can leave on time with Lala."

"Thanks. I'm not looking forward to setting foot back in the funeral home, but Mr. McIntosh is so kind. I think Lala will feel better after she meets with him."

Catrinna poked her head in the doorway. "Our first patient is here. I'll get them set up in room one."

Petal, an eight-year-old, overweight tuxedo cat, had been diagnosed with diabetes four months ago. Her addiction to her crunchies and the never-ending bowl of food had led to her weight gain and eventual diagnosis. Mrs. Harrison originally brought Petal in for a checkup when she started sitting at the water bowl, drinking constantly. Blood tests indicated the need for twice-daily insulin injections and a new approach to feeding. Transitioning her to a canned food diet, a key component in trying to reverse this disease, had come with challenges. After slowly reducing the kibble until she only received ten little pieces per day as a treat, her blood sugar began trending near normal. It had been a week since her last insulin injection, and the monitoring device Emily applied to Petal's skin allowed Mrs. Harrison to check her twice daily to ensure she had been cured of her diabetes.

"That reader has been a lifesaver. She hated it when I pricked her to get her sugar levels. Being able to wave my cell phone over the little round disk on her back has been miraculous. I recorded all her numbers and made a copy for you."

Emily took a moment to review the report. "These results are exactly what we were hoping for. Her blood glucose levels have stayed in the normal range without insulin injections. You must keep her on the canned food diet for the rest of her life. The crunchies have to be doled out as rare treats. There's always a chance her diabetes can return, so if she starts drinking more water, we'll need to recheck her."

"I plan to bring her in every three months, just to be safe. Can we take that disk thingy off her back today?"

"We can, but it will probably fall off or stop working over the next week. It's up to you if you want to continue to monitor her while it's still reading."

"You're right. More information is better. She doesn't seem to notice it, so I'll leave it for now."

"Petal will continue to lose weight slowly by eating only the canned food. That's the ideal scenario. Slow and steady weight loss, not the drastic drop that occurred before we diagnosed her diabetes."

"Got it. Petal and I are both on a health kick these days. She even joins me on the yoga mat. Actually, 'join' is the wrong word. She sits on the edge and watches me, occasionally batting at an arm or leg when I move too close."

Emily laughed. The connection people had with their beloved pets was one of the main reasons she became a vet. Of course, it began with a love of science, but she considered her most important job to be fostering the health of that unique human-animal bond.

After Emily's last client of the morning checked out, she returned to her office to gather her purse. Lala should be arriving soon for their appointment at the McIntosh Funeral Home. She grabbed her phone off the charger and read two missed texts from Lala.

"Oh no. Something must be wrong."

CHAPTER THIRTEEN

Emily charged into Anthony's office. "Lala is already at McIntosh's." She turned her phone to show him the urgent messages asking Emily to meet her at the funeral home. "What does this mean?"

Anthony squinted while reading the text. "There's one way to find out—you should get going. Sounds like Lala needs your help."

Emily took a large breath, in through her nose, out through her mouth. "Okay. I can do this."

"If I could go for you, I would. But I don't know anything about planning a funeral. Lala would end up consoling me instead of the other way around."

"Yeah, I get it. I'll text you when I'm on my way back." Emily put her phone in her bag and walked out of the treatment room door to her designated parking spot.

•   •   •

Traffic slowed as Emily approached the three-lane roundabout in front of City Hall. Coral Shores was about to start its busy tourist season, and for many out-of-towners, the continuous flow of cars through the circular intersection was intimidating. While waiting her turn, Emily chuckled as a yellow Cadillac convertible made its third trip around, the driver's face clouded in panic as he attempted to move into the outer lane. He wasn't trapped in the circle, but Emily couldn't help wondering if he felt caught in some kind of vehicular purgatory.

She took the second exit onto Bay Avenue, driving another mile before turning into the empty parking lot at McIntosh Funeral Home. The immaculate lawn, bordered with lush tropical landscaping of ferns, palms, and bird-of-paradise stretched across the front of a white, stately building, its large columns flanking a covered portico. Nearby benches set around an ornate but tasteful fountain added to the sense of calm and reflection. No matter how beautiful the setting, a wave of dread overtook Emily the moment she stepped inside—as if the air had been pulled from her lungs.

"Breathe, just breathe," she repeated to herself. "It's only a building."

Thick carpets muffled any footsteps, so Emily didn't hear the woman until she stood beside her and said, "Can I help you?"

Emily jumped. "Oh," she exclaimed, flattening her hand against her chest to slow her racing heart. "I didn't see you."

The kind woman's smile immediately put her at ease. "Dr. Benton?"

"Yes," she said in a hushed tone, wondering why even an empty funeral home seemed to demand a whisper.

"My name's Carol. Mr. McIntosh is in his office with Miss Todd. If you'll come with me, they're expecting you."

Grateful that the meeting room lay in the opposite direction of the viewing and reception areas, Emily followed, but her legs became heavy, causing her to shuffle her feet, which kicked up the odd spark of static electricity from the double-pile carpet. She opened and closed her hands to release the tension before entering the office.

"Emily." Lala sprang from her chair in tears.

Emily held her friend until she stopped crying. "What happened?"

Mr. McIntosh grabbed a box of tissues, which he handed to Lala. "Miss Todd received some troubling news this morning."

"Lala," Emily pleaded.

"It's just that…" she hesitated. "Billy's funeral plans have been put on hold. I can't move forward with any of the arrangements."

"Why?" Emily looked at Mr. McIntosh and then back at Lala.

"May I?" he asked Lala, who nodded her consent. "Anomalies were found during the autopsy that have prompted additional investigation."

"I don't understand. I thought Billy drowned."

"At Miss Todd's request, I was to make arrangements for Mr. William Todd to be brought here from the ME's, I mean medical examiner's office, for cremation, but they aren't willing to release his body at this time."

"Em, the deputy I met with yesterday left me a message to contact her. I thought I would drive over so I could talk in person. Would you come with me?"

"Of course. Do you want to go now?"

"Can you? I mean, I know you're working."

"Let me tell Anthony there's a change in plans, but I'm sure I have time. And I'll see if I can help get to the bottom of this."

Mr. McIntosh stood after Lala gathered the paperwork he had prepared for their meeting. "I'll do the same, and here's my personal cell number." He handed her his card. "We're here to assist any way we can."

"Thank you. I was so nervous about coming today, but you've put me at ease, and I appreciate that." Lala had regained her composure and looped her arm through Emily's as they made their way to the parking lot.

"I can drive," Emily said.

"No, I'll be fine. Plus, it's out of your way to come back here."

"Okay. I'll meet you inside the main entrance." Before pulling out, Emily texted Anthony and left messages for Mike and Duncan, explaining why she was coming to see them. Unsure about what had caused a delay in Billy's autopsy, she hoped her brother or her boyfriend could shed some light on the situation.

•   •   •

The front desk at the Coral Shores Sheriff's Department was crowded with a class of first graders waiting to start a tour. While Lala checked in for her appointment with Deputy Garcia, Emily eavesdropped on a teacher explaining to a parent chaperone about the outreach program designed to introduce young kids to the role of law enforcement in their communities.

Lala sat next to Emily on a bench. "They said she'll come here to get us."

Time dragged by while they waited in the deserted lobby. The kids had moved to the first stop on the tour—the police garage. It seemed like each of them had a chance to turn on the siren, as the blaring noise echoed back into the building.

"Miss Todd, thank you for coming in." They were greeted by the same deputy who took Emily's statement on the beach after finding Billy.

Lala stood and shook her hand. "This is my friend, Emily Benton. Is it okay if she comes with me?"

"Of course. Nice to see you again, Dr. Benton." The deputy led them to a conference room in a quiet corner of the building. Once they were seated, she said, "I understand Burt McIntosh advised you that the medical examiner can't release Mr. Todd's body."

"He did, but he didn't say why. I'm very confused," Lala said.

"I'll explain, but first, I have a few questions. Was Mr. Todd having any recent troubles? Had anyone been threatening him?"

"Please call him Billy. And no. He'd been dealing with financial issues, but that's all."

"What type of financial issues?"

"I'm not sure. I think business was slow, and he was struggling to pay the mortgages on both his home and the dive shop. He ended up selling his condo and moving into the store."

"And when was that?"

"I think the condo sale closed about two months ago."

"When was the last time you saw him?"

"This past summer. I came back for his birthday weekend at the end of June."

"And everything seemed normal during your stay? Nothing stood out to you that would cause you concern?"

Lala had been quick to reply to the previous questions but paused before answering.

"Miss Todd, even the smallest detail may be important."

Lala stared down as she fidgeted with her hands, clasping and releasing them. Emily placed her hand over Lala's and said, "It's okay. Whatever you have to say."

Lala looked up, her eyes pooling with tears. "There was nothing specific, but he wasn't his normal, joking self. I'd catch him staring off, lost in thought. He was quieter than usual and seemed distracted, worried even."

Emily didn't understand this line of questioning and asked, "What does all this have to do with his autopsy?"

The deputy leaned forward and spoke in a controlled and empathetic tone. "William Todd didn't drown."

CHAPTER FOURTEEN

"What!" Lala gasped.

Emily shook her head in disbelief. "But I found him in his dive gear on the beach. You were there," she said to the deputy. "His gear was wet. And we both agreed he'd likely drowned in a diving accident."

"Yes. That was our initial assessment. I understand this is a shock. Let me explain."

"Please." Emily moved her chair closer to Lala's and wrapped an arm around her trembling shoulder.

"I agree with you, Dr. Benton. It seemed obvious at the time— an accidental drowning. The ME can better describe the scientific definition of drowning, but essentially it comes down to not finding any salt water in Mr. Todd's lungs."

"Please call him Billy." Lala reached into her purse for a tissue and wiped her tears. Her lips quivered when she said, "I don't understand."

"If he had drowned in the ocean, there would have been salt water in his lungs along with other signs. So, until we determine a cause of death, we are treating Mr. Todd's—I mean, Billy's—death as suspicious. It's now an active investigation."

"Is it possible for me to speak directly with the medical examiner?" Lala asked.

"I'm sure that can be arranged. Excuse me, I'll check to see if he's available."

Once they were alone in the room, Emily stood and began pacing. It helped her to think. "None of this makes sense. How did he end up on the beach?"

"I feel like I'm going to be sick." Lala put her head between her knees.

Emily realized now wasn't the time to pile more unanswered questions onto the conversation and sat next to her friend, gently rubbing her back. "Can I get you anything?"

Lala shook her head but didn't speak. When she finally looked up, her face was pale. "I want to see him."

"Billy?"

She nodded. "They asked me before, but I said no. I didn't want to remember him like that. But now I need to see his face one last time. To say goodbye."

"Are you sure?"

"I'm not sure about anything. I just know that I have to do it." A sob escaped her lips.

Emily grabbed a tissue box from the table. When Lala finished shedding all the tears she had left, Deputy Garcia returned with a grim expression.

Emily wondered how many times the deputy had to deliver devastating news while maintaining her professional composure. As a veterinarian, Emily also had to share a difficult or terminal diagnosis about a beloved pet. It weighed on her, and she empathized with the deputy for the same reasons. These moments took an emotional toll on the ones receiving the news, but also on the ones delivering it.

"I can take you now," the deputy said. "It's in an adjacent building, but we can walk there."

Emily spoke on Lala's behalf. "Could you tell the ME she would like to see Billy?"

The deputy nodded.

Lala stood and faced Emily. "I need to do this on my own. I hope you understand."

"I do, but in case you change your mind, I'll be nearby," Emily said. The two friends hugged and followed the deputy out of the room.

"Dr. Benton, I can have someone escort you back to the lobby."

"That's okay. I know the way."

•   •   •

Emily had no problem navigating the hallways of the sheriff's headquarters. She had been directly involved in solving the murder of Mrs. Eliza Klein and the kidnapping and murder case surrounding Marilyn Peña and her talking parrot, Tiki Lulu. Both Duncan and Mike had offices in the building, but since Duncan had been the first to reply to her text, she headed his way. He was expecting her.

"Hi, Em. Come on in." Duncan greeted his sister.

"I'm glad I caught you. I need your help."

Before she explained why she was there in the middle of the day, he said, "I know you're here about Billy. What did Deputy Garcia tell you?"

"Not much other than the devastating news that he didn't drown. Lala is so distraught. She had been dreading making his funeral arrangements, and now, she has to put everything on hold, prolonging the trauma. What's going on?"

"They can't release the body until they determine a cause of death, but given the circumstances, we're launching an investigation."

"What circumstances?"

"Well, he was a scuba diving instructor found wearing his dive gear. If he didn't drown, it's possible it was staged to look that way. Or he died before entering the water. Either way, there are a lot of unanswered questions."

Emily sat thinking. Something tugged at her memory, so she closed her eyes to concentrate. To bring it into focus. Then her eyes flew open and she asked, "How much air was left in his tank?"

"What?"

"His scuba tank. How much air was left inside?"

"Beats me, but I'm sure I can find out. Is it important?"

"It could be. After every dive, we'd carry our empty tanks to the filling station near the back door of the shop. Billy would then refill the tanks right away and store them on a rack. This ensured empty tanks never got mixed up with full tanks. He was a stickler for following protocols."

"And why does that matter?"

"If his death was made to appear like an accident, the tank would still be full, since he never used it. If the tank was empty or low on air, he either ran out of air on a dive or someone drained the tank. One of those scenarios is almost impossible to believe. He'd never let himself run out. Not unless something terrible happened."

"How much air does a tank hold?" Duncan asked.

"A standard tank holds 3000 PSI. We check our air supply constantly during a dive and communicate our levels with each other using hand signals." Emily demonstrated the signal for 2500 PSI as an example.

"We all enter the water together and surface together, and the person who uses their air the fastest determines when we come up. I often surface with around 1000 PSI left in the tank because I breathe slow and steady, conserving the air. As a safety rule, we never let the tank get below 500, leaving a buffer in case of an emergency."

Duncan pondered the information. "I'm now in charge of the investigation and can check the photos taken at the scene. The tank will be in our possession, so we can verify the air level, assuming the valve was turned off when you found Billy."

"The tank was properly attached to his breathing regulator, and I didn't hear any hissing sounds that would indicate a leak in the seal. I removed most of his gear to start CPR, but I didn't touch the valve on the tank. I released a small amount of air stored in his buoyancy vest in order to get it off his chest, but that wouldn't impact the level in the tank."

Duncan nodded. "There's nothing I can do to speed up the process for Lala. Sorry."

"I understand. Now that you're checking into his death, you can find out how he got out on the water. Has anyone come forward to report him missing or to report an accident? There had to be someone with him."

"Nope, but we're only in the preliminary phase of the investigation. We'll collect some basic information while waiting for the ME. If he finds an underlying medical issue, the case can be closed, allowing Lala to move forward with her plans."

"But that still doesn't explain how he got there. Even if he went into the water alone, there would be a spotter on the boat. In shallow water, the dive boat would anchor and drop a guideline. In deeper water, the captain steers the boat to follow the trail of bubbles given off by the diver's breaths."

"This is the one time I wish I'd taken that scuba course when you did. What's a guideline?"

"It's a rope attached to a buoy with a weight on the end. It marks the boat's location, and if we need to do a decompression stop on our way up, we can hold the line and rest if we're tired."

"Billy's dive boat is registered in his name, and he's the only scuba charter in the immediate area."

"*Diver Down*—that's the name of his boat, and I checked. It's docked in its usual place at the marina."

"Thanks for all this, Em. I'll pass the info along to Deputy Garcia. For now, she'll continue to be the point person on the case."

"Will you call me if you learn anything new?"

He stayed silent, offering her only a faint smile. Recently, they battled over Emily's involvement in solving Marilyn Peña's kidnapping. Following the murder suspect to the Florida Keys without telling her brother had created a rift in their relationship that she was uncertain could be repaired. Nobody got hurt, and her lead helped to solve a high-profile case, so he forgave her. Things had been good ever since.

"I'm serious, Duncan. Lala doesn't have anyone except Anthony and me. We need to help her sort through all this, and that's impossible if you're holding back on me."

"You're a good friend, Em. I'll do my best to share when I can, but you know I can't always talk about an ongoing case. I still think Billy's death won't come to that, but I don't want to jump ahead until we have cause."

Emily knew better. If Billy didn't drown, accidentally or otherwise, his death made little sense. It left her with only one obvious question. Was Billy murdered?

CHAPTER FIFTEEN

Emily checked the time. She'd have to leave right away to make it back to the hospital for afternoon appointments.

"I've got to go, but I have a favor to ask," she said.

"Shoot," Duncan said.

"Lala will be living at the marina. There's a small apartment and office space in the back. It's pretty depressing right now, with marked-up tan walls and dingy curtains. I offered to help her repaint the place and dress it up so it's comfortable for her. Would you and Jane be able to lend a hand? With enough people, we could get it done in a night."

"When?"

"Tomorrow, but I'll have to confirm with Lala."

Duncan referenced the calendar on his phone. "It looks clear, but let me talk to Jane first. Can the kids come?"

"That would be fun. Bring Elvis too if you want. He's a good boy, and Hemingway is great with dogs."

"Speaking of Elvis, are you able to pet sit again next weekend? We'll be leaving for Mac's baseball tournament early Saturday."

"Absolutely. I love having him over." Emily stood, grabbed her purse, and started for the door. "I'll send you the details for the painting party."

Emily had reached the lobby when she received a text from Lala. They were preparing Billy for her viewing, and Lala didn't know how long it would take. She thanked Emily for coming but told her not to wait. She needed some time alone and would catch up with her later.

Torn between being there for her friend and needing to get back to work, she told Lala to call for anything.

Emily understood how she felt. After her mom died, she had gone for long walks alone on the beach to process her grief. Spending time with family and friends helped, but sometimes she had craved solitude.

•   •   •

On her drive to the hospital, Emily ate an expired granola bar she found in her car's console. She parked and raced inside, pulling on her lab coat and wrapping her stethoscope around her neck. Anthony, the lunch fairy, had placed half his deli sandwich on her desk. The attached sticky note said, "Eat!"

After a string of back-to-back appointments, she found Anthony in his office and updated him on the investigation into Billy's death.

Upon hearing the news, he winced. "You think this could be another murder?"

"I wouldn't go that far—not yet, anyway. I think the official police term is suspicious death."

"Excuse my pun—it sounds fishy. And I didn't know Lala saw Billy when I offered to sort through his papers after work. She replied a few minutes ago, saying she's not up to number crunching but would appreciate the company."

"We had talked about decorating her apartment, but that might be too much," Emily said.

"Maybe, but I'll check. I told her I'd work on my own at the desk if she wanted to rest."

"I asked Duncan to join us tomorrow night. I'll order pizza for everyone and pick up the supplies. Can you get Lala to pick a color when you're there tonight?"

"Sure. I have one of those color fans at home from the paint store that I'll bring with me. And, Em—I know being there for Lala is our primary concern, but we need to carve out some time for the turtle center. Sarah is coming into town at the end of the week to do a walk-through with Gus."

Gus Fazio, the general contractor building the Eliza Klein Sea Turtle Center, estimated the turtle medical area to be complete within two months, followed by the interactive welcome center. Marlon and Sharon, long-standing directors of the Coral Shores Turtle Project, would be in charge of daily operations, and Emily and Anthony would serve as co-directors.

After Mrs. Klein's tragic and senseless murder by a corrupt local realtor, her estate became part of an endowment to build a world-class facility. Her daughter, Sarah Klein, dedicated her wealth and resources, with support from a generous donation by local billionaire and wildlife benefactor Marilyn Peña, to bring the project to life. Their mission remained rescue, rehab, and release, and would expand upon decades of community work. Area beaches were established nesting grounds for endangered green and loggerhead sea turtles, and the citizens of Coral Shores took pride in their increasing populations in the Gulf of Mexico.

"I know. You're right. I was headed there the morning I found Billy. Maybe I'll go after work. If you can send me an update from Lala's, I'll stop by when I'm done to get her paint color choice. That way we'll have all the supplies ready to go."

•　　　•　　　•

Leaving work on time was a rare occurrence, so Emily took advantage of the remaining daylight hours and drove directly to the sea turtle center. She moved a traffic cone blocking the parking lot and navigated around equipment. The construction crews had departed for the day, allowing her a quiet moment to survey their progress.

The center had two distinct areas. The front half incorporated the original structure of Mrs. Klein's historic cottage into a welcome center. It would function as an interactive education hub, information desk, and sales center. Sarah had enlisted the help of a designer friend to develop a line of recycled, eco-friendly products to sell.

The back half of the center included a medical facility where injured or sick turtles would be stabilized before transferring them to hospitals equipped to handle their care. To prepare for their new role, Emily and Marlon had spent time at The Turtle Hospital in the Florida Keys, the Loggerhead Marinelife Center in Juno Beach, and the Sea Turtle Rehabilitation Center in Tampa. Still lots of work ahead, but Emily could now envision the completed project. It gave her goosebumps.

She locked up, and after replacing the traffic cones, she drove the short distance along Gulf Beach Road to her cottage. The moment she walked in the front door, Bella made her displeasure at the late dinner hour known.

"Meow, meow, meow," she bellowed as she ran to the kitchen.

The message was clear—Emily was to follow.

"It's not that late," she said to her feline roommate as she opened a can of savory salmon morsels. Bella continued to grumble while eating her delectables.

Emily needed a minute to decompress and moved outside to her beach deck. Her west-facing cottage gifted her with the most amazing sunsets. Her entire life, she'd been watching for the fleeting green flash. The exact second when the red ball of fire dropped below the horizon, sending a green flash of light streaking across the sky. Anthony boasted about his sighting during their high school years, but the moment had eluded Emily. It didn't stop her from staring.

Once her eyes had recalibrated from the solar radiation, she pulled out her phone. Mike's earlier text confirmed he had been out of the office when she came by the station with Lala, and he thought he'd be working late. Emily understood his job didn't come with banker's hours. Neither did hers. You stayed until the work was done. She shared the plans for the painting party, hoping he could be there.

Before she became too tired to move, she texted Anthony for an update and to find out if they had eaten yet. Her empty fridge meant takeout, so she planned to pick up dinner from Sunny's Pit BBQ on her way to the marina.

Anthony replied while she changed out of her scrubs. *Two pulled chicken sandwiches with some fried okra.* The little dots continued on the screen to preview another message. *Lala's still sleeping. I'll wait till you get here before giving her the bad news.*

CHAPTER SIXTEEN

Emily was uncertain if Lala could handle any more bad news. First, she'd learned of her uncle's unexpected death, then lost her job and moved across the country. She now faced an uphill climb to reopen the marina business and the revelation that Billy's death had become an active investigation. That would be too much for most people to cope with.

The street lights in the parking lot helped Emily navigate the dock at night. Anthony jumped up to open the door when he saw her standing outside.

"Thanks for getting here so fast. Lala just woke up." He sniffed the bag. "Smells delicious." He carried the food to the sales counter and began unpacking. "I'm starving."

"Don't keep me waiting—what did you find?"

"Things aren't good. This place is on the verge of bankruptcy."

"Oh, no. Have you told Lala?"

"Not exactly, but I think she knows. We were looking through some recent bank statements, and that's when she decided to take a nap. Seeing Billy's body had to be traumatizing, but she didn't want to talk about it."

They were halfway through their meal when Lala and Hemingway joined them in the shop. The confident tabby jumped onto the counter and stared at Anthony until he wiped the sauce off a bite of chicken and shared a piece. She purred while she enjoyed her snack then moved to her cat bed behind the register.

"She can be quite bossy," Lala said. "Thanks for bringing dinner again. I don't mean to be such a sad charity case."

"The hardest and most important lesson I learned when my mom died was that I didn't need to handle everything on my own. It's okay to accept some help. And it makes us feel better, so you're doing Anthony and me a favor."

Lala smiled, though her heavy eyes betrayed her exhaustion. "If I remember correctly, you were the captain of the debate team, so I'm not going to argue with you."

Emily wrapped her arm around Lala and said, "I know today had to be difficult. We're here for you if you need to talk." Lala leaned her head on Emily's shoulder and nodded.

The three friends kept the conversation light as they finished their meal. While cleaning up the takeout containers, a knock startled them. They all turned to see a man waving at them through the window.

"People have been dropping by to ask about when the business will reopen. Based on Anthony's research, I can't afford to lose any customers. Let me find out what he wants." Lala crossed the room and unlocked the door.

"Hi. Can I help you?"

The man stepped around Lala into the store. He had his ball cap pulled low, but they could see his eyes darting around the room.

"Do you have any bait for sale? I'm hoping to head out at first light and need to stock up."

"No, sorry. We're temporarily closed and won't reopen for a few more days. But there's a gas station down the road that sells bait."

As he moved closer to the counter, Hemingway turned in his direction. Her ears swiveled sideways before flattening against her head. In an instant, her posture changed. The fur along her back and tail stood on end, making her look twice as big. She hissed and emitted a low, guttural growl.

Emily and Anthony jumped to their feet as Lala intercepted the customer, creating a barrier between this stranger and her cat. She gently placed her hand on his elbow and directed him to the door.

"There may be some bait left in the freezer. I'll grab the keys and meet you outside." She glanced back at Hemingway as she escorted the man onto the dock.

Once the door closed behind them, Emily said, "What was that all about?" She shook some cat treats into her palm as a peace offering.

Anthony stood next to Hemingway, gently petting her head. "I don't know, but look at her. She's terrified."

Lala came back into the shop, the corners of her mouth turned down. "Is she okay?"

Hemingway's bottlebrush tail approached normal size, and her ears now faced forward.

"She's better. Do you know that guy?" Anthony asked.

"Nope. Seems he knows Billy, though. He must be a regular customer." She reached behind the counter for a boater's floating keychain labeled *Bait*. "I'll be right back."

They watched as Lala leaned into the chest freezer on the dock by the front door. After pulling the lid shut behind her, she handed the man three packages. He grabbed the frozen bait and headed toward the marina. Lala replaced the lock on the freezer and walked back into the store, waving a twenty-dollar bill. Emily enjoyed seeing her smile again.

"My first sale." She set the money on the counter. "This is for dinner."

Emily pushed the money away. "Dinner's on me. You should frame this to commemorate your fresh start."

"Nice idea," she said, "but given what I've uncovered so far, I might need it to help pay some overdue bills." She pocketed the cash and lifted Hemingway into her arms. Now back to her normal size, the tabby purred loud enough for them all to hear.

"I've never seen Hemingway respond that way to a customer," Emily said.

"Yeah, almost never. I can remember one time when she hissed at an old boyfriend of mine who ended up being a lying cheat. Hemingway proved to be a better judge of character." Lala motioned with her head. "Let's move into the office. I'm going to turn off the store lights so nobody else mistakes us for being open."

Anthony returned to his post at the desk while Emily and Lala walked around the room discussing design ideas. Lala had chosen a soft, buttery yellow paint for the walls and intended to browse the local HomeGoods store for bright, cheerful curtains and bedding. Just a few thoughtful touches would transform the space.

"Anthony, could we borrow Marc's uncle's van to move the furniture from my place?"

"I'll check, but I'm sure it's not a problem."

Emily was concerned Lala might be taking on too much. "You know you don't need to do anything right now except take care of yourself and Hemingway."

"But I need the distraction. I think it would be good for me," Lala said.

"If you're sure, we should be able to finish in one night, but you'd need to get everything moved away from the walls and prepped beforehand. It's a lot of work."

"I can get it done."

Emily pointed to three surfboards polished to a high shine and propped in the corner. "This would be a great spot to put a small chair and table. These are beautiful, but is there another place to move them?"

"Yeah. In the storeroom, but I still need to sort through it all. Do either of you surf?"

Anthony shuddered while Emily suppressed a laugh. "We met at a summer surf camp in middle school," she said. "It didn't end well. Needless to say, it's not Anthony's favorite activity, and I prefer underwater sports."

Anthony jutted out his chin. "In my defense, I've mastered stand-up paddleboard yoga."

"You two crack me up." Lala said.

"If you don't want to keep the boards, you can sell them. I believe the watersports store across the marina has a consignment section for lightly used equipment."

"That would be great. I can't hold on to anything valuable unless it helps keep this place afloat. Anthony, I know you were trying to cushion the blow earlier. It's bad, isn't it?"

He nodded. "There might be more information on the missing laptop, but from what I can piece together, things aren't good. The business was making a profit, but there's a stack of bills and no cash on hand. And I can't find any record of payments from the credit card company into his account. The money was deposited, but the supporting paperwork is missing." He leaned back in his chair, thinking. "Doesn't it cost a ton to fill the tanks on a boat?"

"It depends," Lala said. "It could be anywhere from a couple hundred dollars to a thousand dollars or more. Why do you ask?"

"People don't normally carry that amount of cash on them. Other than smaller purchases in the dive shop, I assume most sales would be processed on a credit card."

"That's right," Lala said. "Hopefully, we can find the missing info when we locate the computer, but the most important thing is that you can see regular cash reimbursements deposited for the credit card sales." She sat next to Hemingway on the bed. "I had a dream this afternoon that I was running this place. It was a happy dream. I only remember vague bits, but I woke up feeling certain this is where I need to be. I have to make this work." Lala reached for each of their hands. "I will make this work—with your help."

"You've got it," Emily said. "I'll head over to the sports store to ask if the owner is interested in these." She snapped a few photos of the surfboards.

"And if it's okay with you, I'm going to take home this paperwork. If we can figure out monthly expenses and sales, you can talk with the bank about a small business line of credit. Something to get you on your feet."

Lala clapped. "Let's do it. But you two already put in a full day before you got here. No more work—it's time to rest."

Anthony gathered the documents and picked up his keys. "I'm glad you'll finally get to meet Marc at the painting party."

"And don't forget about Ava, Mac, and Elvis. Not sure how helpful they'll be, but at least they're entertaining," Emily said.

Emily and Anthony said good night, ensuring Lala locked up behind them. The watersports store still had its lights on, so they crossed the marina, hoping to broker a deal on some surfboards.

As they approached the entrance, the man who had just purchased bait from Lala came out the front door. He stopped when he saw them, then hurried toward the parking lot. Emily looked at Anthony, and they both shrugged.

The store's walls were lined with pool floats, kitesurfing gear, and snorkel equipment. Racks displaying stand-up paddleboards, surfboards, and ocean kayaks filled the floor space. Sitting behind the counter at the back of the room was the same guy they had first met while he was searching for his dive computer on Billy's boat. The harsh expression on his face seemed out of place for a retail setting.

"We're closed," he shouted.

"Sorry," Emily said. "The door was open."

He muttered something under his breath.

Anthony stepped forward. "Is the owner or manager here?"

"No. He'll be back in the morning."

"Could you give him a message?" Emily asked. The guy rolled his finger in the air, prompting her to get to the point. "We have some vintage surfboards in mint condition and wanted to find out if he's interested in buying them or taking them on consignment?"

Without speaking, he handed them a piece of paper and a pen, so Emily wrote Lala's contact information and passed it back.

"If he wants to see them, they're at the Blue Water Dive Shop." Emily pointed across the marina, then they walked outside.

"What a jerk," Anthony said. "Isn't he the same guy we caught picking up his dive thingy from Billy's boat?"

"Yup. Except he acted like he's never seen us before."

"Maybe he's still miffed we cornered him on the dock."

"It's possible. But his attitude can't be good for business." Emily was being charitable with her assessment, but deep down, she thought there was something off about the guy.

CHAPTER SEVENTEEN

"Buckeye! Don't jump."

The friendly Maltese-Shih Tzu mix danced on his hind feet while pawing at Emily's leg. His white fur tinged with caramel highlights around his ears showcased his puppy cut. After reviewing his medical history, Emily concluded the thirteen-year-old dog did not look or act his age.

"It's okay. We love seeing him so happy about coming to the vet." She bent down to pet his head and received a doggy kiss in exchange.

Mrs. Fuller's Ohio State University football jersey complemented Buckeye's collar and leash. Even the attached poop bag holder had an OSU logo.

"We're here for Buckeye's senior physical, plus I'd like you to recheck that fatty lump on his back. He doesn't seem to mind when I pet him there, but he needs to be in top form for the game on Saturday against Michigan." She lifted Buckeye into her arms and squeezed him tight.

Emily had performed a needle biopsy during his previous exam, confirming the mass under the skin was indeed a benign lipoma—a common fatty cyst in older dogs. Mrs. Fuller wanted to avoid surgery unless it was necessary. It didn't bother him or cause any pain, and while there were no concerns that it would spread to other locations, monitoring its growth was essential.

"His lipoma hasn't changed in size," Emily said as she completed his exam. "It's still one cm, which is good news. My only concern is that he's put on another pound."

"I know. It's because of birthday month."

Emily's confused expression prompted Mrs. Fuller to explain further.

"Almost everyone in my family was born in November. I swear, Buckeye thinks he's human. He loves presents and expects one himself, so whenever we're celebrating, we throw a few dog cookies in the bottom of a gift bag. He sort of demands it, and I don't see a way around it."

Emily laughed. "Can you put one small cookie in each bag? Or on the day of a party, he gets less kibble at his regular meals."

Mrs. Fuller put her hand to her head. "Why didn't I think of that? It's so routine to reach for the same amount with the food scooper. I want him to stay lean and healthy, so we'll work on it. Promise."

• • •

Emily and Anthony barely crossed paths during a busy morning of appointments, but connected at lunch when they gathered in Anthony's office.

"I checked with Lala, and everything is a go for the painting party. She worked late last night prepping the walls. Marc will pick up his uncle's van, and we'll load your furniture after work."

"Perfect. I'll touch base with Mike and Duncan to confirm they'll be there." As she composed a group text, Abigail called over the office intercom.

"Dr. Benton, your brother and Detective Mike are here to see you."

Emily could see the whites of Anthony's eyes when they turned to each other, both surprised to learn about their visitors.

"The last time the two of them showed up on a workday, we were dealing with an emergency to remove a fishing hook from Moose Englewood's lip, and they were launching a murder investigation into Mrs. Klein's death. I remember it vividly. This isn't good," he said.

"Let's not jump ahead." Emily knew she didn't sound convincing, since she agreed with Anthony. This joint visit could only mean one thing.

The two men entered the office, their arrival adding tension to the air. Emily and Anthony sat in silence, bracing for whatever shocking news they had to share.

Duncan surveyed their faces and said, "What?"

"What do you mean, what? Why are you here?" Emily asked. "It's not that we don't enjoy seeing you both, but you have to admit, you never just drop by."

Mike moved next to Emily. "You're right. I should do this more often. I enjoy watching you in action, Dr. Benton." He grinned mischievously.

Emily blushed. "You're both welcome any time, but am I wrong to assume this is about official police business?"

"Sort of, but just to ask a question," Duncan said. He handed two photos to Emily. "These are the pictures taken of Billy's dive tank and gear. You can see the air level in the tank is 800 PSI."

Emily studied the images then stared out the office window while gently tapping her finger on the desk.

Mike put his hand on her shoulder. "What are you thinking?"

"I'm trying to work out what Billy's air consumption would be if he dove the reef wall that's just offshore. A diver can track their air usage in PSIs per minute. But it depends on lots of factors like depth, water temperature, currents, and the skill of the diver. Inexperienced divers use air a lot faster than Billy would've."

"And why does that matter?" Duncan asked.

"Billy wouldn't let anyone else put his gear together, which means he assembled it. The tank would have been full before entering the water. Depending on his depth, he could have been diving for thirty to sixty minutes, give or take, before he stopped breathing. That's assuming there was no leak in the tank or seal, and I didn't hear one when I found Billy. You could check the gauge again to see if the level is holding."

Duncan and Mike exchanged a look.

"We can do that," Mike said. "The tank is now at the forensics lab."

"Is there anything in the picture that would indicate this is Billy's dive tank?" Duncan asked.

"Not really, but I've often seen dive masters use steel tanks versus the more common aluminum tanks. Sometimes they carry larger tanks for longer dives, but this one's a standard size. He would've known which tanks were his. Maybe ask Lala."

"We're headed to the marina next. And thanks for your help." Duncan placed the photos in a file folder and turned to leave.

"Hold on a minute. Not so fast," Emily said. "Why all the questions? Do you know something you're not telling us?"

"No. Not yet. We're gathering information to determine how, where, and when Billy might have entered the water. That's all," Duncan said.

Anthony exhaled through his mouth. "Oh boy. Here we go again."

"Really," Mike said. "These are standard questions for any suspicious death."

"But can I ask a favor? Please tread lightly with Lala." Anthony said. "She's barely holding on right now."

"Of course we will," Duncan said. "And we'll all be back later to help with the painting. The kids are looking forward to it."

•　　　•　　　•

After Duncan and Mike left the hospital, Emily asked, "Did you find the names of Billy's former employees in his paperwork? Any pay stubs or tax forms?"

"There's a file, but I didn't get to it yet. Why?"

"I'm trying to think of anyone who could shed some light on what Billy was up to lately. Between his financial troubles and Gamblers Anonymous keychains, someone had to know what was going on and whether he was struggling."

"That's a good idea. We can sort through that stuff tonight. If we can find a name, it might trigger a memory for Lala. It seems Billy kept a lot from her—probably trying to protect her. And she was so far away, it's not like she could pop by and see what he was up to."

"The best thing we can do is help her create a comfortable place to live. I know painting and decorating aren't pressing concerns, considering everything she's going through, but I think it's important. She needs a sanctuary. Somewhere she's proud to call home. Right now, it's a depressing, nonfunctional space. Our small changes will make a huge difference, and it's budget-friendly—a couple of cans of paint and new curtain panels. Add in free labor and some borrowed furniture. A little goes a long way."

Catrinna popped her head into the office. "Dr. Benton, your next appointment is here."

"Thanks. I'll be right there."

"Marc can get off early tonight. If you're okay with it, I'll leave a few minutes before closing so we can load up the spare furniture from your place."

"Sure. Use your keys to let yourself in. I've put the pieces for Lala near the front door. But beware of Bella. She's tricky and will work you until you give her a bunch of treats."

CHAPTER EIGHTEEN

Emily reached the marina in time to catch sight of a man rounding the corner of the dive shop, walk straight to his car, and drive off. With no boats docked nearby, she figured he was just another customer asking about the reopening and dismissed it. Meanwhile, Anthony and Marc were too focused on unloading furniture from the van to notice Lala approaching. But Emily saw it instantly—something was wrong. Lala's face was flushed, and she looked angry.

"What happened?" Emily asked.

Lala stomped her foot while waving a piece of paper in the air. "Some guy tried to strong-arm me into selling *Diver Down*."

Anthony and Marc set down the chair and turned to her. Anthony asked, "Did he threaten you?"

"Not in so many words, but he knew the marina was struggling financially and offered to take Billy's boat off my hands for a ridiculous lowball price. He said if I didn't sell to him, the bank would be taking it next. I don't need to be a broker to know the boat is worth way more." She collapsed onto the chair in the parking lot.

"Was it the guy I just saw leaving?" Emily asked. "A pudgy, middle-aged man?"

Lala nodded.

"That's shady," Anthony said. "What did you tell him?"

"That it's not for sale, then I asked him to leave." She looked up and her face brightened. "Oh, I'm so sorry." She stood and hugged Marc. "I'm glad to finally meet you, and thank you for coming tonight. You must think I'm the most ungrateful host."

Marc smiled. "Not at all. Anthony told me about everything you're going through. I'm so sorry about your uncle."

"Thank you."

Emily asked to see the paper. The letterhead listed Clay Thornton of Thornton Marine Broker as the person making the offer. She'd never heard of them. It felt like an unscrupulous, predatory tactic to swoop in after a death in the family.

Right on cue to shift the mood, her brother arrived. Mac and Ava, led by Elvis on his leash, sprang from the car.

"Auntie Em." Ava jumped into her arms. "We got Elvis a new toy."

Elvis tugged Mac across the lot to meet his adoring fans. Meanwhile, Anthony crouched to pet the little terrier and, pointing to what looked like a stuffed puffer fish, asked, "And who's this?"

"That's Mr. Fish," Mac said. "It's his favorite toy."

By this time, Duncan and Jane had caught up, and Emily introduced everyone to Lala. They all helped unload the furniture and painting supplies, setting everything inside the dive shop. Lala was showing the kids all the cool stuff in the store when Mike walked in.

"Pizza's here. Let's eat."

•   •   •

Elvis sniffed every square inch without realizing Hemingway stood on the counter watching him. When the orange tabby leaped down, Elvis froze and stared at her.

"Should I put his leash back on?" Jane looked to Emily and Lala for direction.

"That's up to you, but Hemingway is accustomed to having dogs in here and has never acted fearful or aggressive. Let's give it a minute," Lala said.

Elvis crouched, inching closer one step at a time. His tail wagged, and his ears perked up—a friendly posture. Once they were inches apart, Hemingway lifted her paw and tapped his head.

"I think she's telling him—you better be good or else," Jane said.

Like a switch flipping, Elvis stood, leaned forward, licked her face, then ran to catch up with the kids. Hemingway groomed her paw then used it to wipe the offending dog slobber off her fur before returning to her cat bed. Lala brought her a few of her favorite treats to reward her stellar hospitality.

"She's amazing," Jane said. "Kids, come say hi to Hemingway. Look at her front feet."

Ava and Mac approached the counter. "Can we pet her?" Mac asked.

Lala said, "She would love that."

"Mommy told us she has extra toes, and that makes her extra special," Ava said.

"I think it's proof she's descended from kitty royalty." Lala smiled. She lifted Hemingway's front paw to show the kids the extra digit.

"Wow," they echoed in unison.

•　　•　　•

With the painting party in full swing, the rapid progress was proof that many hands make light work. Mike and Duncan had covered two walls with the bright and cheerful yellow color using rollers while Emily and Lala concentrated on edging around the trim. Marc moved quickly to tape off the windows and doors then helped Mac roll the bottom half of the room. The only exception to the rule may have been Ava's contribution to the process. She painted fish shapes on the wall and objected when Duncan was forced to cover them up.

"But, Daddy. It's my painting for Miss Lala." She sucked in her lower lip and sniffled.

"Ava, I have a great idea." Lala stepped in to help. "Could you draw me some pictures of fish on paper instead? I can frame them and hang them as art. It'll be way better."

Ava's eyes lit up. "Okay. Mommy, did you bring my art bag?"

"I did." Jane retrieved the requested supplies and motioned for Ava to follow her to the desk. "Anthony, do you have room for a helper?"

"Absolutely." Anthony shifted his chair and papers to make space on the desk. He'd been relieved of painting duty to continue working through Billy's financials.

As the final paint strokes covered the walls, Mac and Ava began to fade, prompting Jane to signal Duncan that it was time to leave.

"Kids, tell Miss Lala, thank you. You've got school in the morning, so we need to get going."

"Oh my. I owe you all a big thanks." Lala twirled around, looking at her transformed space. "I don't think I would've been able to do this on my own. At least not right now."

While Jane gathered the kids' stuff and hooked Elvis to his leash, Emily and Lala washed the paintbrushes and cleaned up the supplies. Emily turned to ask Mike and Duncan for help to move the furniture back into position and realized they had disappeared. She looked out the front window and saw them huddled together on the dock.

Hmmm, Emily said to herself. *What are they up to?* She went outside to join the discussion, but they stopped talking as she approached.

"What's going on?" she asked.

"Em, just because we're talking by ourselves doesn't mean anything is going on." Duncan smiled.

"I get that, but tell me I'm wrong this time."

Mike laughed. "I'm picturing the two of you as kids. Your parents must have had their hands full."

Duncan said, "If you must know, we were talking about Billy's case. We're trying to determine if he left the marina on his boat or someone else's."

"We didn't want to say anything with the kids around," Mike said.

Duncan nodded. "It's dark, but I can see two security cameras covering the marina. Billy owns the dive shop and fuel dock, but a different company owns the marina and boat slips. One of the larger sailboats is a liveaboard, and the cabin lights are on. We'll talk with them after everyone leaves."

"Oh, I didn't realize you'd gotten this far in the investigation—"

Mac ran out the dive shop door ahead of Jane and Lala. "Daddy, can we go fishing?"

"It's too late right now, but if it's okay with Lala, we'll come back another day and fish off the dock."

"Anytime," Lala said. "But if you want to check out something really amazing, follow me."

The kids fell in line behind Lala as she walked to the far end of her dock. Underwater lights mounted on the support pilings cast a glow into the water.

"Look." Lala pointed at the long, powerful fish swimming between the barnacle-encrusted posts. The large tarpon's metallic silver scales reflected the light as small baitfish darted away.

"Whoa," Mac exclaimed. "He's ugly."

Ava stepped back. "What does that fish eat?"

Duncan put a hand on her shoulder. "Little fish and shrimp and insects. They hang out around the dock and eat the scraps tossed in the water from the fish-cleaning table."

"Not people?" Ava asked.

"No, not people," he said with a smile.

Ava moved closer to the edge of the dock to watch the underwater show.

"We call him Big Bob," Lala said. "He sort of lives here."

Now that the fish had a name, Ava must have decided it had to be friendly, and stood next to her brother. Elvis sat between the two kids and followed the tarpon's every movement.

"Okay. Time to go," Jane said.

Ava waved at the water. "Bye, Mr. Big Bob."

Jane packed the kids, the dog, and his puffer fish into the car, then kissed Duncan goodbye. Lala returned to her apartment to join Anthony and Marc. Duncan stepped aside, giving Emily and Mike a moment alone.

"After we talk with the sailboat's owner, I have to drive Duncan home."

"Is there any chance I can join your interview?" Emily asked.

Mike turned to face her. "Sorry, Em. It's official police business."

She was about to say something but caught herself. She didn't need their permission to speak to anyone, including Lala's neighbors. Plus, pushing rarely changed Mike or Duncan's position.

"I'm signed up for turtle watch on Friday night. Want to join me?" She grabbed his shirt and pulled him close. "You can never resist the chance to witness a turtle hatch."

"It's a date." Mike lifted her into his arms for a proper goodnight kiss.

CHAPTER NINETEEN

Lala and Anthony were huddled around the desk when Emily returned to the office. The Murphy bed had been pulled down and made up with the new linens. Hemingway sauntered into the room, and after surveying the changes, she curled up on the cushy duvet.

"I think she approves." Marc sat at the foot of the bed and petted her head. Her purring echoed throughout the space.

"It's amazing how much we accomplished in one night," Emily said.

"Yes, I feel like I can finally take a breath." Lala tapped her hand against the wall next to the window to check the paint. "I'm rushing the process, but can you help me hang these new curtains?"

"Sure." Marc removed the rods from their brackets, and then he and Lala replaced the drab beige curtains with sea-foam green, cotton panels. They stepped back to admire their work.

Anthony turned his chair to face the room. "Looking good."

Lala sat next to the desk. Her downcast expression didn't match the new, sunny decor. "I wish it were as easy to turn the business around."

"Anthony, what did you find in that stack of papers?" Emily asked.

"Well, it looks like Billy had part-time employees until two months ago, then nothing. That timing coincides with the sale of his condo. He must have let them go when finances got tight."

"Did you recognize their names?" Emily asked Lala.

"One of them—Sean. He worked here during high school, but I think he graduated and moved out of state for college. I don't know the other guy, Stewart Jackson, but I recall Billy mentioning a guy he went diving with named Stewie. It must be the same person."

"It might be worthwhile to contact them to find out if they'd seen or talked with Billy recently. But I don't see their address or phone numbers in the file." Anthony picked up the Gamblers Anonymous keychains. "I wonder if Billy had a sponsor—a recovered gambler assigned to help him."

"Maybe." Lala's voice cracked at the mention of Billy's possible addiction. "And I called Billy's old dive buddies. They hadn't heard about his death and were really broken up. It'd been months since they'd seen him last, and they were unaware he'd sold his condo. Seems I'm not the only one he kept secrets from. It makes me sad. It wasn't like him to be so isolated."

Emily thought twice before saying, "You haven't mentioned her much, but what if Billy talked with your mom. Does she know he died?"

Lala covered her face. "No," she sobbed.

Emily squatted in front of her. "You said your mom had changed. She might surprise you, in a good way. And she needs to be told."

Lala looked up and dried her face. "I know I have to call her. I thought I'd wait until I had the final details for the funeral so I only had to contact her once. But I can't put it off any longer."

"She might be able to help you through this. She's still your mom, and I'm sure she loves you." Anthony wiped a tear from his eye.

"Love was never the problem." Lala smiled. "I'll contact her in the morning."

They moved the chair, ottoman, dresser, and carpet into the apartment. A floor lamp bathed the room in soft light, while a table lamp on the nightstand made it feel cozy.

"It's beautiful. Thank you, Em, for loaning me your stuff." Lala hugged each of them.

"I think that's our cue to let you get some rest," Anthony said.

Emily gathered her bag and the remaining paint supplies. Anthony and Marc helped load everything into her car, then they left in the van.

Alone at last to do some reconnaissance, Emily walked to the center of the marina. She located the two security cameras Duncan had mentioned. Based on their angle, it was impossible to tell if there were any blind spots or areas of the marina outside the camera's view.

The sailboat owner was sitting on deck, so Emily went over to introduce herself. Charlie Carney, originally from Rhode Island, had been docked at the marina during the last month of hurricane season, waiting till Thanksgiving to set sail for the Caribbean. He said he told the police the same thing earlier when they stopped by—he didn't have any information about Billy's comings and goings since he'd only been there a short while. But Billy had been a friendly face, sharing helpful tips about the area. Charlie offered his condolences to the family before saying goodnight.

With slumped shoulders, Emily walked to her car, realizing the day ended with more questions than answers. But the transformation of Lala's apartment had brought joy, and that should be celebrated.

•   •   •

The soft tapping against the side of Emily's face pulled her out of a deep sleep. When the tapping increased in frequency and force, she opened her eyes. Bella's whiskers brushed against her cheek.

"Bella, it's still dark out." Emily rolled over, but her hungry cat stepped across her ribs and used her claws to pull the blankets away from Emily's shoulders.

"Okay. You win. I'm getting up."

Not until Emily moved to a sitting position did Bella relent. She then ran to the kitchen, beckoning Emily to follow with a loud meow.

As the coffee machine sputtered to life, Emily presented Bella with her favorite tuna and whitefish medley. Living with Bella made any alarm clock redundant. Most days, she didn't mind the early wake-up call, since she considered herself to be a morning person.

Bella finished her breakfast at the same time Emily filled her mug. The two moved outside to take in the dawn's first light. Sunrise painted the sky with shades of yellow, orange, and red. Palm tree silhouettes traced shadows across her deck. A rare cool breeze forced Emily to drape a throw blanket over her legs. Bella settled in next to her, grooming her paws before curling up for her post-breakfast nap.

Emily sipped her Italian roast while thinking about the week ahead. On top of the demands of running a veterinary hospital, she had a date night planned with Mike, and Sarah Klein would be in town to attend multiple meetings related to the turtle center. That alone would be a lot, but Emily's thoughts kept drifting back to Lala and Billy.

When would the autopsy be completed? Did Billy have a gambling problem? Tracking down any acquaintances that could shed light on the last few months of his life would be important to help explain what may have happened. Lala needed their help to get some answers. Anthony had the financial part handled, so she would concentrate on filling in the remaining missing pieces.

Emily recalled Anthony mentioning the local Gamblers Anonymous group met at a church in town. That would be the best way to track down anyone who knew Billy. She made a mental note to check online for the next scheduled meeting.

She hoped when Lala reached out to her mom, they could find a way forward. Emily's mom had been the most important person in her life. That person she turned to for unconditional love, advice, and support. Her mom was her biggest cheerleader, and she found it hard to imagine how Lala must feel to be estranged from her mom.

"Bella, it's time to get ready for work." The cat refused to move, so Emily slipped out from under the blanket, leaving the patio door open behind her. After a quick shower and a refill of her coffee, Emily was ready to start her day. A knock at the door startled Bella, and she retreated to the bedroom to avoid the unexpected guest.

Emily peeked through the front window and stiffened when she saw Duncan's sheriff's car parked in her driveway. These unexpected stops rarely brought good news.

"Morning, Em. Glad I caught you." Duncan helped himself to a cup of coffee.

"Is everything okay?"

"Well." He took a sip, watching Emily over the rim of his mug. "It's about Billy. The ME determined the cause of death." Duncan read from his phone. "He died of acute intravascular hemolysis and pulmonary edema, not consistent with a saltwater drowning. I have no idea what that means, but toxicology tests are pending, and the coroner has opened an investigation."

"What!" Emily exclaimed. "Toxicology means they're looking for a source of poison. You're basically telling me Billy was…" Her voice trailed off.

"Murdered." Duncan set his empty mug on the counter. "Lala is being notified as we speak. I know you and Anthony are her only support system right now. I figured she'd be reaching out to you."

"But who would want to kill Billy?"

"That's what Mike and I are going to figure out."

"Anthony has been helping Lala sort through all the business financials. It's a mess, but he found the names of two former employees. Might be a good place to start."

"Thanks. We'll be dissecting every aspect of Billy's life. It could get uncomfortable for Lala, depending on what we find."

Emily turned to look out at the water. She concentrated on the repetitive motion of the waves breaking onshore. It helped to center her.

"Can you imagine losing a parent—and that's essentially what Billy was to Lala—then having to deal with a murder investigation?"

"No, I can't. It could be helpful for Sarah Klein to speak with Lala. She dealt with the same emotions when her mom died. Of course, Mrs. Klein was an innocent victim. Until we can determine a motive for Billy's death, it's impossible to say whether he had a role to play in his own demise."

CHAPTER TWENTY

After a quick stop at Savannah's bakery to pick up treats for her staff, Emily drove to work on autopilot. Anthony would freak out at the news of Billy's murder. It wasn't the first time they had landed themselves smack-dab in the middle of one of Duncan and Mike's investigations. She vowed to help Lala learn the truth about what happened to her uncle, even if it was hard to hear.

After dropping her bags on her desk, Emily set the box of pastries in the lunchroom, plated Anthony's favorite, and walked into the lobby.

"Morning, Abigail. Can you tell everyone I brought treats from Savannah's?"

"Thanks, Dr. Benton. The schedule has filled up, and Mr. Englewood called about Moose—he's been shaking his head all night, keeping them both awake. Can I squeeze him in for an appointment between two routine checkups?"

"That's fine. Please tell Mr. Englewood not to clean his ears before he gets here. I need to examine them first."

"Will do."

Anthony stood outside his office, checking the inventory in the pharmacy. Emily held up the plate with the almond croissant for him to see.

"Yum, thanks," he said as they moved into his office.

"Sit down and take a bite. I have something to tell you."

Anthony's face dropped at the ominous warning. "What? And don't keep me waiting."

"Billy was murdered. Duncan dropped by to tell me on his way to work."

"But how? Wait, what about Lala? Has she been told?"

"Duncan mentioned the coroner planned to call her first thing. Since they already proved he didn't die from drowning, they're running tests to look for another cause—specifically, a source of poison."

"I don't understand. You found him on the beach in his dive gear."

"We know they didn't find salt water in his lungs or any other findings consistent with drowning. I haven't been able to do more research." She read aloud the detailed medical cause of death Duncan had shared.

"Lala's going to be devastated. Now, I need some comfort food." Anthony plopped down in his chair, took a bite, and stared at the computer, seemingly lost in thought.

"What's on your mind?"

"I can't put my finger on it, but something is off. Billy's numbers don't add up. The dive shop and fuel dock are making a small but steady profit, but he's behind on paying his suppliers, and there's no cash on hand. I can't figure out where the revenue is going. It's almost like he had two different ledgers. At first, I thought he'd been separating the marina and dive shop business from his charter business, but I don't think that's it."

"If those Gamblers Anonymous keychains were his, that would explain his financial troubles," Emily said. "Wait—does he own *Diver Down* outright?"

"Yes, and it's his only valuable asset. Of course, boats depreciate daily, so it's a diminishing investment. I think we should stop by the marina during our lunch break. Let's check on Lala."

"Good idea."

•   •   •

By mid-morning, Emily realized she wouldn't be able to get away from the hospital. She'd be lucky to have a moment to eat. Squeezing in Moose Englewood's appointment would fill that empty slot, so Anthony planned to see Lala by himself. Emily took the time to do a cursory search on Billy's cause of death.

In veterinary medicine, the most common cause of pulmonary edema, or the accumulation of fluid in the lungs, occurs when a pet's heart disease progresses to congestive heart failure. Hemolysis meant the breakdown of red blood cells, which also happened in pets when their body's immune system attacks their own cells. But what would cause both to happen at the same time and so suddenly? It sounded like something catastrophic had occurred with no early warning signs. The search for a poison made sense.

•   •   •

"Hi, Mr. Englewood." Moose, the almost hundred-pound, chocolate Labrador Retriever bounded over to Emily then sat. "What a good boy." She went to pet his head, but he began shaking and scratching at his ears.

"He's been doing that all night. We're both miserable. And he stinks."

Emily completed the exam. Moose was a healthy, young dog except for the dark brown, sticky wax filling his ear canals. She took a swab and spread the sample on a microscope slide.

"Moose has an ear infection. That's the source of the smell and the reason he's shaking. Has he been swimming lately?"

"He swims every time we go out on the boat. And he loves jumping off the diving board into our pool. We go through a lot of dog towels in our house." Mr. Englewood laughed.

"Moose doesn't have a history of ear infections, but water in the ear canal can be the cause. Drying his ears after swimming will help. By looking at this sample under the microscope, I can determine the cause of the infection and find the right treatment. Catrinna will be in to clean Moose's ears. We need to get that stuff out. She'll show you how to do it—cleaning at home will be part of the plan and prevention from future infections."

Emily walked into the lab and handed Catrinna the slide. After applying a special stain, a microscopic evaluation revealed a yeast infection, a common cause of itchy ears in dogs. Emily dispensed both an ear flush and medicated ear drops and returned to the room.

"That was disgusting," Mr. Englewood said. "I can't believe how much stuff Catrinna got out of his ears." Moose continued to shake his head.

"He has a yeast infection. These drops will treat it, but I would like to see him again in two weeks to ensure his ears are clear."

"Is it contagious? I don't want to end up with that stuff in my ears."

"No, it's not contagious to people or other pets."

Emily showed how to place the drops in Moose's ears and handed the prescriptions to Mr. Englewood. "His ears will feel better in a couple of hours. Keep him out of the water this next week while you're treating him."

"It'll be hard, but I'll try. And thanks for fitting us in today. I don't think we could have gone another night like the last. I'll book that follow-up appointment on my way out."

Emily returned to her office and checked her phone. No word from Anthony, but she expected him back any minute. As she typed a message, the phone rang.

"Em, it's not good," Anthony said.

"What's not good?"

"The police have been carting evidence out of the marina all morning. Lala is so upset, and Hemingway is back in the rafters."

"Oh, no. Are Duncan and Mike there?"

"Yeah, but they're not talking. Are you okay at work if I stay? I can't leave her."

"I'll be fine, but keep me posted. I wanted to check on the turtle center after work in advance of Sarah's arrival, but it can wait a day. I'll get to you as soon as the hospital closes."

Emily did her best to compartmentalize her tasks so she could focus on her patients, but it wasn't easy. After finishing the medical notes for the last appointment of the day, Emily asked Abigail if she could close up the hospital since she needed to leave right away.

"Of course, Dr. Benton. I've got everything covered."

Anthony continued to send regular updates throughout the afternoon. The police had left with the collected evidence, and he and Lala were now trying to coax Hemingway back to ground level. His last message instructed her to be quiet when she arrived at the dive shop.

As she neared the causeway exit to the marina, Emily looked out across the harbor at the stunning ocean view. She drew in a deep breath, trying to steady herself, unsure of what awaited her.

•   •   •

Looking through the window, Emily saw Anthony and Lala sitting on a blanket as Hemingway moved back and forth between them, accepting their pets. She slowly turned the doorknob and walked inside without speaking. Hemingway stopped, looked in her direction, then curled up in Lala's lap.

"Is she okay?" Emily asked.

"Yes, finally." Lala sounded exhausted. "All the commotion scared her. And the police searched every room, so I had no place to hide her. It was horrible."

"I'm so sorry." Emily turned to Anthony and noticed him glaring, his jaw clenched. She rarely saw him angry. "What aren't you telling me?"

"I thought Mike and Duncan would be more forthcoming. They refused to tell us what they were looking for." Anthony reached forward to pet Hemingway.

"What did they collect?"

"Most of the paper files, stuff from his desk, and all the dive tanks in the side yard," Lala said.

"Really? Why would they need those?"

Anthony said, "That's what frustrated me—they wouldn't say. Duncan's like a vault. Can you get Mike to talk—use your feminine wiles or something?" He smiled.

"That rarely works, and you know it," Emily said. "Did anything else happen today?"

"It's hard to keep track. I talked with my mom." Lala smiled as her tears pooled. "It went well. Thanks for encouraging me to reach out to her."

"I'm so happy for you."

"Yeah, I'm happy for me, too. She's getting time off work and will drive here from Tarpon Springs. I'm a little nervous about it, but I'm grateful she's coming."

"Family is family," Anthony said. "You need them at a time like this."

"And in all fairness to your brother," Lala said, "he helped me out this afternoon. As they were wrapping up their police business, two boaters came by to purchase fuel. I planned to send them away, but he offered to help me turn on the pumps and process the sale. He definitely knows his way around boats."

Emily smiled at hearing of Duncan's kindness. "He's a good guy. I sometimes forget they have a tough job to do. It's never personal."

"I understand that. And I had no issue with them coming here as long as it helps figure out what happened to Billy."

Emily wondered about all the reasons they would need to collect the tanks but kept her thoughts to herself. "Were you able to reach Billy's former employees?"

"I talked to Sean. He's a freshman at Florida State with a full-ride baseball scholarship. Billy had cut his hours this summer but didn't tell him why. With his busy baseball season and reporting on campus early for training, he didn't mind. His mom saw a local news report about Billy's death, so he already knew. He sounded pretty upset. I didn't even know it had been released to the public, but I've been in my own little bubble."

"I guess since it's now an official investigation, they can't keep it secret. Sorry you had to hear about it that way."

"That's okay," Lala said. "It might lead a witness to come forward."

"And I couldn't find a number for the other guy, Stewart," Anthony said.

"We need to fill in the blanks about what was going on in Billy's life before he died," Emily said. "I checked online, and the Gamblers Anonymous meeting is tonight at eight. Are either of you interested in joining me?"

"I'm not up to facing that right now," Lala said. "It's been a tough day, and I can't cope with the reality that Billy had a gambling problem. I keep wondering if there was something I could have done to help him."

"I understand," Emily said. "But you know firsthand with your mom—you can't make someone else change. They have to want it for themselves."

"But it's still so hard to accept."

Anthony checked his phone. "I ordered us dinner. Tracking shows it will be here soon. I think I'm going to eat with Lala then head home."

"Yes, you two need to rest and decompress. I'll go alone. I'm not sure what I expect to learn, but I'll start by speaking with the meeting coordinator. It might lead nowhere, but there's only one way to find out. Wish me luck."

CHAPTER TWENTY-ONE

Gamblers Anonymous met in Room 214 of the church on Center Street. Emily's online search confirmed that the meetings offered a space for members to share their experiences, challenges, and achievements while discussing the temptations they faced.

She parked next to the few cars in the lot and entered through the nearest side door. Signs directing her to the meeting room led her down the hallway. There was a coffee and tea station positioned across from an open door. A middle-aged woman with short, curly hair was engaged in conversation with someone whose back was turned to Emily. Noticing her arrival, the woman smiled and stepped forward to introduce herself.

"Hi. My name's Wilma, and I'll be leading tonight's meeting."

"It's nice to meet you. I'm Emily."

"Welcome, Emily. Please fill out a name tag and help yourself to any of the beverages. We'll be starting shortly."

Emily moved closer and spoke in a low voice. "Actually, I'm not here for the meeting. I was hoping you could help me with some information."

Wilma looked up at the newcomer, a questioning look on her face. "What type of information?"

"I'm here about William Todd, or I should say, Billy Todd. Do you know him?"

Her friendly face disappeared. "We only go by first names here—to protect privacy and anonymity. Everything said in the room, stays in the room. I don't think I can help you."

Emily realized she'd made a tactical mistake and changed course. "Let me start over. Billy was a friend, and I'm trying to find anyone he might have confided in lately." She found the website for Blue Water Marina on her phone, zoomed in on a picture of Billy, and held the phone out. "This is Billy Todd. You may not have heard, but he died a few days ago."

Wilma drew her hand to her mouth and gasped. "Oh, no. Not Billy. I talked with him just last week." She stumbled, so Emily grabbed a nearby chair for her to sit. "What happened?"

"He died while scuba diving, and the police are investigating. I'm good friends with Billy's niece, Lauryn. She moved back to take over his marina store, but she's struggling with it all. We found Gamblers Anonymous keychains in Billy's desk, and that led me to you."

Wilma pulled a tissue from her pocket and blew her nose. "He never mentioned Lauryn, but Billy talked all the time about Lala."

"Lala is Lauryn's nickname."

"That makes sense. She's the main reason he kept showing up. He wanted her to be proud of him."

"Lala wasn't aware of Billy's gambling addiction. When did he start attending meetings?" Wilma started to answer then stopped, prompting Emily to add, "I understand you want to protect his privacy, but Lala needs your help."

"Given what happened, I suppose it's alright to talk. He started coming about three months ago."

Emily thought that lined up with the keychains they'd found commemorating his milestones.

Wilma continued. "He didn't share at first but had been opening up lately. He got in a bunch of financial trouble betting on sports with a local bookie and had to sell his house. I'm not sure how bad it was, but you don't need to be a rocket scientist to read between the lines. We all have our weaknesses—mine is online slot machines."

"Was he close to anyone else? Or did he have a sponsor?"

"No sponsor, but I've seen him hanging out with one person—until we banned that guy from meetings a couple of months ago when we realized he was preying on the members. He tried to convince others to join him at the horse track or to go in with him on a bet. He was a real charmer, and people gravitated to him, but he made my skin crawl. I have a sixth sense about these things, and you can trust me when I say, Stewie had a dark side. We're all recovering addicts here, and we don't need predators like him around."

"Wait. Did you say Stewie?"

She nodded. "That's how he introduced himself. Why?"

"Billy employed a Stewart at the marina until recently. Would you know his last name or if it's the same person from the meetings?"

"Sorry, no. But there can't be that many people named Stewie in Coral Shores. Emily, is it okay if I tell the members about Billy?"

"Of course."

Wilma handed her a business card. "Could you share the details of his funeral arrangements? We'll all want to be there. Billy was a kind and caring man and our friend. Please tell Lala how deeply sorry I am for her loss and that she's in my thoughts." She wiped her eyes with her sleeve.

"I will. Thanks for your help."

Emily sat in her parked car, reflecting on Wilma's words. The insight had been crucial in understanding Billy's frame of mind. By sharing it with Lala, she could offer her some sense of closure. Billy had been working hard to stop gambling and made good friends in the process.

But who was this Stewie guy? Based on Wilma's assessment, he sounded like trouble.

It was getting late, and her stomach rumbled to remind her she'd skipped dinner. Bella would be beside herself over the delay, even though she always had access to some dry kibble. Emily called ahead to order takeout from Curry in a Hurry—enough for two people in hopes she could convince Mike to join her.

She and Mike had planned a date night for the end of the week, but the connection to Gamblers Anonymous and Stewie felt too important to sit on. Sharing what she'd learned with Mike might prompt him to share in return. Emily wanted to find out why they took all the scuba tanks from the shop and what they had learned after evaluating the security video from the marina.

"Hi, Em," Mike answered the phone. "What's up?"

"I'm picking up some dinner on my way home and wondered if you've eaten yet."

"Is that an invitation?" She could hear the smile in his voice.

"Absolutely. I'll be home in twenty minutes."

"I'll be there."

•　　•　　•

"Meow. Meow. Meow." Bella squawked at Emily from the top of her cat tree when she entered her cottage.

"My apologies, Bella." Emily grabbed a can of savory chicken morsels from the cupboard and set a dish in front of her impatient cat. She placed the takeout containers in the oven to warm then washed up and changed out of her scrubs. Right on cue, there was a knock at the door.

"Hi." Mike stepped inside and kissed her. "Something smells great. The stale vending machine sandwich I had earlier didn't count as lunch."

Emily took his hand and led him to the kitchen. They helped themselves to chicken tikka masala, aloo gobi, and biryani rice.

Mike grabbed a beer from her fridge and poured her a glass of wine. They moved to the beach deck to dine under the string lights as the sound of the waves played in the background.

Mike finished his plate and leaned back. "That was delicious. I need to add this place to my favorites list." As he drank from his bottle, Emily noticed him watching her intently. She could tell he had something on his mind, so she prodded.

"I had an ulterior motive for inviting you for dinner."

"Oh." Mike set his drink down and took Emily's hand to guide her to the oversized chaise lounge. He sat down and pulled her into his arms, kissing her neck.

For a few minutes, Emily forgot all about her fact-finding trip to the Gamblers Anonymous meeting. After months of dating, Mike could still captivate her. Then an image of Billy lying on the beach flashed before her eyes and she sat up.

"I guess I should say I had two ulterior motives."

Mike studied her face but didn't speak. Emily told him all about the Gamblers Anonymous keychains and what she'd learned at the meeting. She believed this Stewie person might have insight into Billy's financial troubles and urged Mike to talk to him. If he was the same Stewie who had been working at the marina, he might also know who Billy had been diving with lately. Billy wouldn't have trusted just anyone to pilot *Diver Down*. Someone had taken Billy out diving that morning, and the fact they hadn't come forward to report him missing added suspicion.

"Em, I'm only asking because Duncan will want to know, but why did you go to the meeting alone? This is an active investigation."

"You didn't see Lala after your team left the marina. Anthony had to stay behind to console her. Not to mention the fact that Hemingway got scared and climbed back into the ceiling rafters."

"I feel bad about that. We did our best to be respectful and avoid any disruption. Lala was very cooperative, and that helped speed things along. But that still doesn't answer my question."

"I'm trying to get answers. Lala's all alone, and learning that Billy might have a gambling problem shocked her."

"I understand. I do. But can you talk to me first before you do any more investigating?" He smiled to let her know he wasn't angry. "The last time, it involved a kidnapping and a murder."

"And I helped solve that case. Isn't the murderer in jail right now because of me?"

Mike laughed. "Yes, he is. But your actions scared me. I can't bear the thought of anything bad happening to you. And Duncan was beside himself with worry. All I'm asking is that you loop me in next time."

Emily relented. "I'll do my best. You know, if you shared the details of a case with me, I wouldn't feel the need to investigate on my own. To be more specific, why did you collect the dive tanks from the marina?"

"I promise to tell you why, but not until the coroner has spoken with Lala. He'll be calling her in the morning."

"Oh. That doesn't sound good. Do they have the results from the toxicology tests?"

"Em." Mike shook his head and pulled her close to kiss her. "Lala needs to be informed first."

CHAPTER TWENTY-TWO

"Arsenic!" Emily yelled into the phone.

"That's what they told Lala," Anthony said. "I think she went into shock—she wasn't making any sense. When I talked to her, she was already out the door on her way to speak directly with Deputy Garcia. Her exact words were, 'I'm going to camp out at the sheriff's office until someone explains to me what's going on.'"

"Isn't arsenic some old-fashioned poison? My mom took me to a play titled *Arsenic and Old Lace* about two sisters who kill people by putting arsenic in their wine."

"No idea. Let's do some research when we get to work. I'll see you soon." Then Anthony hung up.

Emily had no words. She wished Mike had given her a heads-up so they could have prepared Lala for this devastating news.

Bella finished her breakfast and settled into her favorite nap spot—the window box in the living room. The morning sun streamed in, lighting her gray fur so it shimmered like silver threads.

"Bella, the proverbial cat is out of the bag."

With a full thermos of coffee in hand, Emily hustled to her car. Her commute provided stunning views of the ocean, its sandy beaches, and the vast Intracoastal Waterway—a tonic to start her day. But with so much on her mind, Emily barely noticed the natural beauty passing by.

As she crossed over the causeway, she looked down at the masts from sailboats docked near Billy's dive shop. Something nagged at her, at the back of her mind. When she pulled into the hospital, it hit her. She remembered a case during vet school of cows that died from arsenic poisoning. Emily ran into Anthony's office to share her epiphany.

"A farmer had burned old, pressure-treated lumber and spread the ash around the field as a fertilizer. When the cows grazed on it, they became sick and died. It took a post-mortem exam by the head pathologist at the vet school to figure it out. It was in the wood. The chemical they used to treat the lumber had arsenic in it, and the burned ash concentrated the poison. What if Billy had old lumber on the dock or in the building?"

"Em, take a breath," Anthony said, gesturing to the empty chair for her to sit.

She exhaled. "I'm getting ahead of myself. We need more information." Emily texted Mike to let him know Lala had been informed about the cause of death. That meant he would be free to speak about the details, and she asked him to call.

"I can't imagine they're still using a dangerous poison in the wood you buy at building supply stores. That makes no sense." Anthony searched his computer for information on sources of arsenic.

"It looks like the wood industry stopped treating residential lumber with arsenic over twenty years ago," he said. "And the EPA didn't require old lumber to be removed from building structures. But they suggested sealing it to keep the chemicals from leaching out into the surrounding area."

"That can't be it," Emily said. "Billy's docks are in great condition—likely rebuilt only a few years ago. What about the paint? You know how lead paint is toxic? Is there arsenic in old paint?"

"Let me check." Anthony typed away on his keyboard. "Not since the 1800s. Definitely not the source."

"You're right. And Hemingway is super healthy. If there was a poison in the environment, you'd expect both of them to be sick."

Speculating without all the facts seemed pointless. Emily moved to her office, put on her white doctor's coat, and scrolled through the day's appointment schedule. Routine things so far, but that often changed in an instant. Since becoming a veterinarian, Emily had yet to experience two days alike—and she loved the variety.

Veterinary medicine required an innate ability to multitask— juggling appointments, treating sick patients, and interpreting lab test results, all while running a business. But she and Anthony took on an even larger challenge when they became co-directors of the Eliza Klein Sea Turtle Conservation Center. They had to make every minute of their workday count.

Sarah Klein was flying in from Los Angeles for a weekend of planning meetings to kick off the next phase of the project. Marlon and Sharon would be handling the day-to-day operations, and their latest email included both a status update and an itinerary. Despite Emily and Anthony's packed schedules and time spent assisting Lala, they would need to carve out a moment to focus on the turtles.

·   ·   ·

"Em, have you heard from Lala or Mike yet? I'm getting worried." Anthony leaned on her office door. The hospital was closed, and the doors were locked for the night.

"No. Mike is supposed to be coming over for dinner, but he usually touches base first. He's probably busy dealing with this latest turn of events in the investigation."

"Why don't you reach out to Duncan?"

Emily shrugged her shoulders and gritted her teeth. Her brother often mistook her questions about an ongoing case as meddling.

"I should tell him about my conversation with Wilma from Gamblers Anonymous. I've got her business card and can pass along her phone number. Duncan and Jane will be dropping Elvis off at the hospital tomorrow on their way out of town for Mac's baseball tournament. He's staying with me until Sunday night."

"Okay, but tread lightly, and let me know what he says. I thought about checking on Lala, but I haven't been home much over the past few days, so I'll wait to hear from her first."

"Sarah should be landing soon. I'm looking forward to our meeting. Things are getting exciting."

"Yes, they are, madame co-director." Anthony gave Emily a high five. "Night."

•   •   •

On her way home, Emily made a split-second decision to stop by the marina. She understood firsthand how difficult it was to ask for help. Just because Lala hadn't called didn't mean she wasn't struggling.

Emily saw Hemingway sleeping behind the sales counter and decided against knocking in case it startled the tabby. She texted Lala that she was outside. Lala peeked out of her apartment and waved. She unlocked the door and immediately fell into Emily's arms.

"I'm so sorry," Emily said.

After a minute, Lala stepped back and rubbed her head. "I've had a splitting headache ever since I learned about Billy being poisoned. Until now, I've been in denial that anyone would want to hurt him."

"Did they tell you anything else about how it happened? Anthony told me they found arsenic in his system."

"It was arsine—the gas form of arsenic."

"Oh. Is that why they confiscated the scuba tanks? To test them?"

Lala nodded. "And Duncan said it might take a few days to get the final results."

Emily hypothesized out loud about how someone could be exposed to arsenic gas. She'd never even heard of arsine before. Her curious, scientific mind wondered how difficult it would be to convert arsenic into a gas. What special equipment would you need? It didn't seem like something you could do in your garage.

But when Lala grew frustrated at not having answers to her many questions, Emily shifted gears. She'd do more research later. Her friend needed a boost, so she told Lala about her talk with Wilma, hoping Lala would take comfort in knowing Billy had stopped gambling and wanted to make her proud. He had developed deep friendships at the group meetings.

Lala smiled. "Billy was that type of person. Everyone loved him. That's why I'm struggling to understand who would want to kill him." Her voice trailed off. "I can't even say the word *murder*."

"Can I do anything for you? Anything at all."

"Well, Mr. Haney from the watersports store dropped by to look at Billy's surfboards. He wanted to research one of them, and he just called with a generous offer to buy all three. Do you have time to help me carry them over?"

"Sure, but why don't you let me handle that? Get a big glass of water and go lie down."

Lala looked relieved. "Thank you. I'll let him know you're on the way."

Emily retrieved the surfboards from the storeroom and propped them against the outside wall. Lala thanked her again and locked up behind her.

The boards wouldn't fit in Emily's car, forcing her to carry one at a time across the marina dock. When she arrived at the watersports store, maneuvering the awkward surfboard through the doorway became a struggle. She set it down to free her hands, then wedged her foot to prop the door open. As she bent to pick up the board, the door suddenly swung wide, throwing her off balance. She lurched forward, board in hand, barely steadying herself to avoid crashing to the ground.

"Watch out," a man yelled. He passed by without offering to help.

"Me! You're the one who should watch out. Seriously." Emily couldn't believe his rudeness. She shook off the incident, and as she reached for the door handle, it flung open again. Emily wondered if she deserved hazard pay for delivering these surfboards.

"Stewie, wait up!" The employee who had been so rude on her last trip to the store chased after the guy into the parking lot.

Did he just say Stewie? Emily watched the two men talking and recognized Stewie as the same customer who had come into the dive shop to buy bait on Lala's first night in town—the one Hemingway had hissed at. His voice rose in intensity, and as he waved his arms over his head, a bulky necklace jostled against his chest with each movement.

Standing just out of earshot, Emily could not catch their words. It looked tense, almost heated, but didn't last long—Stewie got into his truck and sped out of the lot, kicking gravel up in his wake. Acting on instinct, she memorized the license plate number on the older-model Toyota.

The employee walked past Emily with his head down, stepping into the store without even glancing in her direction. He didn't acknowledge her presence, let alone hold the door open for her.

What is going on here? She typed the driver's plate number into her phone. If this was Billy's employee, Stewie, why hadn't he said anything to Lala when he bought the bait? If he knew about Billy's death, he should have offered his condolences. And if he didn't know, wouldn't he have asked where Billy was?

CHAPTER TWENTY-THREE

Wilma's words echoed in Emily's head. *How many people named Stewie could there be in Coral Shores?* It was an excellent question. Could the Stewie who almost knocked her down be the same Stewie from the Gamblers Anonymous meeting and the same Stewie who worked part-time at Blue Water Marina? Emily didn't believe in coincidences, so they had to be connected.

She propped the door open with her shoulder, double-checked for oncoming foot traffic, and entered the watersports store. The guy behind the counter stared at her with a blank look, as if she had just appeared out of nowhere.

Tempted to give him a piece of her mind, she exhaled to release her rising tension. She didn't want to say anything to jeopardize the sale. "I'm here to meet with Mr. Haney. He's expecting me."

Without a word, the guy got off his stool and disappeared into a back room.

Emily wondered why any employer would tolerate this behavior, especially in a retail business where customer service meant everything.

A minute later, Mr. Haney approached her. His smiling face revealed deep crow's feet. An exaggerated sunglass tan line attested to time spent outdoors. Emily figured he used his watersports gear often.

"Miss Todd told me you would be dropping by. Let me get that for you." He carried the surfboard to an empty display rack in the corner. "What a beauty." He ran his hand over the board and whistled.

"I'll run and get the other boards," Emily said. "They're still at the dive shop propped on an outside wall."

"You don't need to do that. Trent," he shouted over his shoulder.

The surly employee shuffled into the room. "Yeah."

"Can you go to the dive shop and bring back the two surfboards leaning against the building?"

Trent rolled his eyes and walked past them out the front door.

"I apologize for my nephew's manners." Mr. Haney sighed. "He seems to forget this is an actual job. That's what I get for doing my sister a favor."

Emily considered Mr. Haney a kind man, but she didn't think he was doing anyone a favor.

"I've been eyeing Billy's board for years. I'm still surfing every chance I get and jumped at the opportunity to buy this one. Even though Billy rarely went surfing, I could never get him to part with it. This board is a collector's dream."

"You were friends with Billy?" Emily asked.

"Sort of. Mostly business associates. We shared some of the same customers and helped each other out with referrals, but owning a small business is all-consuming, and neither of us had much free time."

"That makes sense."

"His death is so tragic. And a diving accident at that. I asked Miss Todd to let me know about any funeral arrangements. I want to be there to pay my respects."

Emily nodded. "She'll need all the friends she can get when she reopens the marina."

"You tell her not to be shy. If I'm able to help her, I will."

Trent walked in carrying both boards, carelessly banging them against the door frame.

"Careful. Careful." Mr. Haney rushed to grab a board from his nephew's arms. "These are valuable."

"Whatever," he mumbled under his breath.

Emily stepped forward. "Trent, can I ask you a question?"

His shoulders tensed as he whipped his head around. She waited for him to reply but when he said nothing, she continued.

"I saw you talking to a man. You called him Stewie. Could you tell me his last name?"

A panicked look crossed Trent's face.

His uncle elbowed his shoulder. "Speak up, boy."

"Not sure what you're talking about," Trent said.

"The man you were just talking to in the parking lot," Emily said. "The first time we met, you were retrieving your dive computer from Billy's boat. Would you know if this Stewie person worked with Billy or helped run his scuba charters?"

Mr. Haney looked confused. "But Trent doesn't dive."

"You said—"

Trent interrupted her. "You got the wrong person." Then he stomped out of the room.

Mr. Haney dropped his shoulders and shook his head. "Sorry about that. I wish I could help you, but I didn't see who was here."

Not wanting to get involved in a family squabble, Emily said, "Thank you, Mr. Haney. I'll make sure you're notified about Billy's funeral." She left the store no closer to figuring out who had been diving with Billy. Trent's lie didn't sit well, but she couldn't even begin to guess what it meant.

•   •   •

Running behind as usual, Emily picked up Gulf shrimp kabobs and a few prepared side dishes from King's Seafood. After feeding Bella, she rushed to freshen up. Mike would be there any minute.

After dinner, they planned to walk up the beach to check the turtle nests. A tour of the turtle center would have to wait until the following afternoon, when she and Anthony would be meeting with Sarah, Marlon, Sharon, and Gus Fazio, the general contractor. She could feel the ball dropping on her responsibilities with the center. But right now, supporting Lala remained her primary focus.

Emily wiped down the outdoor chairs and table before dinner.

"Em," Mike called out from the front door.

She leaned into the living room. "Come on in." She waved for him to join her.

When Mike stepped onto the deck, Emily met him with a perfunctory kiss before turning to finish setting the table. He reached for her hand and drew her close, stealing her breath with a kiss.

"That's better." He smiled.

"Much." She hugged him tight. "Are you up for grilling some shrimp while I handle the rest?"

He reached for the BBQ tongs on the table. "I'm your man."

Watching Mike tend the grill through her kitchen window, she placed a hand on her stomach, steadying the flutter of butterflies. Was this what love felt like? Or was it simply the effect of his undeniable handsomeness? She had thought she was in love once before, during her freshman year of college, but it had never felt like this. This was something different.

Mike looked up, caught her eye, and gave her a thumbs-up to signal that the shrimp were ready. Emily brought him a beer and a glass of wine for herself, and they enjoyed a delicious meal as the moon rose over the ocean. He pushed back from the table and sighed. "I'll never get tired of all this fresh seafood."

At the start of the year, Mike had moved from Pittsburgh to Coral Shores for a promotion to detective. After his dad died, his mom bought a home in an active retirement community outside Orlando, and this allowed him to be close by. Since the day Emily met him, she was grateful he made that decision.

"Duncan invited me to go deep sea fishing with a friend of his in a couple of weeks. Looking forward to that."

"That's one major difference between Duncan and me. He prefers to stay afloat, and I prefer to stay submerged."

Emily followed Mike into the kitchen when he stood to clear the dishes. She had hoped he would volunteer the latest developments in Billy's murder investigation, but when that didn't happen, she shifted to Plan B—waiting until after dinner and a drink, when he was relaxed and enjoying a walk along the shore, to press him for information.

"Time for turtle patrol." Emily handed him a flashlight.

Mike's eyes lit up. "Fingers crossed we get a hatch."

They walked up the beach, checking the nests and watching for signs of new ones. As they approached the turnaround point, Emily noticed markings in the sand leading from the ocean toward the dune.

"Yes!" She pumped her arm. "A new loggerhead nest."

"How can you tell it's a loggerhead?"

Emily pointed at the tracks in the sand. "Each species of sea turtle leaves behind unique flipper patterns. Loggerheads have alternating tracks, whereas green sea turtles leave paired flipper tracks. Plus, there are other differences in how they lay their eggs."

They followed the tracks to a mound surrounded by a spray of camouflaging sand. "Definitely a loggerhead. Can you stay here while I grab the supply kit to mark the nest? They're in a storage box near the dune."

When Emily returned, she enlisted Mike's help to rope off the nest and record important information on the wooden stakes, including the identification number, species, date, and hatching window.

"Marlon picks up Sharon's coffee tab every time we log a new nest, and Sharon treats Marlon to an evening cocktail after every successful hatch. They've been alternating for decades." Emily texted them both with the details of her discovery.

"This was great to see this part of the process. So much goes into protecting and monitoring these eggs."

Emily smiled at Mike's genuine enthusiasm. "And it's all run by volunteers. That's why I'm so excited about the new center. We'll have a permanent place for them to record their work and to conduct training sessions."

They walked back to her cottage holding hands. She hesitated, careful not to ruin the mood, before broaching the subject of Billy's murder. *Now or never,* she thought to herself. After all, there was never a good time to stir the pot.

"I want you to know, Lala told me about the arsenic gas."

"Arsine," Mike said, matter-of-factly.

"Right. Is that why you confiscated Billy's dive tanks?"

He nodded.

After an extended silence, she said. "And?"

"All the tanks stored at the dive shop were clean. But the tank he wore when you found him contained arsine gas."

"Oh no. How could that even happen?"

"Someone tampered with his tank. We asked a police diver, and he confirmed the tank Billy wore was a specialized steel tank preferred by experienced divers. Not like the regular, aluminum tanks rented by recreational divers. Anyone who knew Billy and had a knowledge of diving would know which tank was his. And it was the only steel tank we found."

"What about accidental poisoning?" She hesitated. "Or suicide?"

"No way it could be an accident, and while we can't rule out suicide, it's unlikely since we didn't find his boat adrift on the water, and he didn't leave a note."

Emily shuddered to think about Billy's last moments.

"Did he suffer?" she asked.

Mike stopped walking and turned to face her. His grim expression told her everything.

CHAPTER TWENTY-FOUR

Emily changed the subject away from Billy's manner of death to keep from crying. She focused on the practical mechanics of how someone could put poison into a scuba tank.

"One of the important safety steps in setting up your dive gear includes turning the tank on and smelling the air. That's done before you attach the vest or the regulator. Wouldn't Billy have realized something was wrong?" she asked.

"The expert I consulted said the gas is colorless, and while it can take on a fishy or garlic smell, it can also be odorless. The area where Billy stores the tanks already smells fishy since it's at the marina and near the fish-cleaning station. He might not have noticed anything unusual if it had been subtle.

"Where would someone buy arsine gas?"

"It's used to manufacture microchips and other electronic components. The supply is regulated because of its toxic properties."

"Do you have any leads? Any at all? None of this makes any sense without a motive. Why would anyone want to kill Billy?"

"Working on a few, but nothing concrete. We're checking with local arsine suppliers for any recent theft or missing inventory. Em,

I know I don't need to tell you this, but everything we discuss is privileged information. We haven't made an official announcement yet and are trying to keep it quiet for now."

"I know that. I'd never betray your confidence—except with Anthony of course. He doesn't count."

"Yes, I get that you're a package deal." He smiled.

"And I have someone you should check out."

He raised his brows. "Why am I not surprised? You have a nose for this."

"Thank you." Emily reveled in the compliment before telling Mike about her interaction with Stewie. "I'd want to know what he knows, especially if he's the same guy that worked for Billy. Oh, and I got his license plate number. I'll send it to your phone when we get home."

Mike pulled her close. "If you ever decide to make a career change into law enforcement, I'd be out of a job."

She laughed. "I'm certain you have nothing to worry about."

Mike's respect for her made her heart swell. He trusted her and valued her input. Inserting herself in Mrs. Klein's murder case and the kidnapping of Marilyn Peña had created tension, mostly with Duncan, but she'd helped solve those crimes. Not that her brother questioned her skills, but they often got stuck in that big brother-little sister dynamic.

When someone she cared about needed her help, Emily would keep pushing for the truth, no matter whose toes she stepped on.

•   •   •

A tickling sensation on her cheek woke Emily from a delightful dream. She put her hand to her face, imagining Mike kissing her. As she drifted off, something wet pressed against her ear. She rolled over to see her gigantic cat watching her.

"Bella, you have the coldest nose." She pulled the blanket around her head, hoping for ten more minutes of sleep, but Bella could be relentless when breakfast was at stake.

"Okay, okay. I'm up."

She dragged herself to the kitchen, started the brew cycle, and dished up some grilled salmon pate for her waiting roommate. Now wide awake, Emily was grateful for the extra quiet time, so she filled her mug and moved to the chaise on her beach deck to take in the sunrise.

With so many moving pieces surrounding Billy's death, it became increasingly difficult to keep track of everything. During previous murder investigations, she and Anthony had contemplated making a crime board, similar to the ones they'd seen on TV detective shows. A large visual aid to identify suspects, timelines, and clues while breaking the case down using the three pillars of crime solving—means, motive, and opportunity.

Anthony had suggested using a whiteboard at work to organize and prioritize hospital tasks. Maybe it was time to invest in one, since they could repurpose the board after Billy's killer was arrested.

Bella had returned to bed for her post-breakfast nap and ignored Emily as she got ready for work.

·   ·   ·

Saturdays at the Coral Shores Veterinary Hospital required Emily to work in overdrive. The hospital closed at noon and wouldn't reopen until Monday morning, prompting many clients to call for last-minute appointments. It was essentially a full day's work crammed into a half day. Anthony had tweaked the schedule to plan for the unexpected, giving Emily a buffer that allowed her to keep pace.

During her commute, Emily called Anthony, who was already at the hospital, to tell him about the poison in Billy's scuba tank. The compressed workday rarely afforded them a moment to talk, and she hoped he would join her before their turtle center meeting to get started on the new crime board she planned to buy after work.

"I can't believe this. Does Lala know?" Anthony asked.

"I assume so, since Mike told me."

"Let's check in on her on the way to our brainstorming session at your place. Did you see Sarah's email to the Turtle Team?"

Emily smiled at Anthony's nickname for the key players involved in building the Eliza Klein Sea Turtle Conservation Center.

"Yes," she said. "We're meeting Gus onsite at four, then going to dinner with the team to discuss next steps. Oh, I forgot to mention—I have more to tell you about this Stewie guy."

"Tell me now."

"I'm pulling into the hospital parking lot. I'll see you inside."

Emily and Anthony discussed nothing other than veterinary medicine, since two clients arrived even before the doors opened, requesting walk-in appointments for their sick pets. One kitty, Sassy, had chewed on an amaryllis plant and began vomiting. Twyla, a rambunctious Boxer, stole a chicken wing off her owner's dinner plate and developed diarrhea overnight. The hospital suddenly turned into a hub for gastrointestinal cases—bloodwork to rule out serious causes, X-rays of the abdomen, and the administration of subcutaneous fluids, anti-nausea medicine, probiotics, and bland diets to go home.

Emily, who was in an appointment, missed Duncan, Jane, and the kids when they dropped Elvis off with all his stuff. Accustomed to spending the day at the hospital, the confident terrier made himself at home in Anthony's office. He had become an official ambassador when Emily fostered him after Mrs. Klein's murder. He often spent the day on a chair next to Abigail at the front desk, greeting the clients with a doggy smile and a happy, wagging tail.

At closing time, Emily and Anthony convened in his office to make a plan.

With Elvis in her lap, Emily said, "I haven't heard from Lala, which isn't like her."

"I agree."

Abigail popped her head in. "The doors are locked. Elizabeth came by with Phoenix to pick up our gift basket donation for the Yappy Barkday Pawty charity auction and to drop off our dinner tickets. We have two tables of eight."

"That's right. I almost forgot with everything else we have going on. Has everyone signed up?" Emily asked.

"Yes, we've filled one table so far." Abigail handed her the tickets and the list and returned to the lobby to make reminder calls for Monday's appointments.

"Marc would love to come to the event, and I think Lala could use a night away from the marina." Anthony said.

"Great idea. I bet Sarah would enjoy it if she's still in town."

"What about Mike, Jane, and Duncan? That would fill our table."

Emily nodded. "I'll ask. Can you bring Elvis with you to the marina? I want to stop at the office supply store to buy our crime board, and I'll meet you at Lala's."

Anthony scooped Elvis from her lap and connected his leash. "We'll be right behind you."

• • •

Emily purchased her whiteboard, magnets for mounting pictures and clues, and an array of colorful dry-erase markers, then drove to the marina. She scanned the parking lot for Anthony's car and Lala's truck, but neither was in sight. As she approached the dock, the sound of someone pounding on the dive shop's front door caught her attention.

"Excuse me. Is there something I can help you with?" Emily asked.

The man turned toward her, and Emily immediately recognized Clay Thornton, the pushy boat broker who had made a below-market offer to buy *Diver Down* only days after Billy's death.

"Who are you?" he asked abruptly.

"A friend of the owners." Emily put her face to the window and covered her eyes to cut the glare. She couldn't see Lala moving inside, and Hemingway was out of sight or in hiding. She tried the door handle, but it was locked. "I can give her a message for you."

"Tell her my offer is about to expire. I need an answer or—"

Anthony had arrived with Elvis in tow and must have caught the tail end of their conversation when he said, "Or what?" His death stare made it clear the man should watch his tone.

Elvis tugged on his leash, his ears pinned back, a low, persistent growl barely audible. Knowing he would never act aggressively unless threatened, they had learned to trust the terrier's instincts in their previous dealings with unsavory characters. His reaction did not go unnoticed.

"Umm." The broker stammered and moved to create distance from both Anthony and Elvis. "I've been waiting for an answer about my offer to buy the dive boat."

"Do you understand the owner just died, and the family hasn't even had his funeral yet?" Emily asked.

"Yes, and funerals are expensive. I made a very generous offer."

Anthony moved next to Emily and crossed his arms, blocking any access to the front door. "Miss Todd has your business card. We'll let her know you dropped by."

The man grumbled something under his breath.

"Pardon me," Anthony said.

"Tell her the clock is ticking." Then he shuffled sideways past Elvis before retreating to the parking lot.

"I don't like that guy." Anthony petted Elvis to defuse his tension. His ears perked up, and he wagged his tail—back to being the loveable terrier. "And neither does Elvis."

"Really? I couldn't tell." Emily grinned.

"It's such predatory behavior, coming around like this."

"I agree, but it's up to Lala to decide what she wants to do. Speaking of Lala, I wonder where she is."

CHAPTER TWENTY-FIVE

Emily handed Anthony a glass of lemonade and sat in the chair opposite the crime board. Bella looked on from the chaise lounge as Elvis bounded onto the beach deck and jumped up next to her, sitting only inches away. While channeling her authentic, grumpy cat face, Bella turned her back to him but didn't leave her coveted spot.

"Look." Emily pointed at the two of them. "Friends. She takes a few hours to adjust to having Elvis in the house, but she loves him."

"Tolerates him might be more accurate. They're pretty cute, though." Anthony faced the board. "Check this out." The top half outlined the timeline of Billy's death, while beneath it, he had added three headings: *Means*, *Motive*, and *Opportunity*.

"Let's review what we know, starting with the means—arsenic gas," Anthony said.

Emily used a marker to write *AsH3* below the heading.

"What's that?" Anthony asked.

"Chemical formula for arsine. I looked it up." She smiled. "Mike told me it's not technically challenging to put the gas into a dive tank, but sales of arsine are tightly regulated."

Anthony grabbed a red marker and added an arrow pointing to the word, *Supply.* "We need to find out if there have been any recent arsine thefts or reports of missing inventory. I'm sure Mike or Duncan can get a list of chemical suppliers in the area."

He tapped the marker against his chin. "*Opportunity* is wide open. The scuba tanks were stored outside near the compressor. Even though the gate is locked, it wouldn't be too difficult to access them." He drew a dive flag on the board. "But it had to be someone who knew which one was Billy's tank. Unfortunately, Lala's been away too long to know all the people in Billy's day-to-day life."

"And I'm still stuck on *Motive*," Emily said. "Wilma said Billy liked to bet on sports. If he owed a bookie for a gambling debt, it wouldn't make sense to kill him. I don't mean to sound ruthless, but you can't collect money from a dead person." Using a brown marker, she drew a picture of a football and a horse. "Where does someone even go to find a bookie?"

"And what about this Thornton guy trying to buy Billy's boat? I get a bad feeling from him."

"Doesn't make him a murderer, but we should keep him on the suspect list." Emily used a blue marker to draw a boat under *Suspects* then added an orange cartoon-like drawing of a fluffy cat. "And we need to figure out if Billy hired a pet sitter or whoever drove Hemingway to hide in the ceiling. Even if they're not a suspect, they might shed some light on Billy's last days."

"We've eliminated the college student who worked for Billy, since he was away at training camp, but what about the other employee, Stewart?" Anthony said. "And is that Stewart the same Stewie you've run into?"

"Literally. Except he ran into me." She added Stewie's license plate number to the board.

They stood back to take in their handiwork.

"Not bad for our first one," Anthony said.

"It helps to lay it out like this. Don't know why we didn't do it before."

"Every time we get involved in a murder investigation, I think to myself, this can't happen again. And yet, it keeps happening." Anthony sat on the lounger, allowing Elvis to jump into his lap.

"It's not as if we seek out murder cases. They find us. It's not our fault."

"I know, but it's an exhausting trend, and I don't like it."

Emily checked the time on her phone. "Lala hasn't replied to my text. What about you?"

"Nope, and we have to go. Can't keep the Turtle Team waiting."

•   •   •

Construction vehicles filled the lot of the future sea turtle center. Gus Fazio, the general contractor, stood out front talking to his foreperson when Emily and Anthony pulled in. Since parking was limited, they drove together in Anthony's car. Emily considered bringing Elvis along to visit the location of his first forever home with Mrs. Klein, but she decided there were too many hazards and it wasn't safe.

"The entire team is already here," Anthony said as they navigated around the safety barriers.

"Hi, Gus," Emily said.

"Hi, Dr. Benton. Hi, Anthony. Everyone is in the welcome center lobby. We're about to get started." He motioned for them to follow.

"Yeah!" Sarah ran to greet her co-directors with a hug, while Marlon and Sharon, huddled over an architectural drawing, waved.

Sarah pointed around the room. "Gus, you've made amazing progress. Looks like the framing is done, and you'll be ready for drywall soon."

"We're still waiting on inspections for electrical and plumbing, but that should happen this week."

The group gathered as Gus highlighted key features of the future welcome center. The expansive open floor plan was built using the foundation of Mrs. Klein's historic cottage. The front facade would remain intact, preserving its beachy charm.

Emily noticed Sarah turn away to wipe a tear from her eye. It had to be difficult to be in her mom's former home and see it transformed. The two women locked eyes. Emily's concern for her friend eased when Sarah's face lit up and she smiled.

Gus took a break to confer with one of his contractors, leaving the team to explore on their own. Emily walked over to Sarah and asked, "Are you okay?"

"I am. These are happy tears. I had already come to terms with the demolition of the interior of Mom's house, especially since we incorporated the exterior of her cottage into the design. I was just thinking how excited she would be about what we're creating here."

"This center is the best way to honor her memory. I see her everywhere I look. And I can hear her in my head. All those years she mentored Anthony and me in high school."

"Me too." Sarah squeezed Emily's hand.

"What are you two conspiring about?" Anthony joined them carrying floorboard samples.

"Who, us? Conspiring?" Emily laughed. "What do you have there?"

"Gus wants our decision about the flooring so he can place the order." He moved to a workbench and laid out the samples. The three stepped back to study the choices.

"It would be great to restore the hardwoods Mom had in her cottage, but that's not practical with heavy foot traffic. I agree with

Gus that a luxury vinyl plank resembling wood will be the most durable," Sarah said.

Emily and Anthony were inclined to default to her on these decisions, since Sarah owned a successful interior design business in Los Angeles.

"How about on the count of three, we all point to our favorite," Sarah said.

"Okay," Anthony said. "One, two, three."

All three pointed to the light, sand-toned plank at the same time.

"Phew." Emily wiped her brow. "That was too easy. Anthony and I are happy to let you take the lead on all the decisions for the welcome center, and we can weigh in on the turtle intake and triage area."

"That might help streamline things once we get to the final phase of construction, when there are so many options for finishing touches, but I still plan to show you all my choices. Let's agree that we each get a veto vote if it's something you don't like." Emily and Anthony nodded their approval.

The layout of the medical area was designed solely for functionality. The team had consulted with turtle hospitals throughout the Florida and Georgia coasts to understand what they would need. Before moving to Coral Shores, Marlon had spent years as the director of a sea turtle center in North Carolina, and his knowledge would be instrumental in their success.

The center would provide interim care for injured or sick sea turtles until they could be transported to a full-service hospital. At this time, there were no plans to add surgical or long-term care facilities.

"I've now toured a dozen different sea turtle centers to get ideas on what our welcome area should look like and what services we should offer," Sarah said when Marlon and Sharon joined the group.

Sharon said, "And we can incorporate the current programs offered by the Coral Shores Turtle Project. Marlon's 'Walk and Talk' beach tours are quite popular."

"People enjoy seeing the turtle nests up close and are fascinated by the information we gather," Marlon said. "Kids also love my 'Seashell University' Beachwalk, where I teach them about the different species of shells and whelks. When we're done, they get to sort their shells and create scientific displays."

"Exactly. We have so many choices for programming," Sarah said.

Gus approached the group. "Are we ready to move on?" They all nodded.

A hallway connected the welcome area to the turtle triage zone. The back half of the center would be closed to the public except for scheduled guided tours. It included a conference room for training and educational presentations, a lunchroom, restrooms equipped with showers, offices for Marlon, and Sharon, and a third for Emily and Anthony to share.

Marlon helped design the space to maximize efficient workflow, similar to how Emily had set up the treatment area at the veterinary hospital. Smaller open tanks for more critical or baby sea turtles, stainless steel exam tables, refrigerators to store food, and shelves to stock medicine, supplies, and equipment. The back entrance led to an exterior concrete courtyard that would be covered with oversized shade awnings. Two larger tanks could accommodate adult turtles. Special permanent filtration systems would be installed to filter the ocean water, providing an ideal clean water source. They had brainstormed for weeks to ensure nothing was overlooked.

When they finished their walk-through, Gus secured the site for the night, and the Turtle Team moved to Enzo's Italiano for a group dinner. Sarah ordered a bottle of champagne to celebrate.

"If my mom were here, I know she would be so proud. She worked tirelessly with so many animal charities, but sea turtle conservation was her passion. To my mom." Sarah raised her glass in a toast.

They clinked champagne flutes. "To Eliza."

The Turtle Team shared cannoli and tiramisu for dessert when Emily and Anthony's phones started pinging and vibrating from a barrage of incoming texts. Too many to ignore.

"Excuse me," Anthony said. "I think I should get this." He pulled his phone from his pocket. "Oh, no."

CHAPTER TWENTY-SIX

Emily read the messages from Lala. *Hemingway is missing.* She stood and gathered her purse. "Our apologies, everyone. We have to go. It's an emergency."

Anthony shoved the last bite of pastry into his mouth and grabbed his keys.

"Don't worry about us. I just hope everything is okay," Sarah said. "We'll regroup tomorrow. I'm here for a few more days."

Since it was on the way, Emily asked Anthony to stop at her place, and once they were in the car, she called Lala. "Have you found her yet?"

"No." Lala's voice teetered on panic. "And I've looked everywhere. There's more, but I'll wait until you get here. I'll be in the dive shop."

"We're on our way." Emily hung up. "She sounds really upset. It's like she can't catch a break—just one thing after another."

"It feels that way."

Anthony pulled into Emily's driveway. "Do you want me to wait in the car?"

"Yeah. Elvis will need to go out, and I thought he might help find Hemingway. That terrier nose of his is amazing."

"Good idea. Elvis can be our tracker. And Hemingway has met him, so she won't be afraid."

Emily ran to her cottage door. Minutes later, she returned with Elvis bounding beside her on his leash. He stopped for a quick potty break then jumped into the backseat, feet on the center console, tail wagging.

"Hey, buddy." Anthony rubbed his ears, much to the terrier's delight.

"I had to give Bella double the number of treats to make up for the mad dash. She's not happy."

"I have a terrible knot in my stomach about all this."

"I'd be beside myself if Bella were missing. To find a cat, we need to think like a cat."

·   ·   ·

When they arrived at the marina, Emily saw Mr. Haney standing beside his truck. "That's the owner of the watersports store I told you about. I wonder why he's here."

Emily, Anthony, and Elvis approached Mr. Haney in the parking lot as he pulled a piece of plywood from his truck cab.

"Oh, hi," he said. "Dr. Benton, right?"

"Yes. This is my friend, Anthony, and this is Elvis." She pointed to the little terrier dancing in anticipation of making a new friend.

Mr. Haney knelt to pet him. "Miss Lala is inside. I'm sure she'll be relieved you're here."

"What's the plywood for?" Emily asked.

"Seems someone broke a window. She called me for help to secure things until she can get it replaced."

Emily and Anthony exchanged looks and started running. Lala moved to unlock the front door when she saw them. Her hands trembled, and they could see the strain on her face.

She leaned down to pet Elvis, and he responded by kissing her hand. "Elvis, you're the sweetest," Lala said.

"Mr. Haney is right behind us and told us about the window," Emily said. "What happened?"

"I don't know. I came home from a meeting at the funeral home with Mr. McIntosh. Now that they've determined Billy's cause of death, his body will be released. When I returned, Hemingway wasn't in her usual spots, so I started looking for her. That's when I found the broken window near the back door." Her voice trailed off and tears welled up. "I searched everywhere around the marina, but I couldn't find her."

Anthony instinctively looked up into the ceiling rafters to see if Hemingway had retreated to her recent hiding spot.

Lala noticed his gaze. "I checked there, too."

"We'll find her," Emily said with more certainty than she felt. "Is anything else missing?" She surveyed the room and saw no obvious signs that it had been ransacked.

"Not that I can tell, but I've been focused on trying to find Hemingway."

Emily nodded. "The three of us can cover more ground if we split up. Plus, we have Elvis to lead the search."

"Do you have extra flashlights?" Anthony asked.

"I think so." Lala bent down behind the sales counter as Mr. Haney walked into the shop.

"Miss Lala, once I remove the broken glass, I'm going to nail up the plywood to cover the window. Didn't want the noise to startle you."

"Thank you, Mr. Haney. You've been so kind." Lala handed Emily and Anthony a flashlight. "Can you look for her while I help Mr. Haney? I'll join you outside in a few minutes."

"Em, let's let Elvis sniff around here first, in case Hemingway found a new indoor hiding place."

"Good idea. Okay, Elvis, do your thing."

Emily trailed the terrier as he carefully explored every corner of the place. At the back door, they noticed the deadbolt could be accessed through the shattered window. Once outside, Emily and

Elvis turned right, while Anthony went left. "Hemingway," they both called repeatedly, their voices cutting through the air. Anthony shook the bag of treats loudly, hoping to draw her attention.

They used their flashlights to search around the dive shop and the dock. While they didn't board any of the nearby boats, they scanned their decks. Elvis tracked a crab running for cover under the dock and seemed particularly interested in the roosting pelicans, but never picked up Hemingway's scent.

"Anything?" Anthony asked when they reconvened outside the front door.

"No."

"This is Hemingway's home. Even if she got out for a little adventure, she'd be able to find her way back. She's smart. Let's check around the building one more time," Anthony said.

They turned the corner as Mr. Haney loaded his tools into his truck. "It's all sealed up and secure now. Night."

"Thank you for helping Lala," Emily said. He tipped his cap and then drove across the lot to his store.

Lala walked out the back door of the dive shop and joined the search.

Emily asked her, "When you came home, do you remember if the deadbolt was locked?"

Lala stopped to think. "I don't think so, but I'm not certain. When I saw the broken window, I panicked and opened the door. But I know it was locked before I left for the funeral home."

When they reached the exterior fence that surrounded the compressors and scuba tank storage, Emily called out, "Hemingway."

While Anthony checked the lock, Elvis pulled Emily to the gate, sniffed the fence boards, and began digging, as if trying to tunnel his way into the side yard.

"You're right, Elvis. We never checked this area," Anthony said. "Hemingway could easily climb over this fence."

All three friends scrambled inside with Elvis in tow. Lala led them through the dive shop to the door that accessed the outdoor tank area. A single exterior light offered limited visibility.

Elvis dragged Emily to the filling station. She used her flashlight to scan the area, but nothing. When Elvis turned to a storage rack against the wall, he started whining.

"What is it, little buddy?" Anthony asked. They aimed their flashlights on the rack, and a pair of eyes reflected back at them.

"Hemingway," Lala cooed at her beloved cat. "There you are."

Elvis stood with his ears alert, wagging his tail. Emily knelt beside him, petting his head. "Good boy. You did it."

Hemingway's ears were pinned against her head, and her pupils were huge. Emily and Anthony recognized her facial expressions as signs of fear. Lala scooped her into her arms and carried her inside, setting her on the cat bed behind the register.

"Is she okay?" Lala stroked her head. "Emily, can you make sure she's not injured?"

Emily handed Anthony the leash and did a cursory exam. She determined Hemingway's heart rate to be higher than normal based on her pulse, but there were no visible wounds.

"I want to watch her walk." Emily carried the cat to Lala's apartment and set her down within eyesight of her food and water bowls.

Hemingway held her right front paw in the air, and when she took her first step, she meowed and lifted her paw to lick it. Emily took the kitty treat bag from Anthony, laid a trail of treats toward her dishes, and stepped back. Now motivated to walk, Hemingway collected the treats along the way.

"Oh no." Lala put her hand to her mouth. "She's limping."

Hemingway cautiously placed her right front foot with every step but made it to her water bowl and took a big drink.

"We'll let her finish before I do an orthopedic exam."

Anthony handed Lala the leash, and she lifted Elvis to hug him. "I need some puppy therapy right now." He kissed her cheek before she set him down.

Using a blanket from the bed, he covered the desk, creating a makeshift exam table. Emily waited until Hemingway turned away from her dishes, then placed her on top. She moved each of Hemingway's joints through a range of motion to detect any discomfort or swelling. When she reached the right carpus, Hemingway's kitty wrist, the tabby meowed and pulled her leg back.

"I don't feel any fractures, and even with a small, hairline fracture, she wouldn't put it down at all. She'd hop. But there is some swelling in the joint. She may have sprained or strained her wrist, or banged it against something hard, causing the inflammation. I don't see a wound on her skin."

"What does that all mean?" Lala asked.

"With a soft tissue injury, we recommend rest and some pain medicine. If she's not getting better, we can X-ray her wrist, to rule out anything more serious."

"Lala, where did Billy keep Hemingway's stuff, like her flea and heartworm medicine?" Anthony asked.

"In the cupboard next to the fridge. It's in a basket on the shelf. Why?"

"He may have what we need. I remember reading in Hemingway's medical record she had a tooth extracted during a dental cleaning earlier this year. We would have sent Billy home with pain medicine." Anthony moved across the room to search the basket. "Got it." He handed the envelope to Emily.

"This is an anti-inflammatory. Looks like there are three doses left. Each dose will treat her for twenty-four hours, so you'll be covered for the rest of the weekend."

"Can you give it to her so I can watch? I've never given a cat medicine before," Lala said.

Anthony used the pre-measured syringe and showed how to administer the dose. Hemingway took her medicine without issue. "It's not always that easy. This medicine is the only one cats like the taste of. Good girl." He petted her head then carried her to Lala's bed, where she curled up, ready for a nap.

"She seems okay now," Lala said. "What a night. I don't think I can take much more of this." Lala sat down next to Hemingway.

"Do you want us to stay?" Anthony asked.

"You've already done so much. I'll be fine. I'm going to concentrate on Hemingway, and everything else can wait."

"Let us know how she's doing in the morning," Emily said. "If she's still limping, we'll make a plan to do her X-ray. The hospital isn't open again until Monday, but we can go in tomorrow if we need to." Anthony nodded in agreement.

"Thank you," Lala said. "I don't know what I would do without the two of you. You're my guardian angels."

Elvis put his paws up on the bed next to Hemingway and wagged his tail. The orange tabby opened her eyes and made a soft, cooing sound—her way of saying hello.

Lala smiled at their budding friendship. "And Elvis, you're Hemingway's hero."

CHAPTER TWENTY-SEVEN

A heavy silence filled the car as they drove to Emily's cottage. They both agreed it had been an exhausting day, and it had taken its toll.

"Do you think Lala should call the police about the broken window? What if it was an attempted break-in?" Anthony asked.

"She said she would check in the morning for any missing items. It's probably best to wait until then."

"You're right. For all we know, it could have been kids out throwing rocks."

Emily gave him a look to communicate her disbelief.

"And we forgot to tell her about our earlier conversation with that boat broker, Mr. Thornton," she said. "Finding Hemingway took top priority."

"I don't like any of this. I get why Lala wants to stay at the dive shop, but I'm wondering if that's such a good idea. Next time I talk to her, I'm going to offer my guest room again."

Emily smiled at Anthony. He had a heart of gold, and she was thankful every day to have him as a best friend.

"Now that Billy's body has been released, it sounds like Lala will be able to move forward with planning his funeral. I'm sure she's relieved, but it's a huge undertaking."

Anthony turned into Emily's driveway. "I can't wait to crawl into bed," he said. "I'll call you in the morning. Night, Em."

"Night. Let's go, Elvis." Emily connected his leash before he jumped out of the car. They did a quick walk in the neighborhood, and once inside, it took less than ten minutes for the cat and dog to snuggle up next to her in bed.

•   •   •

The early morning sunshine streamed into Emily's bedroom. Grateful not to wake to an alarm, she tried to ease into her day. But when she patted the covers beside her and didn't find any furry bodies, she sat up and looked around. Neither of them was in the room, which was odd.

What are they up to? While she was tempted to go back to sleep, silence was not golden when it came to pets. It usually meant they were getting into trouble.

Emily pulled herself out of bed and headed straight for the coffee maker, scanning for Elvis and Bella. They were sitting inches apart, looking out the sliding doors to the beach deck.

"What are you watching?" she asked. A small green lizard darted under a chair before climbing up a nearby palm tree and disappearing out of view. "Oh, that's what."

They waited for the lizard to reappear, but when it didn't show itself, they followed Emily to the kitchen. She hit the brew button, put a few appetizers next to Bella's bowl, stepped into the nearest flip-flops, and took Elvis outside to do his business. He was back in seconds and ready for breakfast.

With a large steaming mug in hand, she settled in her lounge chair on the beach deck to enjoy the ocean views and morning solitude. Elvis and Bella joined her after finishing their meal.

She tried her best to stay in the moment—to listen to the gentle surf and inhale the scent of the climbing gardenias as a light tropical breeze drifted through her hair. But it became impossible to push away thoughts about Billy Todd's murder, growing threats to Lala's safety, and concerns about Hemingway's injury.

Duncan had his hands full at Mac's baseball tournament, and it was still too early to contact Mike. She would have to wait to get answers to her many questions about the investigation.

"Okay, kids. Time to start our day." Elvis jumped to attention, but Bella ignored her call to action and resumed her nap. "Do you want to go for a walk?" The terrier wagged his tail and ran to the front door, where his leash hung from a hook. Emily changed, carried Bella inside, and placed her on her coveted pillow before making her way toward the water with Elvis.

Aside from a few early morning walkers, the beach was empty. She hesitated before unleashing Elvis, but he needed a good run, so off he went—darting in and out of the surf with a huge smile on his terrier face. After venturing past the same spot where they had found Billy Todd only days ago, she turned for home. Elvis had burned off his excess energy and stepped in line beside her. After a quick wash-up in the outdoor shower, he wiggled as she attempted to towel him off.

"I think that deserves a cookie." Elvis ran to the kitchen and sat, displaying his best manners. Bella joined him but refused to work for her treats—a cat's prerogative.

Now that it was a civilized hour to make calls, she started with Sarah Klein. After running out on dinner last night, Emily had only texted a quick update to let Sarah know everything was okay and to invite her to lunch so she could spend time with Elvis. The little terrier had been Sarah's mother's beloved companion, and Sarah struggled with her decision not to keep Elvis with her after her mom died. Her husband's severe dog allergies made it impossible. When Jane and Duncan agreed to adopt the lovable terrier, it was a best-case scenario. Elvis adored his new family, and Sarah got to see him whenever she came to town.

Emily had learned to wait to push both Mike and Duncan for information about a murder investigation until she could speak with them in person. It was too easy to ignore or sidestep her in a text or phone call. Duncan would be dropping by later in the evening to pick up Elvis, and Mike messaged her with an invitation to dinner.

In case Lala had slept in, Emily texted her first, which resulted in an immediate return call.

"Were you able to get some rest after we left last night?" Emily asked.

"Eventually, but I slept with the lights on. I know—it's silly."

"Not at all. Have you had time yet to check to see if anything is missing?"

"Yeah. Nothing obvious as far as I can tell."

"And how is Hemingway this morning? Is she still limping?"

"She is, but it's so much better than last night. Otherwise, she's eating and grooming like normal."

"I would give her the second dose of the anti-inflammatory pain medicine tonight, and if she's not better by Monday morning, bring her to the hospital, and we'll do an X-ray. Just to be sure."

"I'll do that."

"What's your plan for today?"

"I have to find someone to fix the window, then I'm going to work on Billy's funeral arrangements. I spoke with my mom again last night."

"And how did that go?"

"Better than I expected. She sounded different, in a good way. Of course, she's upset about Billy, and making plans to drive over."

"That's great. I know you haven't had a relationship with her for almost a decade, but maybe it's time."

"I'm cautiously optimistic. But it's up to her to show me things have changed."

"That's fair. If you need help with anything, just ask. Elvis and I can pop by."

"I will. And thanks, Em. For everything."

•   •   •

Lunch with Sarah lifted Emily's spirits. Elvis greeted her with an over-the-top display of puppy love, and they swooned over each other on the couch.

"Sweet boy." Sarah squeezed him tight.

"Mac and Ava have taught him a few new tricks." Elvis showed off his ability to roll over on command, followed by a high five.

Sarah clapped. "I'm so grateful for the home Jane and Duncan have given him. He's so happy."

"He is, and they love him to bits. He has more toys than the kids do." Emily moved to the kitchen to prepare their lunch of chicken salad lettuce wraps and fresh-squeezed lemonade.

"What's this?" Sarah stood in front of the crime board, which was propped up against a chair. "Wait. Are you and Anthony investigating Mr. Todd's murder?"

"We were putting together the facts of the case, trying to organize everything," Emily said.

Sarah's brow furrowed, and she remained silent as she reviewed the various sections. "Em, is this safe? The last time, you both ended up face-to-face with the killer."

"We never go looking to be part of a case. It just ends up that way. We need to be there for our friend, Lala. We're being safe. I promise."

"Okay. If you say so. I understand why you get involved. I did the same thing when Mom was murdered. But I also learned how good Mike and Duncan are at solving crimes. You should leave the detective work to them."

Emily agreed about the fact they were exceptional at their jobs, but that didn't mean she planned to sit on the sidelines.

"I'd love for you to meet Lala. I think it would help her talk with someone who's been through the same type of loss. We're all planning to attend a local charity event at the end of next week to raise money for the animal shelter. It's the shelter where your mom organized all the volunteers. It's called the Yappy Barkday Pawty, and the hospital sponsored a table. If you're in town, would you like to come?"

"I'll plan to be there. Just send me the details."

Over lunch, the two friends brainstormed the next phase of development for the sea turtle center. Sarah showed Emily samples she had brought of the branded merchandise they planned to sell in the welcome center. T-shirts, recycled water bottles, straws, and bags made from plastic pulled from the ocean. A line of dog collars, leashes, and bandanas were adorned with baby sea turtles. Puzzles, books for all ages, and jewelry featured sea turtles and ocean conservation.

Emily and Anthony had been working with Marlon and Sharon on the more technical parts of the facility. They had developed intake protocols for injured turtles, and training programs for the volunteers had been scheduled for the upcoming months.

"I'm still in awe of everything we've accomplished," Sarah said. "Before you know it, we'll be planning the grand opening ceremony."

"The Eliza Klein Sea Turtle Conservation Center will bring people from all over to Coral Shores. I can't wait."

CHAPTER TWENTY-EIGHT

Emily had a few free hours before she planned to meet Mike. He had invited her to join him for an early dinner at their favorite beachfront seafood shack, Barnacles. Duncan wouldn't be there to get Elvis until eight o'clock, so she had plenty of time.

By midafternoon, the winds had settled, so Emily changed into her bathing suit, grabbed her life jacket, and carried her stand-up paddleboard to the water's edge. Once she'd cleared the surf break, she paddled parallel to the shore, working hard against the current. After thirty minutes, she turned back toward home, the water carrying her with little effort.

Looking out at the horizon, Emily saw a small head pop out of the ocean before disappearing. She kept scanning for any signs of movement when, suddenly, a sea turtle appeared just beneath the surface.

"Hello, friend." Emily watched as the juvenile green sea turtle passed under her board before turning toward the open sea. "Safe travels." She resumed paddling at a leisurely pace until she reached the beach in front of her cottage. She surfed ashore, washed her gear, and left it outside to dry. Elvis and Bella had their noses pressed against the glass, following her every move. They didn't like it when she did stuff without them.

•   •   •

While studying her crime board on the dining table, Emily marked the dive shop's broken window on the timeline. The more she thought about it, the more it bothered her. The window might be a key breakthrough in Billy's case, and she couldn't wait until dinner to bring it up with Mike.

Emily left him a message that she had something important to tell him. He replied right away by text. He was wrapping up a tennis match with a work friend and would stop by on his way home. She glimpsed her reflection in the mirror—her hair matted to her head by sweat and seawater, so she darted to the shower. By the time Mike pulled into her driveway, she looked fresh-faced and ready for the day.

"Hi, Em." He leaned in to kiss her. "You smell nice."

Emily swooned when she saw Mike in his tennis clothes, his wavy brown hair curled up around the base of his hat.

"Thanks. I just got back from a paddle and spotted a sea turtle swimming inside the reef."

Mike walked to the kitchen and poured himself a glass of water. "That's amazing. I'd love to join you next time you go out. Speaking of turtles, how was your board meeting at the turtle center?"

"Great. We accomplished a lot. Sarah's in town for a few more days to work on the design of the welcome center with our contractor."

He nodded. "So, what's up? I got here as fast as possible."

When he turned toward the dining room, Emily realized she forgot to put away her crime board. Not that she intended to keep it from him. Mike often welcomed her input in solving the previous cases she'd become entangled with, but only to a point. He never wanted her to be in harm's way, and that's when he would often push back on her involvement.

"Are those the turtle center plans?" He walked around the kitchen island to get a better look as Emily scrambled after him. It was too late to hide her work, so she left him to study the board without speaking. He turned to face her. "Is this what I think it is?"

She said nothing.

"Em, have you and Anthony been investigating William Todd's murder?"

"Of course we have. But I wouldn't say investigating. More like brainstorming. And that's why I wanted to talk to you. Our turtle meeting got cut short last night because Lala called in a panic. She came home from the funeral home and discovered a broken window at her back door and Hemingway missing."

"What?"

"She's okay. We found Hemingway outside near the scuba tank air compressor, and her neighbor came over to board up the window."

"Did she report it to the police?"

"Not yet. We were so focused on finding Hemingway. As far as she could tell, nothing was stolen. We wondered if it might have been kids out throwing rocks, but you know I don't like coincidences. What if someone broke in? Can you collect fingerprints from around the door?"

He didn't answer and continued staring at her board.

"Who's Clay Thornton?"

"He's a pushy boat broker. He keeps dropping by, trying to pressure Lala to sell the dive boat."

"But why did you add him to the board?"

"A gut feeling. He kind of threatened her when he said the bank would take the boat if she didn't sell to him. That's not how a reputable business operates. Plus, how did he find out about Billy's financial troubles?"

"Has Duncan seen all this?"

Emily looked at him, then her gaze slipped away. "He's been busy."

"Em, I can't keep this from him."

"I understand. I'm not hiding anything. Lala is my friend, and she doesn't have anyone other than Anthony and me to turn to. She's already been through a lot, and things keep happening. I'm worried about her safety."

Mike pulled her close. "I know you are. And you're right. This break-in or attempted break-in needs to be investigated. I'll send a deputy to the marina."

"She was trying to find someone to come fix the window, but it's Sunday, so I doubt she had much luck."

Mike nodded. "I'll reach out to her and ask her to put that on hold."

"I was thinking this morning. The security cameras at the marina might have picked up movement behind the dive shop last night. Were they helpful in figuring out how Billy got out on the water with his dive gear? Did he leave the dock on *Diver Down*?"

Mike frowned. Emily sensed he was holding something back. As always, she pushed for more details.

"Well?" she said. "Did he go out that day on *Diver Down* or not?"

"He did. The cameras captured him loading his dive gear on deck before pushing off from the dock. But—"

"But what? What happened?"

"His boat headed inland after leaving the marina. We expected him to turn left toward the Intracoastal Waterway, since that was the only way to reach the open water of the Gulf. Instead, he turned right."

Emily paced around her dining room table with her head down. "Where could he have been going?" Then she stopped cold. "He must have gone to pick someone up."

Mike watched as Emily processed the news.

"That's our working theory. But we don't know where he went. Because the canal beyond the marina is out of the camera's view, we can't confirm the time he made his return trip, heading to open water.

Emily continued to pace. "But we found the boat docked in the marina the day we found Billy. Someone had to drive it back. Isn't that captured on the camera?"

He caught her arm, turning her to look at him.

"The camera aimed at the dock near *Diver Down* was disabled later that morning. We don't know what time the boat returned."

A gasp escaped Emily as she clapped a hand over her mouth. "That means the murderer had help. Or maybe they figured out a way to turn the camera off from the water?"

He shook his head. "The cable to that specific camera had been cut."

"Which camera was that? I mean, where was the camera mounted?"

"On the roof of the watersports store."

"So, you don't know who brought the boat back to the dock?"

"Not yet."

"Any other leads you can share?"

"I can't say right now. Not while we're actively investigating. Sorry, Em."

She paused before responding. Based on experience, pressing the issue would only put him on the defensive. When he could tell her, he would. Until then, she planned to do her own fact-finding.

"I've got to go. I need to get someone over to the marina ASAP." He turned for the door. "But I'll be back for our dinner date. And I know you. You'll want to call Lala as soon as I leave. Can you give me some time to speak to her first?"

Emily put her hands on her hips, prepared to challenge his assumptions. Then he disarmed her with a grin. She relaxed her arms and he pulled her close, kissing her softly. When he stepped back to gauge her reaction, they both laughed.

"Okay, you've got an hour." She smiled. "But that's all."

He nodded and turned to leave. Over his shoulder, he said, "You need to show Duncan that crime board when he comes by later. Tell him about your interactions with the boat broker."

Emily waved as he pulled out of the driveway. "Oh boy," she said. Sharing the details of her secret investigation with her brother could prove tricky.

The last time she had become embroiled in one of his cases, she followed the suspected kidnapper and murderer across the state without telling anyone. But in the end, her brother acknowledged her pivotal role in solving the case, and she apologized for keeping him in the dark. Since then, things had been good—but that was before she became involved with another murder.

CHAPTER TWENTY-NINE

Enough time had passed for Mike to speak with Lala about the break-in. If Emily rushed, she could get to the marina and back before he returned for their dinner date.

"Want to go see Hemingway?"

Elvis jumped to attention and ran to the door.

"I guess that's a yes." She attached his leash. "Bella, we'll be home soon." Her Maine Coon flicked the tip of her tail, the only acknowledgment of their departure.

During the short drive along the beach, Elvis stood with his front paws on the handle while sticking his nose out the window. Emily opened it only a few inches to let him enjoy the ocean air while keeping him safe. When she arrived at the marina, she noticed Deputy Garcia walking toward the crime scene van parked next to her patrol car.

That was fast, she thought. The little terrier leaped from the car and pulled Emily to the dive shop.

"Elvis." Lala smiled as she moved to unlock the door. "Hi, Em. Mike told me you might be dropping by."

Emily snorted. He knew her too well. "Be good, Elvis." She removed his leash, allowing him to greet his friend. Hemingway jumped down from her bed on the counter, and after she landed, she lifted her injured paw off the ground for a few seconds. When she walked over to Elvis, Emily noted an almost imperceptible limp.

"Can you bring Hemingway to the hospital in the morning? I'd like to get an X-ray of her leg. Anthony and I can meet you before appointments start so it will be quiet."

"We'll be there. She seemed a little better when she woke up, but it's hard to keep her from jumping."

Elvis got into the play bow position, his front legs stretched forward and tail up. His version of downward dog. Hemingway tapped her oversized paw on the top of his head. Her way of saying, *behave.* He wriggled his body and licked her face. She didn't object, and the two walked shoulder to shoulder to the window to watch a pelican that had landed on the dock.

"They're so cute," Lala said. "And speaking of cute—Mike is quite the catch, Em. I'm happy for you."

"Thanks. He's pretty great. I haven't even asked if you have anyone special in your life."

"Not right now. I had a serious boyfriend until about a year ago, when we both agreed we were better off as friends."

Deputy Garcia stepped inside. "We're all done here. You can arrange for the window repair."

"When will you know if you found anything helpful?" Lala asked.

"That's up to the crime lab. Likely a couple of days."

"Thank you."

After the deputy left, Emily asked, "How are you holding up?"

"I'm not sure I am. Holding up, that is."

"Is there something I can do to help?"

"Actually, yes. I need to plan Billy's celebration of life ceremony, and I wondered if you could tell me what you did for your mom. But I understand if you'd rather not."

Emily often struggled to express her emotions about her mom's death, but over time, it became easier. After hesitating for only a moment, she said, "I'd like to help."

They moved into Lala's apartment and spent the next hour discussing ideas about how to honor Billy. After living his life on the water, Lala was adamant that her uncle wanted to be buried at sea. Since the dive shop remained closed, it could be used as the venue for the ceremony. McIntosh Funeral Home would provide Billy's ashes in an urn and arrange for a public announcement about his service. After listing everything she had to organize, including renting chairs and catering refreshments, a date of Tuesday seemed tight but doable.

"I'll update Mr. McIntosh," Lala said. "But I have one problem. I can't pilot *Diver Down*. Do you think Duncan would drive the boat out to the reef for me so I can spread his ashes? We could do it right after the ceremony. He was so helpful at the fuel dock a few days ago, it's clear he knows his stuff when it comes to boats."

"I'll ask him for you. I'm sure he'll say yes if he's available."

Lala hugged her friend. "I've been saying 'thank you' a lot lately. But I mean it."

"You're welcome. What about your mom? Is she still planning to come?"

Lala smiled. "Yeah. She should be here tomorrow. I feel both excited and anxious about seeing her. It's been so long since we spent any quality time together."

"You need your family right now."

Lala agreed.

•   •   •

Since Lala had a lot on her mind, Emily decided not to burden her with the latest details about the missing security footage. Plus, Mike had shared the information in confidence. Mr. Haney had been so kind to help Lala board up her broken window, so Emily wanted to drop by and thank him. Truth be told, it would give her a chance to inquire about the camera on his roof.

While standing on the dock, Emily studied the two cameras mounted on light poles at opposite sides of the marina. They captured most of the boats and the parking lot. The camera attached to the watersports store's roof was aimed at the main channel, the only access point in and out of the marina. She positioned herself against the wall under the camera and used her hands as binoculars to focus her view. Since *Diver Down* was permanently docked next to the dive shop, this would be the only angle to capture activity at the boat, dive shop, and fuel dock. All three were located closest to the main channel.

Once she finished her reconnaissance, Emily entered the store. Trent, Mr. Haney's nephew, glanced up from his phone but said nothing.

"Hi." She tried to sound friendly. "Is your uncle around?"

"He's busy."

"I'd like to talk to him. It's important."

He grumbled something then got off his stool and walked away. A few minutes later, Mr. Haney came out to greet her.

"Hello again." He bent down to pet Elvis, then said, "Is everything okay with Miss Lala?"

"Oh, yes. I wanted to thank you for last night. That was kind of you."

"Of course. That's what neighbors do." His warm smile communicated his authenticity.

"I hope you don't mind me asking, but I'm aware there was a lapse in the security footage. Do you have any idea what might have happened?"

He hesitated before answering, so Emily formulated a white lie. "Lala thought about adding a security camera outside the dive shop, and I told her I would check with you first."

"Well," he said. "Since the police have already been here, I guess it's okay to talk about it. The camera mounted on my roof picks up Lala's section of the marina. It's out of service until the company comes to run some new wires."

"Can you reach it from inside your store or only from the outside?"

"I have access since my air conditioners are up there and need to be serviced."

"Could you show me?"

He waved for her to follow. As they rounded the corner near the sales counter, Emily caught Trent ducking behind a wall at the entrance to a nearby office. Elvis saw him too and pulled to the end of his leash, his hackles up. The doorway was close enough for the nephew to have overheard their conversation.

That's suspicious. She redirected Elvis and wondered. *Was he eavesdropping on us?*

Mr. Haney stopped at a metal ladder mounted to the wall on the far side of the storage room. It accessed a drop-down in the ceiling.

He pointed upward. "That's how we get onto the roof. You can tell Miss Lala the repair company will be here next week. I don't think she has to spend money on an additional system. When this one's up and running, it will cover her area."

Emily looked around for Trent but didn't spot him.

"Thank you. I'll let her know. She'll be relieved not to have an added expense right now."

Mr. Haney led Emily and Elvis to the sales floor.

"Billy's service will be held this Tuesday at the dive shop," she said. "McIntosh Funeral Home will post a notice with the details.

"Thank you. I plan to be there. It's not the same around here without Billy. Will Miss Lala be reopening the store and fuel dock? People have been asking."

"That's her plan. I think she wants to get through the funeral first."

"Understandable."

Emily faced a wall-mounted sunglass display rack. A mirror next to the display reflected the area behind her. Once again, Trent peered around the corner, covertly listening in on their conversation.

What is he up to? If she had to hazard a guess, it was nothing good.

CHAPTER THIRTY

Emily exited the causeway, pulling into the right turn lane for Gulf Beach Road. That's when she first noticed a car following close behind. She didn't remember seeing it earlier, but she had been daydreaming about her dinner date with Mike.

Residents of Coral Shores drove as if they had all the time in the world—the complete opposite of city drivers. Plus, unneighborly behavior on the road would stand out in a small town. That's why it seemed so out of place to have someone riding her bumper.

"Dude, what's your rush?" Elvis looked over his shoulder at her, his head cocked to the side. "Not you, little dude." She rubbed his head, and he returned his gaze out the window.

The narrow, two-lane road had a posted speed limit of thirty miles per hour, and Emily was doing thirty-two. That didn't satisfy the driver behind her. She glanced in her rearview mirror, but the driver had the visor pulled down, blocking their face. When she turned into her driveway, the car sped past, sounding in need of a new muffler. Emily noted the older model blue Camaro with primer paint on the trunk.

"C'mon, Elvis." Inside the front door, she unhooked his leash and he ran to Bella, who scowled as he planted a sloppy, wet kiss on her cheek. She then used her paw to groom away his greeting.

After updating Anthony on the latest developments regarding the broken window, the accidental reveal of their crime board, and Trent's eavesdropping, Emily spent the rest of the afternoon catching up on everyday tasks, like laundry, and a quick pass with the vacuum. Living at the beach meant there was a constant influx of sand—it clung to your feet after every walk, leaving behind a fine layer of grit on the floor.

She had to choose between reading from her backlogged stack of veterinary journals or spending time with her four-legged roommates. While it was important to keep up with all medical and surgical advancements, she opted for brushing Elvis and Bella on the deck until they were the fluffiest versions of themselves. Emily was serving them an early dinner when Mike arrived.

"Hi, Em." He kissed her when she opened the door.

"Let me grab my purse, and we can head out."

"I've been thinking all day about the seafood platter at Barnacles. I skipped lunch and I'm starving."

On the drive to their favorite restaurant, Mike seemed to have something on his mind. He kept glancing over to Emily, then back to the road ahead.

"What's up?" she asked. "You can tell me."

"Yeah, but I think this time you're going to be mad."

She couldn't imagine anything he might do or say to make her feel that way. Then it dawned on her.

"You told Duncan about the crime board, didn't you?"

He looked at her sheepishly and nodded. "I didn't intend to. I wanted to let you do it. But I called him about fingerprinting the dive shop's back door and mentioned adding Thornton, the boat broker, to our person of interest list. Duncan asked me about my sources, and I told him the truth. Sorry, Em."

"Was he angry?"

"Not really. More quiet at first."

"I hope you reminded him I was the one who got the lead on Stewie and told you about the window."

"I did. And I think it's good he has a few hours to absorb the information before he picks up Elvis."

"You're probably right. He's never liked surprises, even as a kid."

Mike pulled into the parking lot for Barnacles.

"Let's focus on enjoying our dinner," she said.

"Good plan. And thanks for understanding about my slip of the lips."

Emily leaned across the front seat. "Speaking of lips." She kissed him, letting him know she wasn't upset. Mike's inability to tell a lie made him even more attractive. She trusted him to always be honest with her, and that meant everything.

By the time they finished dinner, a line of people waiting for a table had formed outside. True to form, Mike polished off his entire seafood lover's platter while Emily enjoyed blackened grouper tacos. When the bill came, Mike received a call.

"Sorry, Em. I've got to take this." He stepped onto the beachside deck. Emily studied his body language for a clue to the reason behind the call. When he returned to the table, he had a pensive look on his face.

"Something's come up. After I drop you at home, I'm headed to work. Trust me—I'd rather spend the evening with you, but this can't wait."

"Is it about Billy?"

Mike didn't reply. He paid the bill and held out his hand for Emily to stand. When they were alone, he said, "We got a match from the fingerprints collected this morning from the dive shop's door frame. I can't say more until I check it out. I hope you can understand."

She understood but didn't like it.

"Is Lala in any imminent danger? I need to know." Emily wondered if Anthony should ask Lala again to stay with him until it was safe.

"Not directly, but we've put extra patrols around the marina. Just in case."

"Oh. That sounds serious."

He pulled onto the road, and they traveled the few short miles back to her cottage in silence. Mike held her hand until they were parked.

"We'll have to schedule a do-over," he said.

"Most definitely."

Mike walked her to the door, kissed her goodnight, and turned to leave. He stopped halfway to his cruiser, looked up the beach road, then headed in that direction instead.

"Where are you going?" she asked.

"Stay there, Em." She ignored him and ran to catch up. He had crossed into the neighbor's yard, approaching a car idling two doors down. The moment Emily came into view, the driver squealed their tires and sped away. She immediately recognized the Camaro—the same one from earlier. She tried to read the license plate, but a plastic cover distorted the letters and numbers.

"Did you see the driver?" Emily asked Mike. "That's the car that followed me home this afternoon, riding my bumper the whole way."

"What?" Mike's eyes narrowed. "Why didn't you tell me?"

"At the time, I didn't think much of it—I just assumed it was an obnoxious driver."

"Are you sure it's the same car?"

"One hundred percent."

"And you've never seen the car before—on your street or around town?"

Emily shook her head.

"Let's go inside. We need to make a new plan. I'm not leaving you alone."

Elvis and Bella provided a momentary distraction from the recent drama. Mike made a call, telling whoever was on the other end he would be late.

"I don't want to interfere with your work. I'll be fine with the doors locked," Emily said. "Plus, Duncan will be here soon for Elvis."

"Nope. I'm not going anywhere."

He seemed to be overreacting, but considering Emily had been threatened in her own home when Mrs. Klein's murderer tried to break in, his response was understandable.

"What if Anthony comes over till Duncan gets here?" Mike didn't answer, so she said, "And I promise to call you if I see anything suspicious."

"All right. That will give me a chance to track down that vehicle."

•   •   •

Anthony arrived in record time. He didn't need a long, drawn-out explanation of the risks—this wasn't the first instance either of them had landed in the crosshairs of a criminal investigation.

Mike had taken Elvis down the street for a quick walk, and when he returned, he said, "Thanks again for coming. I hope we didn't mess up your night."

"No worries. Marc and I were having dinner and a movie at home. He's making his famous Bolognese sauce and can bring us some if you want."

Emily smiled. "Sounds delicious. I wish I hadn't eaten already."

Mike kissed Emily and headed for the door. He paused and looked back at her, concern on his face.

"We're fine. Now, go catch Billy's killer," she said.

•   •   •

"Em, I think I noticed a few gray hairs on Mike's head. Worrying about you investigating another murder is aging him." Anthony nudged her shoulder and grinned.

"Stop," she laughed. "No, it's not, and don't act like you're not involved in these cases, too."

He settled on the couch, inviting Elvis to join him. "If you had to guess, who do you think was driving the Camaro?"

"No clue, but if I were profiling the owner of a beat-up hot rod, it would be a younger guy."

"Or someone who restores old cars."

"Don't know anyone who does that."

"Hmm. You should get one of those video doorbell systems so you can record any suspicious activity."

"I forgot to mention something. Duncan knows about our crime board."

"Ouch."

"Mike wants me to tell him about our interactions with Thornton. And speaking of the broker, we have some time before Duncan gets here. Want to take a drive? We can stop at The Cone Zone for a soft serve on our way."

"On our way where?"

Emily tapped away on her cell phone then passed it to him.

"Thornton Marine Brokerage," he said. "Seriously?"

"It's closed on Sundays, so we can check the place out on the down-low. See what type of operation he's running. I don't like how he's been pressuring Lala. While it's a bit of a stretch to think getting his hands on *Diver Down* could be a motive for murder, maybe we're missing something."

"So, just a drive-by?"

"Promise."

"Okay, but I have one request. Cone Zone first, snooping and mayhem second."

CHAPTER THIRTY-ONE

The Cone Zone, an iconic Coral Shores establishment built in the 50s, had resisted the trends of modern frozen yogurt places with their fancy toppings bars. They offered only one product—soft-serve ice cream. The giant cone-shaped building had a small takeout window for service. Anthony opted for a double-dipped, and Emily chose "The Swirl," a twisty combination of chocolate and vanilla. They sat at a nearby picnic table to enjoy their treat.

"It's a good thing I don't have to drive by here on my way home from work," Emily said. "I'm always starving by then and would end up eating ice cream as an appetizer."

Two causeway bridges at the north and south ends of the barrier island where Emily lived connected the beach to the mainland. Emily's route to work took her south, and The Cone Zone sat next to the north bridge.

"The best part is the soggy tip soaked in melted ice cream goodness." Anthony popped the last bite into his mouth then picked up his phone to study the map. "Looks like Thornton's place is on the inland side near the north causeway, in that industrial area along the Intracoastal."

"Seeing the place in person should help us get a handle on this guy. We better get going. Duncan will be at my place in an hour."

·   ·   ·

They drove past boat dealers, repair shops, and yacht purveyors before arriving at Thornton Marine Brokerage. Emily had expected to see a fancy building, like a luxury car dealership, but instead, they found a rundown construction trailer parked at the back of a gravel lot. A backwater flats boat sat next to a couple of faded and weatherworn paddleboats and a single jet ski.

"This is more like a flea market than a brokerage," Anthony said.

"Doesn't scream successful businessman." She looked around. "It's hard to imagine Thornton has the money to buy *Diver Down*, but it does explain why he was pushing Lala to accept an unfair offer. It's likely the only offer he could afford."

Emily walked to the far side of the lot. "I can't see if any boats are docked on the canal behind the trailer. I wonder if there's another way to get back there."

"Hold up. A chain-link fence blocks the access."

"I'm only going to take a peek."

"Famous last words." Anthony jogged to catch up to her. "But isn't that trespassing?"

She stopped to think. "You're right. Let's check the office first— to make sure nobody is here."

Emily climbed the wobbly front steps and knocked on the door while Anthony peered inside the window. After no response, they returned to the side yard. A padlocked gate prevented their easy access to the canal, but a small gap in the fence next to the trailer allowed Emily to squeeze through. Anthony's robust size made that an impossibility.

"Em, there's no way I can get through there."

She turned and smiled. "I'll be right back." Then she disappeared before he could object.

There wasn't much to see. The yard held a rusty boat lift and a single kayak propped against the outside wall of the trailer, but no boats or equipment of any kind. She stood with her hands on her hips, staring at the empty canal. "Strange."

As Emily turned the corner near the fence, she found Anthony pacing in a circle, talking to himself while waving his arms in the air. When he saw her, he said, "You can't do that to me. No more sneaking off by yourself."

While tempted to remind him she had been less than fifty yards away and could have called for help, she opted for, "Sorry. I promise."

"Can we get out of here? This place is depressing."

•   •   •

They arrived back at Emily's cottage and found Marc standing at the front door, holding a large cooking pot and a duffel bag.

"Hey. I was about to text you to find out where you'd gone," Marc said as they approached.

Neither Anthony nor Emily volunteered the reason for their absence. Marc scanned their faces, then said, "You've been sleuthing, haven't you?"

"Guilty as charged," Anthony said. "But mostly just a drive-by to check out a local business."

"Uh-huh. Sure." Marc's raised brows communicated his disbelief. "As long as you're being safe and sticking together. Especially after Emily's Camaro stalker incident."

Emily wanted to change the subject. "What do you have there?" She pointed to the pot.

"My pappardelle Bolognese. A particularly good batch. And an overnight bag for Anthony. Just in case you need backup."

"Perfect. I haven't eaten yet, and I'm starving." Anthony looked at Emily. "Ice cream doesn't count."

Emily watched Marc and Anthony side-by-side in the kitchen, prepping their dinner. Their relationship made her smile. When they started dating, she'd been protective of her friend until she got to know Marc, and then she fell in love with him, too. They were a great couple and proved that opposites attract. Equally tall, Marc's white-blond hair contrasted with Anthony's Cuban and Puerto Rican heritage. He was smart, an engineer, and his calm, even-keeled personality balanced Anthony's more emotional and impulsive side. They brought out the best in each other. Emily supported their decision to move in together earlier this year, taking their relationship to the next level.

She couldn't resist having a small serving of the delectable pasta and joined them at the kitchen island while they ate their dinner. They were clearing the dishes when she received a text alert.

"Duncan asked if I could keep Elvis one more night. They got back late from the tournament, and everyone was wiped out. Jane will pick him up at work in the morning."

"Looks like you and I are staying over." Anthony pointed to the attentive terrier.

"Are you sure?" Emily asked.

"Has Mike sent any updates about tracking down the Camaro's owner?" Anthony asked.

"No."

"Then that's that. It's not up for debate." He placed his overnight bag in the guest room.

Emily didn't push back. Not because she felt threatened by a random driver, but because she enjoyed the company.

"Should Lala be alone—with a possible break-in and a hotrod driver on the loose?" Marc asked.

"Probably not," Emily said. "Maybe we can convince her to accept your offer to stay at your place? I can keep Hemingway here for a few days, but I'll have to separate her from Bella so there's no friction or stress."

"It's worth a try," Anthony said. "Let's talk with her about it in the morning."

The three friends gathered on her beach deck to have a nightcap. Once Marc headed home, they watched some TV before calling it an early night. Lala planned to meet them before opening for Hemingway's X-ray.

•   •   •

They told Lala to park behind the hospital and knock on the door when she arrived, but Hemingway's bellowing meow made that unnecessary. Elvis had been resting on his dog bed in Emily's office when he heard the tabby's distress call. His ears perked up, and he ran into the treatment area. When Emily rescued Elvis, he spent the first few weeks coming to work with her every day, and he now moved around the place like he owned it.

"She sure hates car rides." Lala set the carrier on the exam table. "It took me ten minutes to lure her in there. Hi, Elvis." The terrier had his paws up on the table, trying to get a glimpse.

"That's pretty common. I can give you tips to make that easier next time." Emily opened the door and looked inside. Hemingway's eyes were as wide as saucers. She extended her finger in front of the cat's nose, using it to lure her outside. When Hemingway saw Elvis, a familiar face, she walked out of the carrier with confidence. The terrier wagged his tail enthusiastically. The two were becoming fast friends.

Emily repeated her orthopedic exam of Hemingway's injured leg. The swelling had improved, but she still resisted the full range of motion of her carpus or wrist.

"So, I have news," Lala said.

Anthony and Emily's faces dropped. After a streak of bad news, they assumed the worst.

Lala laughed. "I should have said good news. My mom and I talked for a long time last night—she'll be at the marina for dinner."

Anthony exhaled. "That's amazing. I'm so happy for you."

"Thanks. I was nervous about seeing her again, but now it's different. In a good way, you know."

Emily felt a lump in her throat, thinking about the prospect of being able to see her mom one more time. Mostly, she was grateful Lala wouldn't be alone.

"And I appreciate you fitting Hemingway in this morning. I have tons to do to get ready for her visit."

"Then let's get this taken care of." Anthony set up the X-ray machine and returned wearing his protective gear. "It'll only be a few minutes." He stroked the nervous cat until her posture relaxed and she began purring, then he carried Hemingway into the X-ray room while Emily gowned up. Lala waited outside with Elvis on her lap.

They turned off the lights, using only the overhead alignment beam on the machine to position Hemingway's extended leg over the X-ray plate.

"Wait a second," Anthony said. He removed his protective gloves and unclipped Hemingway's collar. "Don't want this showing up on the image." He set it on an adjacent table.

They gently held Hemingway's paw and snapped two images—one with her leg straight and one turned to the side. It was essential to get both images to create a two-dimensional view of the injury. Otherwise, they might miss something. She meowed a few times but didn't resist. When they finished, they turned on the overhead lights. Emily took off her gear and carried Hemingway back to Lala in the treatment area, while Anthony finalized the images.

"She's the best patient," Emily said. "Let's move to an exam room. It has the largest screen for me to show you the X-rays. Plus, we can let Hemingway and Elvis hang out while we talk."

"I hope she's okay," Lala said. "She seemed much better this morning."

"The swelling has gone down quite a bit."

Anthony joined them and placed a bowl of water and a blanket on the floor. When he reached into the treat jars on the counter, both cat and dog sat, waiting for their snack. Elvis licked Hemingway's cheek, his way of saying "Hey, friend," and they settled together on the blanket.

Emily examined the X-rays, zooming in and out. "Good news. There's only evidence of minimal swelling." She indicated the area on the screen. "These are the bones in her joints, and they're okay. No fractures and no signs of arthritis."

"That's such a relief," Lala said.

"You have the last dose of pain medicine to give her today, and I think with a week of rest, she should be back to normal. But if she needs more medicine, I can bring some by."

"Did you hear that, Hemingway?" Lala said. "You get to rest, but of course, that's what you do most days." She leaned over and stroked her fur. "Her collar is missing."

Anthony stood up. "We took it off for her X-rays. I'll get it." He returned a few minutes later with Hemingway's collar and a puzzled look on his face.

"What's wrong?" Emily asked.

"I tried to clip her collar together, and it wouldn't click shut. That's when I found this lodged inside the clasp." He opened his hand to reveal a tiny device the size of an eraser head.

Emily leaned in. "What's that? And why was it in her collar?"

CHAPTER THIRTY-TWO

The friends took turns examining the device that was no bigger than a watch battery and flatter than a paperclip. Its sleek, black, rectangular shape had three round edges and a flat metal end resembling a USB connector.

"Could it be the microchip to identify lost pets?" Lala asked. "Could it have fallen off?"

"No, those chips are implanted under the skin over the shoulders, and they're shaped like a tiny tube. Let me double-check Hemingway's chip." Emily reached into a drawer for a microchip scanner and waved it over the tabby's back. It beeped, revealing a fifteen-digit number on the screen. Emily compared it to the number in her file, and it was a match.

"That's a relief, especially after she got out the other night. I couldn't handle it if anything happened to her." Lala picked up her cat and hugged her tight before returning her to Elvis on the blanket.

"This metal end looks the same as a flash drive, like the ones used to transfer files from work to my computer at home." Anthony reached for the ophthalmic light mounted in the charger on the counter and used it to examine the inner workings of the clasp on Hemingway's collar.

"That's weird." He passed the collar and light to Lala. "There's a little pocket inside the clip about the same size. But the whole thing looks handmade. Most cat collars have a plastic clip, but this one is metal."

Lala studied the clasp before Emily had a turn.

"Someone welded a tiny pocket inside the clasp," Emily said.

Lala leaned against the counter and looked up at the ceiling in thought.

"Was Billy a welder?" Anthony asked.

"Not by profession, but he was a tinkerer. He could fix anything. I remember him using a welding gun to repair a broken deck railing in high school, and I found some equipment in the dive shop's storage room when I was rearranging things."

Anthony's eyes lit up. "If this thing were plugged into a computer, you'd never see it. It would sit flush against the side. Should we check what's on it?"

They exchanged glances, then Emily said, "Why not? But that's up to you, Lala."

She replied, "We really have no choice. Let's do it."

"I'll grab my laptop. I don't want to plug it into the hospital network in case there's a virus." Anthony retrieved his personal computer from his office. He inserted the device into the standard USB port on the side of his laptop. A whirling sound indicated power to the drive, and the device lit up with an LED light. An icon representing the flash drive appeared on the home screen.

He moved his cursor over the file and looked back at Lala. She nodded, so he double-clicked the icon, and a pop-up window asked for a password.

"Try *Hemingway*," Lala said. Anthony entered a combination of capital and lower-case versions but continued to receive an error message.

"What about this?" Lala searched her phone before turning the screen to face Anthony. "It's the boat registration number for *Diver Down*. I had to find it for the insurance company when I called about his policy."

He tried the twelve-digit combination of numbers and letters, but it also delivered an invalid password alert.

"Why did Billy put a computer file in her collar?" Lala asked.

"He wanted to hide something," Emily said. Based on the look on their faces, she didn't need to point out the suspicious nature of the whole situation. "The police should have tech specialists who can hack into the file."

Anthony lifted his hands, realizing he had contaminated evidence in a murder investigation. "Our prints are all over that thing now."

"It's what's in the file that matters the most." Emily picked up her phone and sent her brother and Mike a text.

Hemingway appeared antsy, pacing the exam room, so Lala decided to take her back to the marina. Plus, she had to prep for her mom's arrival and Billy's service. She opened the carrier, and the orange, fluffy cat stepped in without a fuss.

"She never does that when I'm trying to get her inside to come here. It's a complete battle royale. Like she's Houdini, escaping my attempts."

Emily laughed. "That happens all the time. I think they know they're going home."

Elvis pressed his nose against the carrier and whined. Hemingway rubbed the side of her face against the door.

"They're so sweet together. Elvis, I'm sure you'll see her again soon," Emily said.

"Call me after Duncan gets here," Lala said on her way out. "And thank you for taking such good care of Hemingway."

Emily and Anthony sealed Hemingway's collar and the mysterious flash drive in a lab sample bag, their version of an evidence bag, as Catrinna leaned into the office.

"Your first appointment is here."

•   •   •

When Emily walked into the exam room, she saw a mound covered by a blanket on the table.

"Fluffy likes to hide when she's scared," Mrs. Merkin said. "This is her favorite blanket from home. I thought the smells would comfort her."

"That's a great idea. Whatever allows Fluffy to feel secure."

Emily peeked underneath. Two golden-hazel eyes, their pupils fully dilated, stared back at her. She slid her stethoscope beneath the covering and listened intently, moving the device around to assess lung sounds in all areas of the kitty's chest, while watching the clock on the wall to count Fluffy's respirations and heart rate.

When Emily removed her stethoscope and stepped back, Mrs. Merkin asked, "So, is it better? Please say it's better."

Emily smiled, immediately putting her at ease. "Much better. Has her coughing improved?"

Mrs. Merkin put her hand to her chest, exhaled, then reached into her purse. "Yes, I record every time she coughs, so I can keep track. Her coughing spells were more than six times a day before we started the medicine, and in the last two days, she's only coughed once. And no more coughing attacks. I canceled all my appointments this week and never left the house, so I'm certain I didn't miss any." She handed the spreadsheet to Emily.

"Thank you. This is very helpful. What about her appetite? Is it back to normal?"

"Yes, and she's grooming again. And playing with her toys."

"Those are all important signs she is feeling better. Especially since cats love to hide their illnesses from us. Catrinna mentioned you had questions about her inhaler."

Fluffy had been diagnosed with asthma the prior week. Chest X-rays confirmed that the wheezing and crackling sounds Emily heard with her stethoscope were caused by inflammation in the lungs. Fluffy had a history of a rare cough that would occur when she ran around chasing her cat siblings, but the recent construction of a new house next door to the Merkins had kicked up a lot of dust into the environment and triggered an asthma attack.

Fluffy had arrived at the Coral Shores Veterinary Hospital, struggling to get air into her lungs. Since cats only breathe through their nose unless they're in respiratory distress, her open-mouth breathing prompted a set of emergency protocols. She was immediately put in the oxygen chamber and administered emergency drugs. After her breathing stabilized, she was discharged later the same day.

Long-term management of her asthma required using an inhaler with a special mask designed for cats, called an AeroKat. It could be fussy to administer the medicine while holding a squirming cat. Emily had provided Mrs. Merkin with helpful hints and links to websites where she could see other cats receiving their inhaler.

"I think I'm doing it right, but I want to be certain. It's time for her treatment, and I thought we could do it together. To make sure she's getting a full dose."

Mrs. Merkin handed the inhaler and the AeroKat to Emily. The blanket was pulled back just far enough to expose Fluffy's head and her chest. Her sable fur and markings on her face were beautiful. Mrs. Merkin gently held Fluffy and talked softly to her.

Emily shook the inhaler and attached it to one end of the chamber. Mrs. Merkin placed the mask over Fluffy's nose and mouth to create a seal as Emily pressed the inhaler, releasing the puff of medicine.

"She needs to take five to six breaths to get a full dose. It's easiest if you watch her chest move up and down with each breath."

Together, they counted to six. Fluffy accepted her treatment without an issue.

"She did great," Emily said. "Since Fluffy takes impeccable care of her fur, you can use a damp cloth to wipe her face when you're done to remove any medicine residue. She may always need an inhaler, but it's possible that once the construction is over, she may be weaned off slowly. But for now, continue using it once a day, and we'll recheck her in two weeks. Of course, if anything changes, come in right away."

Mrs. Merkin wrapped Fluffy in the blanket and put her inside the carrying bag. "Thanks, Dr. Benton. I'm so relieved. Let's go, Fluffy—some new tuna treats are waiting for you at home."

Emily emerged from her appointment and followed the sound of Duncan's voice into Anthony's office.

"This case keeps getting stranger and stranger." Duncan wore gloves as he examined the inner clasp on the collar. "Hi, Em." Elvis sat at his feet, leaning on his leg. "I appreciate you keeping Elvis for an extra night. We were all asleep within thirty minutes of arriving home."

"Anytime." She pointed at the collar. "So, what do you think?"

"Your guess is as good as mine. The computer whizzes will have to work their magic to access those files."

"I hope they don't find anything that might disparage Billy's memory. Lala can't take any more bad news," Anthony said.

"When is his memorial service?" Duncan asked.

"Tuesday at five o'clock at the marina. Why?" Emily asked.

"Mike and I will be there."

"Oh," Anthony said. "That whole *returning to the scene of the crime* theory. The murderer might show up. Is that what you're thinking?"

"I think you and Em watch too many detective shows." Duncan smiled. "And no, it's not just about the investigation. We want to show our respect."

Emily wore a pensive expression as she stared at her brother. "First, there's no such thing as too many detective shows. Second, have you been able to uncover any irregular arsine gas purchases or figured out what equipment is needed to put that gas in a dive tank?"

He returned her stare but didn't say anything, so Emily continued.

"And what about all the information on the paperwork you confiscated from Billy's office? Anything interesting turn up?"

Before he could reply, Abigail called over the intercom. "Dr. Benton, your next appointment is here."

"Perfect timing. I'm headed to the station, but Jane will be here to get Elvis after dropping the kids at school. Bye, little buddy." He reached down to ruffle the fur on his head, then left the office.

"That was unsatisfying," Anthony said. "More questions without answers."

Emily stared out the window. Palm fronds swayed in the gusty wind, casting shifting shadows into the room as the sun slipped behind a cloud.

"Em, I don't like that look on your face."

She turned to face him. "We can't hack into a file, but that doesn't mean we can't help Lala. We need more info on this Stewie guy. I told Wilma from Gamblers Anonymous I would let her know about Billy's service. I'll check if she's free to meet after work."

"Count me in. And speaking of work—" He motioned to Catrinna standing in his doorway, signaling the next appointment.

CHAPTER THIRTY-THREE

Having finished work a few minutes early, Emily and Anthony left Abigail to lock up for the night and drove together to the Gamblers Anonymous meeting.

"I forgot to tell you," Anthony said. "When Jane came by for Elvis, she told me she's planning to come to Billy's service, since the kids have some after-school activities. I mentioned Elvis and Hemingway's budding friendship, so she might bring him along. I thought that would be okay with Lala."

"I think so, but we can check with her."

They pulled up by the church's side entrance, and as they walked toward the door, Anthony asked, "What are you hoping to learn here?"

"Anything to help us figure out how to find Stewie. Wilma comes early to set up before the meeting. This way, we can talk to her in private."

The Gambler's Anonymous meeting coordinator walked into the hallway with her arms full.

"Hi, Emily. I mean Dr. Benton." She placed the pot of coffee on the table. "After you left last week, I realized I'd seen you before. I helped a neighbor of mine bring her big dog to the vet hospital.

He'd hurt his leg, and it took the two of us to load him into the car. I waited in the lobby, so we weren't introduced."

"I remember," Anthony said. "You came in with Dasher."

"That's right. It's Anthony, isn't it? You were so kind to help us get him back into the car."

"Yes." He extended his hand. "Dasher's a sweet boy."

"Your message said you had information about Billy's funeral? I told the group, and there are a handful of us who plan to come."

"That's one of the reasons why we stopped by. His niece is having a memorial service at the dive shop tomorrow at five o'clock. Anyone is welcome to speak, and there will be light refreshments served."

"I'll be there and can help get the word out." Wilma resumed setting up cups and snacks. "But I feel bad you had to drive over to tell me."

"There's something else we wanted to talk to you about."

Wilma set the creamer on the table. "Is this about Stewie?"

Taken aback, Emily didn't answer right away.

"Yes, it is," Anthony said. "But what made you say that?"

"Well, Stewie dropped by after you were here, and I let him know about Billy. I thought he'd be upset since I was under the impression they were friends. But he didn't say much. He asked me how I knew, and I told him about you and Billy's niece. I assumed he was trying to rejoin our meeting group, and when I reminded him that nothing had changed and he still wasn't welcome, his tone became aggressive. I didn't pay it much attention at the time—he's always been a bit prickly with me—but now that you mention it, I'm starting to wonder."

"Wonder what?" Emily asked.

"He didn't seem at all surprised, but I thought he might have seen it in the news. I've stopped judging people's emotional responses to trauma. It's all over the map, and there's no one way. Everyone processes things differently."

Billy's name hadn't been released to the media at the time of Wilma's conversation with Stewie, but Emily kept that piece of information to herself.

"Could you describe what he looks like?" Emily asked.

"Sure. He's about forty years old, six feet tall, with sandy brown, straight hair, and brown eyes. He looks like a washed-up high school athlete—muscular but with a paunch around the middle. He always wears a thick, gold-link chain necklace."

Wilma's description of Stewie matched the man who knocked her over at the watersports store, right down to the jewelry.

"Did he talk about working with Billy at the marina?" Emily asked.

"No, sorry. He never said where he worked. We don't require any personal information to join the group. You just need to come with an open heart and good intentions."

"Thanks, Wilma. If you think of anything else, please call me."

"Will do. I'll see you both at the memorial service."

•   •   •

"So?" Anthony asked.

"It's the same Stewie that knocked me down at Mr. Haney's store. But we don't know if it's the same Stewart Jackson that worked for Billy. Especially since he didn't mention anything the night he bought bait from Lala. Are you sure his contact info wasn't listed in any of the papers you found on Billy's desk?"

"Not that I remember, but I didn't get through them all before they were confiscated as evidence. I'm sure Mike or Duncan can find out."

"Mm-hmm." Emily continued driving in silence while Anthony read an incoming text.

"Lala invited us to drop by the marina to meet her mom. Well, not meet her, since we knew her as kids, but I don't remember what she looks like."

"She might want backup depending on how things are going. I'm nervous for her."

Emily turned the car in the marina's direction. When they entered the lot, she saw another car disappear behind the back of the watersports store. Based on the primer paint visible on the trunk, it was the same Camaro that had followed her home.

"Gotcha," Emily said before executing an abrupt turn and backing into a space next to a garbage dumpster behind the dive shop.

"What are you doing?" Anthony asked.

Emily pointed. "The Camaro just pulled in ahead of us. I don't want the driver to know we spotted them."

Anthony craned his neck. "I don't see a Camaro."

"It's behind the watersports store. I think there's only a loading dock on that side." Emily grabbed her phone and texted Mike to tell him she'd found the car. He replied right away that he was on his way.

"So, why don't we drive around and check it out?"

"I don't want to spook them before Mike gets here. Let's stake it out—"

Before she could finish her sentence, a truck pulled into the lot. Emily immediately recognized Stewie at the wheel. Trent ran out from behind the watersports building and jumped into the passenger seat.

"That's Stewie!" Emily put her car in drive and inched forward, waiting to see which way they turned.

"Who?"

"The guy driving that old truck."

When she caught Anthony tightening his seatbelt, she said, "This isn't some high-speed car chase. We're just going to follow him to find out where he lives."

"You know that's not a plan, right?"

The truck headed toward town. Emily remained a few car lengths behind, and at the first red light, she flipped down her visor and asked Anthony to do the same.

"Let's stay incognito until—" Emily's phone rang. It was Mike.

"Hey," she said. "You're on speaker with Anthony."

"Where are you? I'm at the marina, and you're not here."

"Well…we're following Stewie and a guy from the watersports store, Trent."

"You're what?"

Anthony frantically gestured, trying to convey his panic, but Emily just shook her head, rotating her palms up to show she had no idea what he meant.

"We're hoping they lead us back to Stewie's house," she said. "So we can figure out who he is."

"Oh, no, you don't. Em, we already know who he is. Please turn around and come back to the marina. I'll tell you everything."

She didn't reply, prompting Mike to say, "Anthony, I need your help here."

Anthony whispered, trying to prove his loyalty to Team Emily, "Maybe we should let it go."

Stewie signaled his left-hand turn into a neighborhood named Isle of Venice. Emily followed, noting a No Thru Street sign at the entrance.

"Does he live on the Isle of Venice?" Emily asked.

"Yes."

"Okay, we'll turn around. See you in a few." Then she hung up.

"This doesn't look like you're turning around," Anthony said.

"It's a dead-end street. Let's drive by, and then we can do a U-turn."

Anthony stared at the open water flanking both sides of the street, where sailboats were docked bow to stern along the canals. "I think Marc's aunt used to live here. She spends most of the year sailing the Caribbean but would rent a short-term place during hurricane season. Lots of liveaboard sailors call this area home. It's very transient."

Stewie pulled into a parking lot next to a small two-story apartment building. Emily ducked when she passed by so Stewie and Trent couldn't see her when they exited the car. After continuing another quarter mile before reaching the cul-de-sac, she put the car in park and opened the map on her phone.

"I'm pretty sure it's a straight shot from here to the inlet, and you'd have to pass by Blue Water Marina before reaching open water." She pinched her fingers together on the screen to expand the aerial view. "I was right." She handed her phone to Anthony. "Billy headed inland on *Diver Down* after leaving the marina that last day. He could reach this location in no time."

"I dropped a pin to mark the apartment building. Let's go before Mike sends in a SWAT team." Anthony grinned. "You sure have a knack for getting him to talk."

She pointed to Anthony. "There are two of us here."

"I know, but I need to be Switzerland between you, Mike, and Duncan. A neutral party to keep the peace."

"I plan to hold Mike to his word. This case is more advanced than we realized. Billy's memorial service is right around the corner, and Lala needs answers if she's going to get any closure."

CHAPTER THIRTY-FOUR

When they arrived at Blue Water Marina, Lala stood on the dock next to a woman. From a distance, it looked like Lala's mom, but after more than a decade, Emily couldn't be certain.

A truck emblazoned with *Shoreline Catering Co.* had parked near the dive shop, and two women unloaded tables and chairs from the back. Emily pulled alongside Mike's empty police car. She wanted to hear what he had to say about Stewie but felt conflicted, knowing he would have a definite opinion about her recent surveillance activities.

She exited her car and turned to scan the lot. "Where is he?"

"I'm sure he's nearby," Anthony said.

Lala waved for them to join her.

Anthony waved back. "Let's say hi to her mom before we talk with Mike. Should we say anything about Stewie?"

"Not right now. Plus, we have nothing concrete to share. Not yet, anyway."

Lala and her mom were holding hands. They could have been sisters. Emily remembered Claire Todd as being very thin, almost frail, with sunken cheeks and a downcast expression. The woman in front of her exuded health. Although both women had been crying, Claire's bright eyes and rosy complexion beamed when she smiled.

"Mom, you remember Emily Benton and Anthony Torres."

"Yes, of course." She hugged them both. "Thank you so much for being there for Lauryn. She told me everything you've done to help her and Hemingway."

"It's nice to see you again," Anthony said. "We're so sorry about Billy. I'm sure it's difficult being back at your brother's place."

"Thank you. I'm still in shock and struggling with what happened. There are so many things I wish I could say to him. To tell him what an amazing brother and uncle he was and how much I loved him." She put her arm around her daughter and pulled her close. "But I believe Billy would be smiling down on us right now. It's all he ever wanted—for us to be back in each other's lives."

Emily turned away and wiped a tear. Her heart broke all over again, wishing she could feel her own mom's arms around her.

Anthony squeezed Emily's shoulder, his way of letting her know she wasn't alone. "Lala mentioned you've been living in Tarpon Springs."

"For a year now. I've been helping a friend start up a new jewelry design store. I also work the odd shift at a Greek restaurant near the Sponge Docks."

Emily returned to the conversation to watch Lala's face, trying to gauge her reaction. It appeared inviting her mom back into her life had been the right decision. Lala looked like someone who'd had a great weight lifted off her shoulders.

"Is all this for Billy's service?" Emily pointed at the catering truck.

Lala nodded. "I've rented some chairs and a few tables. They're also catering some refreshments after his memorial service. I got their name from Mr. Haney. He's been super supportive."

Just then, Emily caught Mike walking out of the watersports store. It was impossible to gauge his mood from this distance. She excused herself and met him halfway.

Aviator sunglasses shaded his eyes, but when he removed them, his brows were knitted together, the intensity of his stare giving her pause.

"Hi, Em." He held her hand loosely and leaned in, speaking in a low but controlled voice. "We need to talk. But not here." He motioned for her to follow him to his car.

From the passenger seat, she watched Mike staring out at the water, waiting for him to speak. When she couldn't take the silence any longer, she blurted out, "What's going on? And why were you at the watersports store?"

"Hold up. First, can you tell me why you thought it was a good idea to follow a suspect on your own?"

"But I wasn't on my own. And I didn't have time to do anything other than react. Not if I wanted to get some answers." Emily informed him about her conversation with Wilma and Stewie's strange reaction to the news of Billy's death.

He tightened his jaw and took a deep breath. "I know you want to help Lala, but you need to stand down. Do you realize how dangerous that was?"

She ignored his question. "Can you please tell me what's going on? You said you already knew where Stewie lived. Is he the same guy who worked for Billy?"

Mike nodded.

"Twice, I've seen him with Trent, the nephew of the man that owns the watersports store, Mr. Haney. Is he involved, too? Is that why you were there just now?"

"I can't say. It's an active investigation, and I'm not the only one working on this case."

"What does that mean?"

"There are other law enforcement agencies involved. Em, that's all I can tell you. Please, let it go."

"Wait. Does it have something to do with the arsine gas supply companies? I assume the Environmental Protection Agency would want to know about the theft of a toxic substance. Does the EPA have their own investigators?" She looked out her window in thought. "Of course, they do. Even the vet hospital undergoes workplace and hazardous materials inspections with OSHA. And they're part of a federal agency."

Mike's grin broke through as he listened to Emily unravel her hypothesis.

"And what about the Thornton Marine Brokerage company? Do you have any leads there?"

"Em, you'll have to trust me. All my department's resources are focused on solving Billy's murder."

She trusted him, and realizing she'd hit a brick wall, she pivoted.

"Will you be able to come to the memorial service? That's Lala's mom standing next to her." Emily pointed across the marina.

"I'll be there." He smiled then leaned over to kiss her. "I've got to go, but tell them I said hi."

•   •   •

With no choice but to accept her bystander role in the investigation, at least for the time being, Emily joined her friends. The caterers were in the process of assembling a white event tent next to the dive shop.

"What did Mike have to say?" Anthony asked.

"Not much." She motioned with her eyebrows toward Lala, not wanting to risk upsetting them with a discussion of Billy's murder investigation. But Lala noticed.

"Em, it's okay. You don't need to shield me from the truth. Or Mom either."

"We want to help catch the person who did this to Billy," Claire said. "That's what I told Detective Lane when he called me a couple days ago."

This was news. Emily couldn't quite control her expression.

"Mom, that's Emily's boyfriend. The man she was just talking to. He's the lead detective on Billy's case, alongside her brother, Deputy Sheriff Duncan Benton."

"And I know they won't stop until they arrest the person responsible," Emily said.

"I'm reassured learning they're the ones on the case. Please tell Detective Mike how much I appreciated his sincerity and kindness when he called to tell me about Billy."

"I will."

"Is there anything we can do to help you tomorrow?" Anthony asked.

"Most everything is handled, but thank you. Mom and I are going to work on our eulogy. She's staying here with me for the next two days. And Joe Fazio came by earlier to clean *Diver Down* and run the engines, making sure the boat is ready for us to spread Billy's ashes on the reef."

"Did you say Fazio?" Anthony asked.

"Yes. I got his name from Duncan. He came highly recommended as a boat captain."

Anthony looked at Emily. "That's Gus's son." He turned to Lala and her mom. "Gus is the contractor building our sea turtle center. I'm sure you're in good hands."

"I think so, too," Lala said.

Emily smiled, thinking about her brother's good deed in helping Lala find a boat captain, then asked, "What about Hemingway? How's her limp?"

"So much better. I've only seen her favor it for a few steps after she wakes up from a long nap. Otherwise, she walks normally."

"That's great to hear," Emily said. "Try to keep her from jumping down from heights this next week, but it sounds like her mild sprain is healing well."

"Thanks to the best vet team in the world," Lala said.

At the mention of Hemingway, Emily checked her watch. Bella would be unhappy about the late dinner hour.

"Anthony, we should get going," Emily said. "But we'll be here early tomorrow and can help with anything you need."

Lala hugged them and walked with her mom inside the dive shop.

•   •   •

As Emily drove to the vet hospital so Anthony could pick up his car, he said, "I'm so happy for them both. Lala's mom seems different than I remember. In the best possible way."

"I agree. And they need each other right now."

"So, are you going to tell me what Mike said?"

"It wasn't much. He confirmed Stewie is Stewart Jackson, Billy's former employee. We have to stay on alert in case we see him lurking around the marina. I'm sure he's connected to this. Why else would he avoid offering his condolences? Plus, I keep seeing him with Trent. They're up to something. Oh, and other agencies are working on this case, but Mike wouldn't say which ones. I thought EPA investigators might be involved because of the missing toxic gas."

"Had he mentioned he already spoke to Lala's mom?"

"No. And it didn't feel good finding out the way we did."

"You can't be mad at him. He's doing his job, and if anything, he's more willing than Duncan to share things."

"I hear you, but I'm not going to apologize for getting involved. This is personal for us."

She pulled in next to Anthony's car.

"Try to rest," he said. "Work will be hectic since we had to double-book some morning appointments to leave early for Billy's service."

She squeezed his hand. "Night, Anthony. And thanks for riding shotgun."

"Forever partners in crime." A mischievous grin spread across his face as he waggled his eyebrows up and down.

CHAPTER THIRTY-FIVE

Something nagged at the edge of her conscious mind, forcing her awake an hour before her alarm. Emily felt around in the darkness for Bella. She was sleeping on her favorite pillow and only responded with a cooing sound to Emily's gentle touch.

That's a first. I'm up before Bella. She tiptoed out of the bedroom, feeling her way to the kitchen before turning on a light. While waiting for the coffee to brew, she sat in a chair facing the crime board.

Finding a motive for Billy's murder had eluded her. If the case now involved outside law enforcement agencies, something else must be going on. But what?

Emily grabbed the dry-erase markers and placed a yellow star beside Stewie's name and the word "EPA" under *Means* since she considered them the most likely agency to be investigating the toxic gas theft. The more she stared at the board, the more confused she became. Bella's solitary, booming meow forced her to change course.

"Good morning to you, too."

The enormous Maine Coon sat next to her empty bowl. Emily opened the cupboard and chose a can of flaked ocean fish while the tabby wove a figure eight around her legs, the purring vibrating against her skin.

"You're so fickle." She set the dish in front of Bella then trailed her fingers along her back to the tip of her tail. Bella continued to purr while she ate.

After packing a separate outfit for Billy's service, Emily dressed in her usual scrubs, filled her travel mug, and left for work. She took advantage of the extra time to stop for breakfast for the staff on her way. Arriving earlier than normal would allow her to get a head start on her day.

•   •   •

Emily let everyone know there was food in the lunchroom then joined Anthony in his office.

"Even when I'm early, you're already here." Emily pulled two sausage, egg, and cheese bagels from a bag. "I have a feeling we'll be missing lunch, so I wanted to front-load at breakfast."

He set his sandwich on the counter and continued gazing outside. The palms barely moved in the light breeze as the sun streamed through the window. The corners of his mouth turned slightly downward and faint lines crossed his forehead. Not his normal exuberant and energetic self.

"You okay?" she asked. "There are plain bagels in the lunchroom if you prefer."

He smiled. "No, the sandwich is great. I was just thinking about Lala and Uncle Billy. I wish I still had access to his papers to sort out how he got into financial trouble. If it was to pay a gambling debt, what type of gambling? Lala said he sometimes wagered on sports, so I checked. There's only one legal online sports betting place in Florida, and it's run by the Seminole Tribe of Florida. Otherwise, he'd have to connect with a local sportsbook or a bookie. How would you find someone like that?"

"I bet Duncan would know. He's in law enforcement, and he grew up here. But it still doesn't work as a motive for murder. In the movies, the bookies always beat up the people who can't pay. They don't kill them. That guarantees they won't get their money."

"You're right. Let's focus on supporting Lala. We can put the crime solving on the back burner for a day."

• • •

Dressed for the occasion, Emily and Anthony arrived an hour before the start of Billy's memorial service. They found Claire helping the caterers arrange flowers and chairs under the event tent.

"Lauryn's inside," she said. "Can you check on her while I finish out here? It's been a difficult morning."

"Sure," Emily said.

Lala was sitting on a stool behind the sales counter, petting Hemingway, when they walked in. She looked pale, her eyes heavy with sadness, but she managed a little wave.

Emily wrapped her arm around Lala's shoulder as Anthony retrieved a glass of water from the apartment.

"Can we do anything?" Emily asked.

"Just sit here with me. Mom has everything else covered."

"Why don't you lie down for a while before people arrive?" Anthony said.

Lala shook her head. "I might not get up again. And I ran out of tears. I've been keeping myself going by planning what comes next—starting tomorrow."

"But that can wait a day, can't it?" he asked.

"Don't think so. I've made my final decision. I'm fully committed to getting Blue Water Marina up and running. Mom and I were up late last night talking. She's going to discuss it with her friend at the jewelry store, but she plans to move back to Coral Shores to help me get the business off the ground. At least temporarily—but I have to admit, I'm hoping it's permanent. Mom is healthy and taking great care of herself. It's all I ever wanted for her, and for me. A fresh start as mother and daughter."

Anthony put his hand on Lala's shoulder. "I'm relieved you're not tackling this on your own. I know you can do it, but it's a lot for any one person."

"It's the best way I can think of to honor Billy's memory." Lala drank the glass of water, stood to brush the wrinkles out of her sundress, and smiled. "Today needs to be a celebration of Billy's life. I want everyone to feel free to laugh and share their fondest memories."

•   •   •

Marc had arrived and was helping Emily and Anthony hand out memorial cards to Billy's friends, allowing Lala and Claire to greet everyone. The keepsake featured a photo of Billy behind the wheel of *Diver Down*, under the caption, *The ocean was your sanctuary, and now its waves carry your spirit forever*. Instead of flowers, Lala requested that a donation be made in Billy's memory to the Coral Reef Alliance, a nonprofit charity committed to ocean conservation projects and protecting the reefs. The number of attendees exceeded expectations, and the caterers scrambled to add additional chairs under the tent.

Emily introduced Wilma, from Gamblers Anonymous, to Lala and Claire then excused herself so they could talk in private. It would be important to hear firsthand how committed Billy had been to quitting gambling.

Mike and Duncan arrived together. After expressing their condolences, they stood on the periphery, watching.

Anthony pointed in their direction. "What are they up to?"

"To show their respect, of course, but I'm pretty sure they're working. You said it—the murderer may return to the scene of the crime."

Anthony shivered. "Can you imagine having the nerve? You have to be a sick person to gloat about something like this."

Emily felt a wet lick on her ankle and turned to look. "Elvis!"

"Hi." Jane reigned in the fluffy white terrier's leash as she approached. "How's Lala doing?"

Emily pointed at the crowd of people standing around Lala and her mom. "All this outpouring of love for Billy helps."

"Lala encouraged me to bring Elvis so he could spend time with Hemingway, but I don't want to interrupt her. I'll find a seat at the back so he doesn't get in the way." She glanced at her husband, huddled in close conversation with Mike. "They look serious."

"Yup," Anthony said. "I have an idea. Marc and I will take you to Hemingway after you say hi to Duncan. Maybe you can help us find out what they're discussing."

"You're asking me to spy on my husband?" Jane smirked. "I'm on it, but don't get your hopes up. You know Duncan. He'll never betray the badge, not even for his wife."

With the service about to start, Emily scanned the parking lot for stragglers before making her way under the tent. That's when she noticed Mr. Haney and Trent walking along the dock from the direction of the watersports store. Despite Trent's surly expression, she thanked them for attending and handed them each a memorial card. What she really wanted to do was interrogate him about Stewie and find out why he had been following her. But now was not the time.

Mr. Haney took his card and said, "After I pay my respects, I'll find us a seat."

Trent didn't move. Once he was alone with Emily, he said, "You and your cop boyfriend need to mind your own business, or someone's going to get hurt. And it ain't gonna be me."

Emily's jaw dropped. "Who do you think you are? Showing up here and making threats."

"No threats. Just facts. You can do whatever you want, but don't say I didn't warn you." He walked away and joined his uncle but continued to stare at Emily—a menacing stare.

She contemplated asking him to leave, but didn't want to create a scene right as the service began. She tried and failed to make eye contact with Mike and Duncan. Still seething from her interaction with Trent, Emily compartmentalized her emotions so she could be present for Lala. Out of respect for Billy, she took a seat under the tent.

●　　　●　　　●

The memorial service was a true celebration of life. Lala and Claire each spoke, followed by Wilma and two dive master friends of Billy's. They shared stories about his life, his kind heart, and his adventurous spirit. There wasn't a dry eye under the tent. Lala extended an invitation for everyone to enjoy light appetizers and refreshments. Emily searched the crowd for Trent, but he had slipped out during the service. *Coward*, she thought.

Mike and Duncan disappeared without a word as soon as the service ended, leaving Emily no chance to share Trent's warning. Each time she tried to step away to call Mike, another guest drew her into conversation. Surrounded by Billy's friends, the sense of danger gradually faded.

Once the crowd thinned, Lala and Claire prepared to board *Diver Down,* captained by Joe Fazio. He would drive just the two of them out to the reef so they could spread Billy's ashes. Marc returned to work, but Emily and Anthony had committed to remaining behind while the caterers cleaned up. Jane stayed inside with Elvis to keep Hemingway company.

While the tent and chairs were being loaded into the truck, Emily walked around the dock to ensure no cups, plates, or garbage had blown away. That's when she saw him. Clay Thornton, of

Thornton Marine Brokerage, pushing a dock cart down the main ramp to the marina. He appeared unaware of her surveillance.

Where's he going? She moved to follow him to his intended destination. And then the second shockwave occurred. She recognized a man sitting on the deck of a liveaboard trawler, reading a book. He looked so familiar, but she struggled to place him. When he turned in her direction, it came flooding back. Special Agent Franklin Bonaventura of the FBI tapped the brim of his hat, acknowledging her with a nod, then pressed his index finger to his lips in a quiet warning.

CHAPTER THIRTY-SIX

"What the?" Emily stutter-stepped, unsure what to do next. She wanted to follow Thornton but would have to pass by the FBI agent to do so. Was he working a case or enjoying some downtime? She respected his cue to be quiet and avoided saying or doing anything that could reveal his identity.

The first time Emily met Agent Bonaventura, he had been posted as an undercover agent outside her veterinary hospital. Assigned to monitor Tiki Lulu the talking parrot's social media followers and paparazzi that had swarmed her parking lot, he embedded himself as the leader of the group to gain intel on Marilyn Peña's kidnapping case. Franklin had been her ally in keeping the peace.

Now, Mike and Duncan's behavior at the memorial service made sense. They'd kept their distance because they were working. Was it the FBI, and not the EPA, that Mike had referenced as the outside agency investigating Billy's murder? And if so, why? According to the crime dramas she watched on TV, the FBI didn't meddle in local matters.

She turned and sprinted toward the tent, waiting until she was sure the agent couldn't see her before calling out in a hushed shout, "Anthony!"

He stepped from behind the catering van. "What?"

Emily grabbed his hand and pulled him aside so they could talk in private.

"Em, you're freaking me out."

She took a deep breath to collect herself before filling him in on both Thornton and Agent Bonaventura's presence at the marina. He peeked his head around the corner to get a glimpse while Emily called Duncan then Mike. She struck out and had to leave them both an urgent message to contact her.

"It might have nothing to do with Billy's case," he said.

Emily gave him a look. "Do I need to say it?

"You're right. It's not a coincidence."

"And there's more. Before the service started, that creep, Trent, threatened me. Said if Mike and I didn't mind our own business, someone would get hurt."

"He said that? Did Mr. Haney hear him?"

She shook her head. "He'd already taken his seat."

"What is going on here? I think Mr. Haney should be told about what his nephew is doing, and I'm pretty sure Lala doesn't have a clue about any of it, or she would have said something."

"But until we know more, I don't want to alarm her or her mom. Plus, they'll be emotionally exhausted when they return from their sea burial."

Emily's phone buzzed. "It's Jane. She needs to pick up the kids and asked if we could take over babysitting Hemingway." Lala had been concerned the noise outside might upset the tabby and wanted to avoid another escape to the ceiling rafters.

The caterers loaded the last set of chairs and waved as they pulled out of the marina. Emily and Anthony tiptoed inside to keep from startling the cat. They found Jane sitting at Billy's desk with Elvis and Hemingway curled up next to each other, napping on the bed. Hemingway's oversized front feet were pressed against the terrier's side, and they could see her flexing and extending her toes—or making biscuits, as Anthony called it.

"They're adorable," Emily whispered. "Looks like Elvis is enjoying his kitty massage."

"I feel bad about taking him home," Jane said.

Emily smiled at the sleeping furballs. "I can drop him off later if you want."

"That would be great. I need to get Mac some new baseball cleats and can't leave Elvis in the car while we shop. We'll be home in an hour." She grabbed her purse and keys and started for the door. "Please tell Lala and Claire again how sorry I am for their loss. It was a beautiful service."

"We will," Anthony said.

Cat and dog continued sleeping, so Emily and Anthony moved into the shop to monitor any marina activity through the windows.

"What types of crimes do the FBI get involved with?" Anthony asked.

"Well, we know firsthand they handle kidnapping cases. I saw in a movie that they investigate bank robberies and, of course, terrorism plots." She executed a quick internet search. "No recent bank robberies in the area."

"And nothing on the local news about any larger threats," he said. "Did you offer to bring Elvis home so you can corner Duncan?"

"Well, if he doesn't return my call, it's the only way to find out what's going on. To force him to talk. Plus, Mike is ghosting me, too."

"Good plan. Devious, but brilliant."

Emily grinned. "And I didn't want to break up Elvis and Hemingway's bonding moment."

She walked around and noticed the small changes Lala had made. The shelves and racks were dusted and polished, and the merchandise rearranged to maximize the use of the sales floor.

"We need to do something," Emily said.

"Like what? If we approach Thornton, there's a chance we could mess up an undercover operation."

"Do you still have the business card Agent Bonaventura gave us during Marilyn's kidnapping case?"

"It's at work. And what makes you think he would tell you anything when Mike and Duncan won't?"

"You're right." She dropped onto the stool and let her chin sink to the counter. Elvis trotted into the room, padded over to the door, and let out a single, sharp bark.

"Do you need to go out, little buddy?" Emily asked. Elvis shuffled his feet in a doggy dance. "I'll take him for a quick walk," she said to Anthony.

• • •

Emily led Elvis around the perimeter of the marina. She couldn't see either Thornton or Agent Bonaventura. After Elvis did his business, she headed back as *Diver Down* turned into the marina from the main channel. Claire sat with her arm around her daughter on the port side bench.

Emily met them as Joe Fazio secured the dive boat. They stepped onto the dock and hugged each other. Emily hesitated before approaching, not wanting to interrupt, but Elvis had other plans. He pulled on his leash to get to Lala.

"What a sweetie." Claire leaned over to scratch his ears.

"Hi, Em. Thanks again for helping with the caterers." Lala squatted to rub the terrier's belly.

"Anthony handled most of it. How are you doing?"

"Not good. I'll never be okay with losing Billy, but Mom and I got to say our goodbyes."

"Miss Lala." Joe handed her the keys. "I'll rinse off *Diver Down* and be on my way. You can tell me when it's a convenient time to drop by to discuss the next steps."

"I will. And thank you again for today."

"What's that about?" Emily asked.

"Joe's going to take over running the scuba and snorkel charters. He's a licensed captain, and his wife is a scuba instructor. We'll do a trial month to make sure it works for both of us, but I feel real good about this."

"Joe is fantastic," Claire said. "And we'll have our hands full with the dive shop and fuel dock."

"We?" Emily asked.

Claire put her arm around Lala's shoulders.

"Mom's committed to helping me run the business."

"I'm heading back to Tarpon Springs first thing," Claire said, "but should return within the week. I found a studio apartment to rent close by."

"And I'll continue living here with Hemingway. At least for now."

"I'm so happy for you both," Emily said.

"Thanks. It feels good, you know," Lala said. "But all I want to do right now is curl up in bed with Hemingway."

"Anthony's inside keeping her company. Let's go tell him the news, then we'll leave you to get some rest."

•   •   •

Emily dropped Anthony at his car before driving to Duncan and Jane's place to return Elvis. When she made the last turn in the road, Elvis perked up, having realized his proximity to home and bumping Emily's arm with each wag of his tail.

She parked next to Duncan's sheriff's car. He couldn't avoid her now.

"Hi." Emily let herself in and unlatched Elvis's leash. He ran toward the bedrooms to find the kids.

"Thanks for bringing him home." Jane waved at her from the kitchen. "How are Lala and Claire doing?"

"They're as good as to be expected, just emotionally exhausted." Emily saw Duncan outside tending to some chicken kabobs on the grill.

"That's understandable," Jane said. "You're welcome to join us for dinner. The kids are having a bath, but food should be ready in fifteen."

"Thanks, but I'm pretty wiped out, and I need to feed Bella. After I talk with Duncan, I'm headed home."

"Em, I can tell from your face," Jane said. "If it's about Billy's murder, I'll forewarn you. Duncan had a tough day."

"I'll tread lightly." She stepped outside and closed the door behind her.

Her brother took one look at her and said, "What happened?"

"You'd know if you returned my call."

"I planned to after the kids went to bed. I've been in the weeds all day."

"Working an FBI undercover operation?"

He fumbled the BBQ tongs, his mouth hanging open. "How did you find out?"

"I saw Agent Bonaventura at the marina. And that's not all. Clay Thornton, the marine broker, is up to something, and Trent, the guy from the watersports store, threatened me."

"What! He didn't hurt you, did he?"

"Nope. But it would have been nice if I could have talked with either you or Mike about it."

He ignored her dig. "Did you speak with Bonaventura?"

"No. He made it clear he was undercover, so I backed off. C'mon, Duncan. Spill it. I'll find out one way or the other."

He turned down the temperature on the grill and invited Emily to join him at the table. Seeing the exhaustion on her brother's face gave her pause. She contemplated letting him off the hook until Billy and Lala came to mind. They deserved justice.

"I'll go first." She recounted her interactions with Trent, the FBI agent, and the pushy marine broker, Thornton.

Duncan stood and paced around the table with his hands on his hips. Emily knew her brother well enough to give him a minute to sort through his thoughts without interrupting. When he sat back down, he said, "You're going to continue investigating, aren't you?"

She nodded. "Unless you can give me a good reason not to."

"If I do, will you promise to stay out of it?"

"I'll do my best."

He let out a harrumph and smirked. "I don't even know why I ask, but here goes. We think Billy's murder is linked to a credit card skimming syndicate, and the FBI is assisting in the investigation."

CHAPTER THIRTY-SEVEN

Now it was Emily's turn to pace around the table.

"Does Lala know about this?"

"Mike's there right now briefing her and her mom. And you don't need to say it—the timing is terrible."

"How is Billy involved in all this?" She stopped and looked at her brother. "Was it from the evidence you collected from the mini-USB drive we found in Hemingway's collar?"

Duncan nodded.

"Well…what was on it?"

"A list of credit card numbers, including names and PINs. We're still cross-checking with the banks, but many of them matched reports of credit card fraud filed by the cardholders."

"But there's more. Isn't there?"

"Stewart Jackson has gone from being a person of interest to our primary suspect. He's a local bookie, and the fraudulent credit card charges coincide with the dates of his employment at Billy's dive shop."

Emily sat down. "Oh." Her voice sounded distant. "Anthony and I were going to ask you where to find a bookie, but I guess we don't have to now. Still, I find it hard to believe Billy had anything to do with this."

"But the evidence was hidden on his cat. He had to know."

"This will break Lala's heart. And she's already heartbroken. There just has to be another explanation. Wait—what about Clay Thornton? His business is a dump, yet he offered to buy *Diver Down*. Where was he getting the money? Is he in the syndicate?"

"How would you know his business is a dump?"

"Umm, Anthony and I may have checked it out."

"Em—"

"You don't have to say it. And you were away at Mac's ball tournament."

"That's no excuse." Duncan shook his head disapprovingly. "Thornton has delusions of grandeur about becoming the next big name in yachts. He's trying to start his own charter boat business and has been hanging around the marina trying to buy a boat. That's how he found out about Billy. He doesn't have the means to buy much of anything. He's odd, but he's not a murderer."

Jane opened the patio door. "Almost done? The kids are hungry and climbing the walls."

"Coming." Duncan set the kebabs on a plate and turned off the grill. "Em, this case has lots of moving parts, and we're still working through Billy's documents. Trust me when I say, we've got things handled." Then he walked inside.

She was forced to take him at his word.

•   •   •

Bella skillfully corralled Emily from the front door to the kitchen by darting through and around her legs. After presenting her cat with a savory dinner, Emily poured herself a glass of wine and carried the crime board outside to the beachfront deck. She propped it against a coconut palm tree and collapsed into her favorite chair.

Left with so many unanswered questions after her conversation with Duncan, she texted Mike on her way home, inviting him for a nightcap. She now understood why Mike had distanced himself ever since the memorial service—he'd been working. But whatever the reason behind his late-night meeting with Lala and her mom, Emily planned to find out.

She fixated on the *Motive* heading on her crime board, struggling to understand Billy's role in a credit card fraud scandal. It didn't match with her impressions of the man. Had a gambling debt forced him to make bad decisions? To do something out of desperation?

She put an X through Thornton's name on the suspect list, but added Trent's. Since Trent and Stewie were friends, that made Trent's threatening message more ominous.

While contemplating a second glass of wine, she received an apologetic text from Mike. He was tied up at work and couldn't stop by.

It had been a long day for everyone, but if Emily didn't share the latest break in Billy's case with Anthony, he'd never forgive her. He didn't pick up, so she texted him and promised to update him in the morning. Since Claire would be returning to Tarpon Springs to pack her stuff, Lala would need their support now more than ever.

On top of their commitments to the veterinary hospital, they had to prepare for Sarah arriving in a few days for a turtle center board meeting and for Phoenix's Yappy Barkday Pawty fundraiser. Emily and Anthony were stretched thin, and if they didn't take care of themselves, they'd be no help to anyone.

The only smart thing to do would be to get a good night's sleep. Emily carried her crime board inside, washed up, and climbed into bed. Bella was already curled up on the pillow and refused to make room, forcing Emily to position herself diagonally across the bed. Sleep did not come easily. Unresolved questions and persistent threats caused her to toss and turn. At least as much as Bella would allow. Each nudge of her pillow triggered a shrill meow of objection.

•　　•　　•

At the crack of dawn, Emily woke to the sensation of Bella's cold nose pressed to her ear—one of her cat's signature moves.

She pulled the duvet over her head. "Bella, not yet. I need to sleep."

Bella stepped across her body, and when Emily peeked out from under the covers, she sat only inches away, looking determined to hold a vigil until she'd been fed.

"You win. Again."

Emily shuffled to the kitchen, placed an entire can of cat food on a plate for Bella, and brewed her coffee. Once she had a fresh cup in hand, she returned to bed to savor the first sip.

Leaving the room in the dark, she tuned into the local morning news, curious if there were any reports about credit card fraud or updates on Billy's murder investigation. While listening to the weather forecast, she checked her phone.

"Oh no." Since her phone reverted to *Do Not Disturb* overnight, she'd missed two calls from Lala. Only Anthony, Duncan, Jane, Mike, and the hospital security alarm company could override the setting. While Emily listened to Lala's message, Anthony called.

"Good. You're up." He was on speakerphone in his car.

"I didn't see Lala's message until right now."

"It's okay. I talked to her last night and will be at the marina in a few minutes. I'm not sure about the protocol for an undercover operation, but I brought donuts."

"I'll be there as soon as possible. Save me one."

•   •   •

When Emily pulled into the lot, she noticed Jane's SUV parked behind the dive shop and assumed Duncan had swapped cars with his wife to maintain his cover.

Her brother, wearing a T-shirt, shorts, and a ball cap, stood chatting to a boater while filling their tanks. He locked eyes with her, then turned away, making it clear she should not approach or acknowledge him.

Emily walked into the shop and found Lala and Anthony seated behind the cash register, enjoying their donuts, while Hemingway napped in her kitty bed.

"Hi." Emily scanned the store to ensure they were alone then pointed at her brother. "I wish he told me about this last night."

"Don't be mad at Duncan. It was late when I finally agreed to Mike's plan to station an undercover officer at the fuel dock."

"But this is a lot. Billy's service ended only hours ago."

"I know, but there's nothing I wouldn't do to catch his killer. And I need to get this business reopened. It forced me to take that first step, and that's all right."

"Is Claire here?"

"No, she left early this morning, but only after Mike reassured her of my safety. She'll pack up her stuff in Tarpon Springs and move into her new place next week."

"But I still don't understand why they're undercover at the marina. I thought the credit card skimming ended when Stewie stopped working here."

"It had until this past week. They're not staking out the dive shop—they're watching the watersports store."

Emily gasped. "Not Mr. Haney. How could we be so wrong about him?"

Anthony nodded. "It's hard to believe. Maybe he's a victim and doesn't know what's happening."

Lala shrugged. "Mike didn't say either way."

Emily wiggled the credit card machine sitting on the sales counter. It seemed sturdy enough and resembled the one they used at the veterinary hospital. "So, how does the skimming device work?"

Anthony jumped off his stool. "It's quite ingenious. The criminals install a second keypad on top of the existing one and place a keyhole camera nearby to capture the PIN the customers enter onto the pad. That's why they always tell you to cover the keypad with your hand when you punch in your secret code. So that criminals can't steal your info."

"Do you remember that extra card machine Anthony found on Billy's desk? The one that fell apart when he picked it up?" Lala said. "Well, that machine had been tampered with to install the skimming device. A specialist came last night with Mike and double-checked this one—it's legit." Lala smiled.

Emily thought her response seemed out of context and asked, "Okay, but why do you look so happy?"

"It means Billy wasn't stealing credit card information when he died. I just know in my heart he tried to do the right thing." She wiped away a tear.

Anthony wrapped his arm around her shoulder. "And we think that might be the reason he was killed."

"He must have hidden the information on Hemingway's collar to keep it safe. Mike told me the fraud reports stopped months ago. About the time Billy started attending the Gamblers Anonymous meetings. He wanted to turn his life around," Lala said.

Emily selected a chocolate glazed from the box of donuts and chewed absentmindedly. With her free hand, she grabbed a strawberry donut covered with sprinkles.

"Uh, Em." Anthony pointed at her double-fisted sugar bomb of a breakfast.

"See what happens when you don't get any sleep." She alternated bites between the two flavors. "Did Mike tell you about the FBI agent stationed in the marina?"

"He did. That's how he convinced both me and my mom that everyone would be safe. They've got the place covered."

Duncan walked inside and waved a device in his hand. "The customer already paid me for two bags of Ballyhoo bait."

"What's that?" Emily pointed to the black box he was holding.

"It's the portable credit card terminal," Lala said.

"Can I see it?" Emily asked.

Duncan looked over his shoulder toward the fuel dock then handed it to her.

"This looks almost identical to my dive computer." Emily turned the unit around for Anthony to see. "Look familiar?"

Anthony's eyes lit up. "It's the same thing Trent collected from *Diver Down* the day Billy died. He told us he'd left his computer behind on a recent scuba trip."

"And he refused to acknowledge ever being on the boat when I asked him about it. But more importantly, Mr. Haney told me Trent doesn't dive."

"They do look similar," Lauryn said. "Billy used the smaller handheld device to process sales at the dock when the store got busy or for extra equipment rentals on dive charters. It's like the ones waitstaff use table-side in restaurants. Not having to run inside saves time."

Emily now understood the motive behind Billy's murder and the reason for the current undercover operation. "You're not watching Mr. Haney. You're watching Trent—to see if Stewie shows up."

CHAPTER THIRTY-EIGHT

When the customer from the fuel dock approached the front door, Duncan turned to Emily and said, "Not now. Not a word."

"I get it." She executed a zipper motion across her lips.

Duncan resumed his role as an employee and opened the door so Lala could greet her first customer.

"Welcome to Blue Water Marina," she said as Emily and Anthony moved to make room at the counter.

The man filled his arms with snacks and drinks for the boat. "I've been coming here for years, and I can't tell you how happy I am that you're back open."

"We'll be here seven days a week. And if there's anything we don't have that we should stock in the store, please let me know." As Lala rang up the sale, she chatted with the boater about the current marine forecast and wished him "tight lines" as he left. Duncan followed the customer outside, but not before giving Emily a warning look, one that only a big brother could give a little sister.

"Yay!" Lala raised her arms over her head in victory.

"Congrats. Looks like you're off to a great start," Anthony said. "And speaking of starts, Em, we need to get to work."

"Lala, will you promise to call if anything happens? We'll be back the moment the hospital closes."

• • •

Emily and Anthony huddled together every time Lala sent an update. She reported hourly, but there wasn't much to tell. Duncan was doing a phenomenal job as a dockhand, but otherwise, things were quiet at the marina.

Abigail walked into Anthony's office. "The last appointment of the day is here—a new puppy. The client, Dee Holt, couldn't give me a name for the pup. She said it's a long story. Oh, and I finalized our tables for the fundraiser." She handed over the list. "I've confirmed with the staff who are attending, as well as Sarah Klein, but haven't spoken to the others."

"They'll be there unless something unexpected comes up." Emily knew anything could change during an undercover operation, but she kept that to herself.

"Catrinna left early for a doctor's appointment, so I'll be your tech for the appointment." Anthony walked to the lobby to greet the new puppy.

• • •

The problem wasn't that "Puppy" Holt didn't have a name, but that he had too many names. Dee Holt and her four-year-old grandson introduced Emily to their puppy, Dilly.

"Well, his name changes based on my grandson's favorite food. It started as Tater Tot, but when cheese quesadillas became his latest culinary obsession, we changed it to Dilly. Quesadilla was too tricky to pronounce. But I'll forewarn you, he asked me for a hot dog today, so you never know what it'll be the next time we come in. The strange thing is—the puppy responds to every one of them."

Emily laughed. "Most people have multiple names for their pets."

"My family dog growing up responded to Johnny, JD, The Bud, Sir Johnathan, and Mr. Handsome Boy," Anthony said. "I'm sure there were more that I've forgotten."

"Well, I wish my grandson would call the puppy 'Broccoli' or 'Spinach' because I'm struggling to get him to eat his vegetables."

They all laughed.

The pup slept through most of the exam. The breeder had performed the initial vaccines, so the next booster was scheduled in two weeks. Today's exam was for a wellness checkup, fecal test for intestinal worms, and to introduce Dilly to the hospital. Lots of training treats helped to create a positive experience.

•　　•　　•

Ending the day with a healthy puppy meant the entire staff could leave on time—a rare occurrence.

"Ever since Dilly's appointment, I've been craving Mexican food. Why don't I pick up dinner for all of us, and I'll meet you at the marina. I'll text Lala and Duncan to get their order."

"Sounds perfect. I'm eager to find out what's happening."

"You know," Anthony said, "in the movies, stakeouts are usually super boring."

"It's different when it involves friends, and the threat is real."

"You're right. Nothing is boring about any of this."

Emily followed her staff out the treatment room door and locked the hospital for the night.

•　　•　　•

Instead of parking close to the dive shop, Emily drove a slow loop around the perimeter, checking for signs of Agent Bonaventura or Clay Thornton. She couldn't find either of them on deck. Before turning at the far side of the lot, Trent ran out the front door of the watersports store, carrying a small bag similar to the one he retrieved the day she met him on *Diver Down.* Then he disappeared out of sight.

Now what? Emily searched for Duncan, but a large fishing yacht obscured her sightlines. She lurched to a stop and jumped out of the car before darting to the side of the watersports building. She peered in the front window but didn't see Mr. Haney or any other customers. Emily ran around the back of the store, sticking to the wall for cover.

As she neared the loading dock door on the opposite side of the building, Emily heard angry voices. She inched closer to listen.

"You need to get this thing outta here," Trent said. Emily recognized his whiny voice.

"You're gonna do what I tell you to—or someone will get hurt."

Emily couldn't identify the second voice and continued moving closer to the back corner of the building, staying hidden from view.

"But my uncle is acting all suspicious. He knows something's up."

A loud banging noise startled Emily, and she dropped to the ground.

"Stop. You're gonna break my arm," Trent pleaded with his attacker. "Okay, I'll do it. I'll put it back."

Emily crawled the last few feet and peeked around the corner. *I knew it.* Stewie had Trent in an arm-lock, his face pressed against the wall.

Just then, a low-flying pelican passed close to Emily before landing on a nearby piling. Startled, she involuntarily gasped, causing both men to turn in her direction. Emily moved back, but not quickly enough.

"Who's there?" Stewie yelled.

Emily jumped to her feet and sprinted toward the main section of the marina. She didn't need to turn around to know she'd been followed, since she could hear footsteps in the gravel accelerating behind her.

Once she reached the front of the store, she made a sharp right and started shouting, "Help!"

Stewie gained on her with every step. Her distress calls brought Duncan running out of the dive shop at the same time Agent Bonaventura moved onto the deck of the trawler. But neither of them was close enough to stop what came next.

Stewie lunged for her scrub top, but she stayed just beyond his reach. Knowing he wouldn't miss a second time, she sprinted at full speed. At that moment, a massive shadow shifted in the corner of her eye, unleashing a blood-curdling war cry. Seconds later, a tsunami-like splash erupted as two bodies plunged into the canal.

Emily turned to see Anthony holding Stewie underwater as he thrashed his arms, gasping for air.

Duncan arrived on the scene, his gun aimed at Stewie, as Mike sprinted to the dock from across the parking lot. Agent Bonaventura started after Trent, who was running to his Camaro.

When Anthony saw the firepower, he kicked hard to distance himself from Stewie and swam to a nearby ladder.

Wild-eyed, Stewie blinked and continued to gasp for air.

"Stewart Jackson, you're under arrest for the murder of William Todd." Mike commanded him to get out of the water.

The words had a sobering effect on Stewie. He accepted the lifesaving ring tossed to him, allowing the law enforcement officers to pull him to safety. Duncan rolled him face down on the dock and cuffed his hands behind his back.

"Em, are you okay?" Mike turned to her while keeping his gun pointed at Stewie.

She nodded. "I'm fine, thanks to—"

Anthony stepped onto the dock soaking wet, and Emily ran to him, almost knocking him into the canal.

"That was fun." His grin spread across his face, and they both laughed—a nervous, *holy crap, we almost died* kind of laugh. "But let's promise not to do that again."

Agent Bonaventura placed Trent in cuffs and secured him in his vehicle before talking with a shell-shocked Mr. Haney, who stood outside, his hand covering his mouth. Mr. Haney's body language confirmed everything Emily believed to be true about his innocence.

Mike moved his unmarked police car next to the dock and loaded Stewie into the caged back seat. He conferred with Duncan, then walked with purpose to Emily, pulling her into his arms. The intensity of his embrace caught her off guard.

"I have to go, but I'll call you as soon as I can. I need to talk to you."

She nodded, and a minute later, he drove out of the marina.

"What's that about?" Anthony asked.

"Not sure."

Lala had joined them in time to see Stewie's arrest. After he was taken away, she sat on the dock, tucked her head to her knees, and sobbed. Emily and Anthony settled on either side of her, each slipping an arm around her back, staying silent until she had let everything out.

CHAPTER THIRTY-NINE

In short order, the three friends were alone on the dock. The few stragglers who had wandered into the marina drawn by the police presence had dispersed. Duncan locked the fuel pumps for Lala, and once he confirmed they didn't need anything, he left for the station to join Mike and Agent Bonaventura.

Anthony pointed toward the bag of food sitting in the parking lot. "I somehow saved dinner before tackling Stewie into the canal." He stood and offered his hand to his friends, pulling them to their feet.

"You totally missed your calling—you should've gone out for football in high school instead of joining the band," Emily said, nudging him in the ribs.

"When Stewie tried to grab you, I lost my mind. I didn't think— I reacted."

"Like the superhero you are," Lala said. "At least to Em and me."

"All that action made me hungry." He picked up the takeout and waved for them to follow.

•   •   •

While waiting for word about the arrests, Mr. Haney came by to offer his sincerest apologies. Despite not understanding Trent's full role in the skimming operation or Billy's death, he looked devastated. He promised Lala that he'd make it up to her even if it took him the rest of his life and became tearful when he excused himself to call his sister to inform her about the arrest of her son.

"I wish we could be there when they interrogate Stewie and Trent. I need to know what role they played in Billy's death. It's the only way I'll find any closure," Lala said.

"You'll get answers to all your questions once Duncan and Mike finish with them," Anthony said.

Hemingway descended from her kitty bed behind the register, stretched her body, yawned, then walked into the apartment.

"I think I'm going to follow her lead. For the first time since getting to town, I feel truly safe. Fingers crossed that translates into a good night's sleep. Until Mom returns, I'm working on my own. But if business keeps up like today, we'll be able to hire some part-time help. Unless Duncan is looking for a second job."

That made Emily laugh. "I'm sure you'll find the right person."

"Do you think you're up to joining us at the Barkday Pawty fundraiser this weekend?"

"I wouldn't miss it," Lala said. "After all these years away, I'm excited to reconnect with the Coral Shores community. But your friendship is the most important thing to me. There's no way I would have survived this past week without the two of you. And forget the fact that you both put yourselves in danger trying to solve Billy's murder. To echo Mr. Haney, I'll spend my life repaying you for your kindness."

"Well, you won't have to. That's not how we roll. You're now one of us." He circled his finger between them. "But be careful what you wish for—we can be trouble."

"But good trouble." Emily grinned.

•   •   •

Emily stayed up for Mike, and it was close to midnight when he confirmed he was on his way. Bella had already gone to bed while she waited on the couch.

After a gentle knock on the door, Mike leaned inside. "Em?"

"I'm in the living room."

Mike's stubble and the dark circles under his eyes made it clear he'd been working nonstop.

"I'm going to grab some water. Do you want anything?" He moved to the kitchen and helped himself.

"I'm good. Come sit." She patted the couch beside her.

He drank the glass in one gulp, then joined her, wrapping an arm around her shoulders.

"I'm sorry I couldn't call or update you about what was happening. I've been staked out across from the marina for two days now, waiting for Stewie to show up."

"How did he get there without being seen?"

"We found his truck parked a mile away. He must have traveled on foot, keeping along the waterside of the canal."

"So, can you tell me how all this is linked to Billy's murder?"

"You figured out some of it and guessed at the rest. Stewie wasn't talking until he found out Trent, who was petrified of facing a lifelong prison sentence, started singing. They're both accusing the other of being the mastermind, offering their complete testimony in exchange for leniency."

"They better not get off easy. They should never again see the light of day."

"Agreed. The DA has made no commitments that I'm aware of. So far, we know Billy owed Stewie, his bookie, over some gambling debts. Stewie pressured him to install the credit card skimming devices at the marina to recoup his money. But Billy kept track of all the data, and when he had repaid the debt, he told Stewie he wanted out."

"But I'm guessing Stewie didn't accept no for an answer."

He shook his head. "That's when their friendship, or whatever you want to call it, fell apart. Stewie was forced to bring Trent in on the plan when he needed someone to cut the security camera to the marina. Trent said that during one of their last dives together, Billy gave Stewie an ultimatum and confessed to keeping all the credit card data as evidence—as an insurance policy."

"And Trent told you all that?"

"Yup. Trent agreed to help Stewie for a payout. But he swears up and down he had no clue Stewie planned to kill Billy. He thought he was just going to rough him up. When he heard the news about Billy's death, he confronted Stewie, but by then, he'd become an accomplice. That's when Stewie blackmailed him into installing a credit card skimmer and keyhole camera at the watersports store."

"I don't have any sympathy for Trent. He's not a victim."

"They both got greedy. The FBI had given up on the case when it went cold about two months ago. The recent flurry of fraudulent activity led them to the watersports store, reviving the investigation."

"That matches the time Billy joined Gamblers Anonymous," Emily said. "But what about the arsine gas? Was that Stewie?"

Mike nodded. "He often dove with Billy, so he had to know his routines. They both logged their dives using the same dive app, so we could match them up. We're still tracking down a few leads, connecting Stewie to some missing arsine at a local chemical company. But he was stupid enough to brag to Trent about how easy it was to put the gas into a scuba tank."

"So, Billy put an end to it. He stopped gambling and tried to get out of the deal he made with Stewie. But I don't understand why someone would resort to murder over some credit card fraud? It sounds like Billy just wanted out."

Mike nodded. "Likely because of the 'Three Strikes' law. Stewie already had two previous felony convictions, so a third conviction would mean he automatically faced an extended prison sentence. The stakes were bigger this time."

"That must be who kept coming into the dive shop and broke in after Lala changed the locks. Stewie needed to retrieve all the evidence. And that's why we couldn't find Billy's laptop—he took it."

"Yes, we executed a search warrant for Stewie's apartment this morning before dawn—the same place you followed him to. Among his belongings, he had a countertop and a portable handheld credit card terminal from Billy's dive shop, along with an air compressor, the missing laptop, his sports betting ledger, and several other electronic devices used in skimming operations."

"And you're sure Thornton wasn't involved in all this?"

"We're sure. He's abrasive, but he's just a boat broker trying to build a business. Agent Bonaventura confirmed Thornton plans to offer fishing charters from that old trawler he recently purchased."

"Well, he's going to need a serious attitude adjustment if he wants Lala to sell him any bait or fuel—he owes her an apology," Emily said, standing up and pacing the room. "At first, we thought Billy had hired a pet sitter for Hemingway, but that never quite added up. Still, how did Stewie figure out the credit card data was hidden on Hemingway's collar?"

"We may never know unless Stewie decides to tell us," Mike said. "The techs confirmed the incriminating data Billy had gathered wasn't on the laptop—that's why Stewie kept searching. Maybe he saw Billy welding the collar." Mike took her hand and gently guided her to sit beside him.

"You should've seen how Hemingway reacted to Stewie the one time he walked into the dive shop, pretending to be a customer buying bait. She arched her back and hissed—something she never does. Still, I have to believe Billy didn't think she'd be in any danger."

"It's possible the keyhole camera Stewie installed to capture customers' PINs when they entered them into the credit card machine may have picked up Billy tinkering with Hemingway's collar. You said she usually stayed behind the register during business hours."

"That makes sense. I'm grateful Hemingway's strong survival skills told her to escape to the rafters. What would Stewie have done if he got his hands on her?" Emily shivered at the thought.

Mike drew her in and placed his finger under her chin, turning her to face him.

"Em, when I saw Stewie chasing you…" His voice caught in his throat. "To think anything bad could happen to you, well, I never want to feel that way again." He kissed her gently.

"That was a close call, but Anthony and I always have each other's backs. I don't want you to worry."

"You're not kidding. He was like an angry bear, charging at Stewie. But that's not my point." He stood, walked to the kitchen for another glass of water, then came back and asked her to stand. "I don't know why this is so hard."

Emily felt panic rising. He seemed so serious.

Mike cleared his throat and continued. "What I mean to say is, I want to be the one who always has your back. Today and forever."

Emily swallowed but failed to find her words. Mike made it easy for her.

"I want us to be each other's future," he said. "I can't imagine spending my life with anyone else. I know we promised to take it slow, but I'm not sure that's what I want anymore. Taking it slow, I mean. I'm committed to you, Em. And just you."

CHAPTER FORTY

The next few days leading up to the Yappy Barkday Pawty fundraiser were chaotic. Emily and Anthony spent their evenings at the dive shop helping Lala get things up and running. They focused on restocking shelves, cleaning, and working the sales counter, since neither was trained on the fuel pumps. The pace was not sustainable, but Claire would be there soon to help her daughter. Lala planned to run the business in partnership with her mom.

Jane and Duncan came by the marina with Elvis and the kids. While Duncan taught Mac and Ava how to fish off the dock, Elvis insisted on following Hemingway around, inviting her to play by bowing down and yipping for attention. Since her paw had fully healed, Hemingway obliged, and they took turns chasing each other across the apartment in a game of cat and dog tag.

Ava's squeals of joy drew everyone outside. She reeled in a nice-sized mangrove snapper, and despite Duncan's attempts to convince her it was a tasty fish to eat, she named the fish "Princess" and forced her dad to release it back to its family. Mac rolled his eyes but congratulated his sister on her catch.

Emily had been on cloud nine since Mike's declaration. She didn't need to put a label on it—not yet anyway. Knowing their commitment had moved to the next level made her happy.

Anthony picked up on her change in mood. When he and Marc declared themselves to each other before moving in together, Emily had been there to cheer them on. He told her he wanted her to have the same happiness.

Sarah Klein arrived in town the day before the fundraiser. The Coral Shores Humane Society had been one of her mom's favorite charities. Before her death, she had donated much of her time to support their causes, almost as hard as she worked for sea turtle conservation. Sarah's commitment to the Eliza Klein Sea Turtle Conservation Center included a renewed connection to the community, despite living on the opposite coast in Los Angeles. A Turtle Team board meeting was added to the weekend schedule to sign off on all the design choices for the interior of the welcome center.

•   •   •

When Mike picked up Emily to escort her to the event, she let out an audible gasp as she opened the door. It was the first time she'd seen him in a suit, and his movie-star charm left her speechless.

They arrived at the Coral Shores Community Center and were greeted by Phoenix and Elizabeth, who stood at the entrance, similar to a receiving line at a wedding. Phoenix wore a brand-new, pink peony flower on her collar, perfectly coordinated with her leash. Donation bins placed throughout the room were filled with dog and cat food, blankets, bedding, toys, and more.

Decorated with streamers and balloon arches, the center had been transformed into a magical event space. Music played in the background, but not loudly enough to scare the celebrity canine attendees. The keynote speaker, a famous actress known for her animal rescue work, dazzled the guests as she circulated throughout the room.

Anthony and Marc arrived arm-in-arm at the soiree wearing matching bow ties—Anthony's adorned with cats, while Marc's featured dogs.

Sarah Klein and Lala were huddled in conversation at a table. Emily could see Lala's face as Sarah spoke. Her features relaxed, and she smiled. Knowing Lala had someone to talk with who understood how it felt to lose the most important person in your life to a violent crime made them a small but exclusive club. Emily witnessed the beginning of a new friendship.

Jane and Duncan were seated as the guest of honor took the stage. Elvis stayed home with the kids and their babysitter since this was Phoenix's night to shine, and Elvis had a knack for stealing the spotlight. Plus, Jane told Emily she was desperate for an adult night on the town. They toasted each other with a glass of champagne.

Once the speeches, silent auction, and keynote address had wrapped up, Elizabeth revealed the grand total to the room full of supporters. They had set a record, raising over twenty thousand dollars for the Humane Society. The place erupted with applause. Once the tables were cleared, the band picked up, drawing everyone onto the dance floor. Marc and Anthony were the center of attention, showing off their signature moves. After a string of fast songs, Emily grabbed Mike's hand and pulled him into a quiet corner.

She looked up at him with a smile. "I couldn't find my words the other night, after Stewie's arrest, but I want you to know I feel the same way." She paused and placed her hand over her chest to calm her fluttering heart. He kissed her gently without breaking the moment.

She continued. "From the day I met you, I knew you were the one for me. There's no one else I want to be with."

"That's all I need to hear." Mike lifted her into his arms and kissed her as if the world had stopped. When he set her back on the floor, he whispered in her ear, "I love you, Dr. Emily Benton."

THE END

ABOUT THE AUTHOR

DL Mitchell is the author of the Coral Shores Veterinary Mystery series and a 2024 Nominee for Georgia Author of the Year. She received the 2024 Killer Nashville Silver Falchion award for best cozy.

She brings her unique perspective as a practicing small animal veterinarian to the world of mystery fiction. With experience in big-city hospitals, her transition to a house call concierge veterinary practice has enriched her storytelling with firsthand encounters and insights into the human-animal bond.

She loves spending time with her husband, daughter, and their menagerie of pets, planning the next travel adventure, and running nearby trails. She's a scuba diver but gets seasick, and when she's on the road, she travels with her espresso machine and stand-up paddle board.

OTHER TITLES BY
DL MITCHELL

The Coral Shores Veterinary Mystery series

The Mick Nassau Key West Mystery series

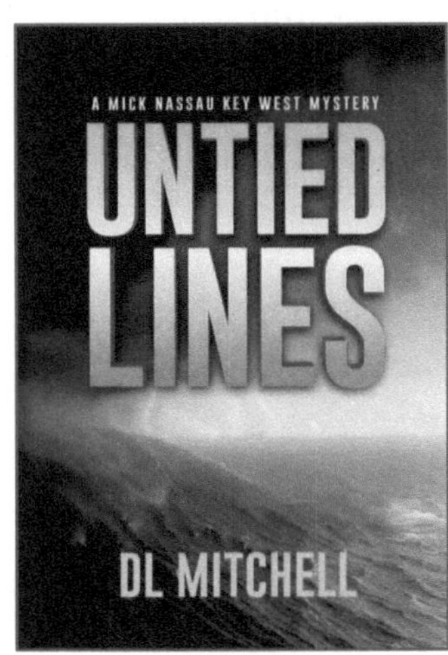

NOTE FROM DL MITCHELL

Word-of-mouth is crucial for any author to succeed. If you enjoyed *Marina Mews*, please leave a review online—anywhere you are able. Even if it's just a sentence or two. It would make all the difference and would be very much appreciated.

Visit my website at DLMitchellMystery.com for information about book signings, new releases, and more.

Thanks!
DL Mitchell

We hope you enjoyed reading this title from:

www.blackrosewriting.com

Subscribe to our mailing list – *The Rosevine* – and receive **FREE** books, daily deals, and stay current with news about upcoming releases and our hottest authors.
Scan the QR code below to sign up.

Already a subscriber? Please accept a sincere thank you for being a fan of Black Rose Writing authors.

View other Black Rose Writing titles at
www.blackrosewriting.com/books and use promo code
PRINT to receive a **20% discount** when purchasing.

www.ingramcontent.com/pod-product-compliance
Lightning Source LLC
Chambersburg PA
CBHW061549210726
48287CB00006B/2121